Praise for *Christopher Walsh's works*:

"*As Fierce as Steel* is quite an admirable work of writing for a first-time novelist, and it is with great eagerness I anticipate its sequel, *The Worth of Gold*. Highly recommended for fans of the genre." – **James M. Fisher, *The Miramichi Reader***

"If you're a fan of epic stories with mythology, politics, interesting characters, and an imaginative world, then the Gold and Steel Saga should be on your reading list." – **Ali House, author of *The Six Elemental***

"Walsh is a part of a new breed: He grew up on the fantasy of his generation and has decided what of it works and what of it doesn't, and has produced his own spin on things. This is a unique novel in the fantasy genre, a genre which has not seen innovation since the last crop of visionaries came through the pipeline in the late 80s." – **Matthew LeDrew, author of the *Black Womb* series**

Works by Christopher Walsh

The Gold & Steel Saga
Vol. I: *As Fierce as Steel* (2016)
Vol. II: *The Worth of Gold* (2020)
Vol. III: *The Strength of Steel* (TBA)

Short Works from the world of Gold & Steel
Stealing Back Freedom (2016)
In Defense of Our Home Pt. 1 (2017)
The City That Hid From Time Itself (2017)
In Defense of Our Home Pt. 2 (2018)
In Dangerous Company Pt. 1 (2019)

Short Work collections from Gold & Steel
Legends & Tales: Volume I (2018)

The Gold & Steel Saga's Legends & Tales Volume I

By

Christopher Walsh

THE GOLD & STEEL SAGA'S LEGENDS & TALES: VOL. 1
by CHRISTOPHER WALSH

Second Paperback Edition

ISBN 978-1-9995001-7-7

Cover design by Christina Hamlyn

Cover illustration by atrtinkcovers.com

Maps by Sarah O'Rourke-Whelan

Edited by Erin Vance

Written in Canada by Christopher Walsh

The Gold & Steel Saga's Legends & Tales Volume I

By
Christopher Walsh

THE GOLD & STEEL SAGA'S LEGENDS & TALES: VOL. 1
by CHRISTOPHER WALSH

Second Paperback Edition

Stealing Back Freedom © 2016
The City That Hid From Time Itself © 2017
In Defence of Our Home Pt. 1 © 2017
In Defence of Our Home Pt. 2 © 2018
The Worth of Gold © 2018

ISBN 978-1-9995001-7-7

Cover design by Christina Hamlyn

Cover illustration by atrtinkcovers.com

Maps by Sarah O'Rourke-Whelan

Edited by Erin Vance

Written in Canada by Christopher Walsh

This book is for Kyra,
I love you to the moon and back

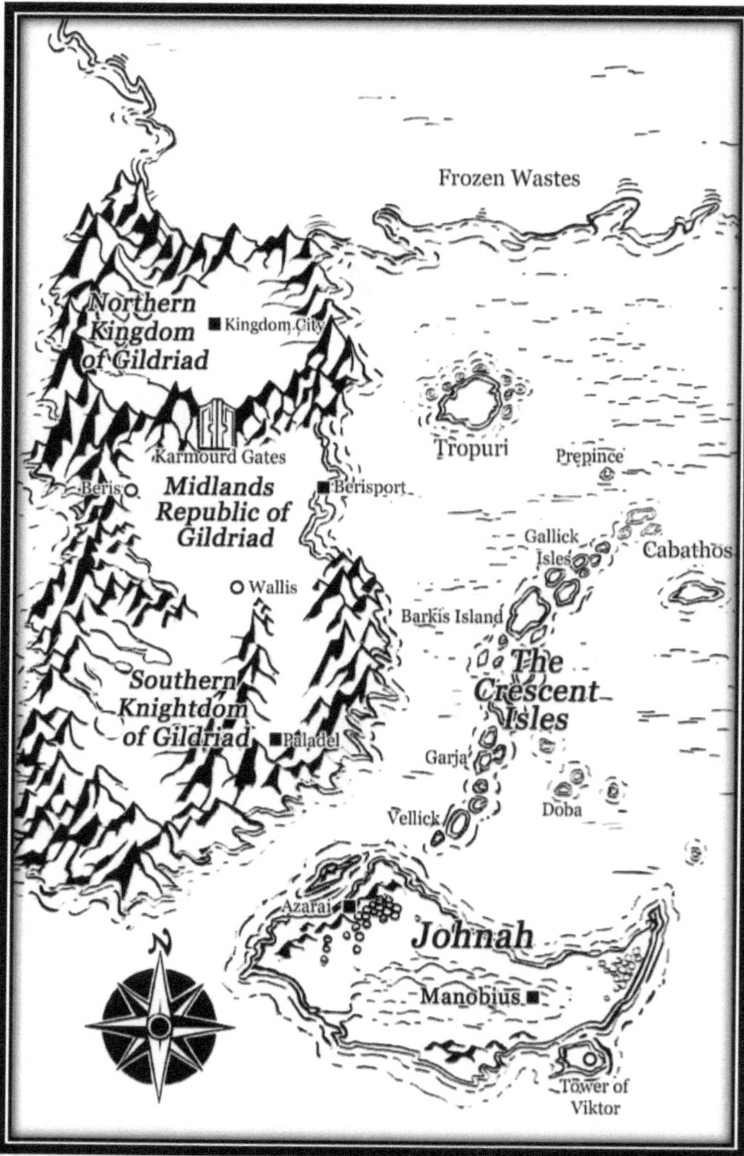

Frozen Wastes
Northern Kingdom of Gildriad
Kingdom City
Karmourd Gates
Beris
Midlands Republic of Gildriad
Berisport
Tropuri
Prepince
Gallick Isles
Cabathos
Wallis
Barkis Island
The Crescent Isles
Southern Knightdom of Gildriad
Paladel
Garja
Doba
Vellick
N
Azarai
Johnah
Manobius
Tower of Viktor

Drake
Snowy Lands
Gondarrius
Elven Forest
Kushika City
Calimfaire
Shatoya
Mount Graelin
Fuwachita City
Tusker's Cove
Axel's Islands
Portsward
Atrebell
Daol Bay
Hercalest
Biddenhurst
Daol Forest
Western Realm
Eastern Realm
Pelican Harbour
Illiastra
Weicaster Bay
Farmourd
Fort Layn
Aquas Bay
Southlands
Phaleayna
The Warrens
The Storming Sea

TABLE OF CONTENTS

STEALING BACK FREEDOM

Original publication:
***Sci-Fi From The Rock* (2016)**

Stealing Back Freedom takes readers to mere months before the beginning of the events of ***As Fierce as Steel***. In the sweltering summer heat of Aquas Bay, deep in the Southlands of Illiastra, Lady Orangecloak and a select few members of the Thieves are about to undertake a protest in the city square during its peak traffic hours. Though expected to be a routine demonstration, they learn that a dangerous presence has been detected. How will Orangecloak and her team react to the threat? Read on to find out.

From the Author: "My first short story! (In print, anyway) I wrote this one right in the midst of finishing ***As Fierce as Steel*** and I did so for two reasons: 1. I wanted to produce some material to show readers how Orangecloak and the Thieves operated before the events of ***As Fierce as Steel*** fractured the group. 2. I was told about the ***Sci-Fi From The Rock*** anthologies and wanted to try my hand at writing in shorter form than I had been at this point. The end result of those two goals was ***Stealing Back Freedom***."

Trivia: ***Stealing Back Freedom*** is an event that should be familiar to readers of the first book of the series, as it is brought up throughout.

Stealing Back Freedom

They were three, left alone in a darkened woodshed to wait. Though abandoned, the shed remained full of sawn spruce and birch that emitted a calming, pleasant scent that Orangecloak always welcomed in such stressful times.

Although, it appeared that there was at least one among them didn't find the aroma so soothing. "Myles, for the love of all things, sit. You're going to wear a hole in the damn floor," she said to her friend. He had been pacing since the scouts had gone out, working himself into a ball of nerves like he always did.

Myles chose to remain standing, but at least came to a stop before the short row of wood Orangecloak had commandeered as a seat. "I saw a lot of guards when we snuck into town, Orangecloak. I think you should call off the protest for the day," he stated, as she knew he would. Myles was cautious by nature and protective of Orangecloak at the best of times.

From beside her stirred Coquarro, her other constant companion. "It's Aquas Bay, Myles. We're in the home of Illiastra's naval fleet. There's always a heavy presence of guards. I tell you this every time. Red asked you to sit and I agree with her. Spinning in circles isn't going to improve our situation," Coquarro told

Myles. Red was the only name that Coquarro had ever known Orangecloak by, going back to the day they had met on the island refuge of Phaleayna all those years ago. One of his thick, callused dark hands found its way onto her knee. "Have you thought about what you're going to say today?"

"Something similar to what I usually say, I think," Orangecloak answered with a shrug. "I haven't given it much thought."

Myles wagged a finger at her. "You're too lackadaisical, Orangecloak. You should have your speech ready in the back of your head. We won't have much time for a protest today, and every second you waste trying to think of things to say on the spot is time the guards will use to move in on you."

"Calm down, Myles," Coquarro said with a shake of his head.

"No, I won't calm down, Coquarro," Myles responded, making visible effort to keep his frustration from getting the better of him. "You heard what people are saying: There's a ship from Daol Bay docked in port from Lord Tullivan's own fleet and the Master of Blades himself was seen disembarking from it. He's here, Coquarro and if he knows Orangecloak is too, he's going to come after her. Who's going to stop him? Are you naïve enough to think you can fight off Tryst Reine? I know I can't."

In truth, the news had been weighing on Orangecloak's mind as much as it had Myles', but she was Field Commander of the Thieves, whatever worries burdened her, she could not show them. "We don't know that it will come to that, Myles. It's a fairly large city, the Master of Blades might be anywhere within its walls. If our scouts see him in the market, where we are to protest, then we will call it off."

Myles remained unconvinced. "I still don't think it right that we go through with it, Orangecloak. If the Master of Blades is in town, then that means that Lord Master Grenjin Howland might be here as well and he travels with the Honourable Guardsmen about him."

"If the Lord Master of Illiastra were on that ship, people would be talking more about that than they would the Master of Blades, Myles," Orangecloak pointed out. "It would seem that Tryst Reine came alone. He's probably here for a vacation. In fact, I bet he's on his way to the Red Isles for some rest and relaxation as we speak."

"What if he's not?" Myles offered as a counterpoint. "By the gods, what if he knew you were coming here and was sent alone to do the deed of killing you himself? We should be on our way out of the city and heading for the ruins of Amarosha right now before he has his chance to do anything, Orangecloak."

Coquarro groaned and leaned forward from the high row of wood he had been using as a backrest. "For goodness sake, Myles, do you even hear yourself? We've been in Aquas Bay half a hundred times doing this very thing and you've never been craven before. It's not going to be any different now. The Master of Blades is just one man in a city of tens of thousands."

That drew a scoff from Myles and he threw his hands up. "Tryst Reine is the *Master* of *Blades*," he argued, putting heavy emphasis on those two words above all. "He is the best swordsman in the Known World, the sworn protector of the Lord Master and given to serve with full authority and full immunity from all laws. That man can do whatever he so pleases in the name of the

Lord Master, and Orangecloak is the most wanted person in all of Illiastra. Do you think it coincidence that they're in the same city together? I'm telling you both, he knows she is here and he has come to make the arrest."

Despite knowing how stubborn Myles could be, Orangecloak knew she must try to reason with him. "They call Tryst Reine the Master of Blades, but that is a title only earned by students of the University of Combative Arts in the nation of Drake. How many have there been that were called Master of Blades? Only two or three in a thousand years, right? We all know who the first Master of Blades was: Segai, the Great Hero of Phaleayna. We've seen his bones and the remnants of his plate armour in the crypts behind Great Valley Lake. I don't think you can earn the name Master of Blades if you don't somehow embody his heroic traits. Besides, this Tryst Reine is a sell sword. He's sworn no oaths, said no vows, and his loyalty to the Lord Master is made of paper. I doubt he spends his days worrying about pleasing Grenjin Howland. Also, consider that if he was all he's made out to be and he wanted to find us, it would not have taken him four years to do so."

"Red speaks sense, Myles," Coquarro said in an attempt to assuage Myles' concerns. "If she is not worried, then you should not be either."

It did worry Orangecloak, though. Not that she could say as much, but the notion that Tryst Reine was in the city was one she found troubling. If what she had heard about him out of Atrebell, Illiastra's capital, bore any truth, then he was a monster, as morally depraved as he was skilled with a sword. Oftentimes, stories that made their way across the Varras River and into the Southlands had a way of becoming exaggerated along the way, but Orangecloak could not dismiss them outright. Some among her ranks believed the tales of Tryst Reine to be mere fabrications, knowing that the Lord Master and his Elite Merchant Party frequently spread such lies, all of it done to bolster fear in the populace of Illiastra toward their government. Fear that Orangecloak and their Thieves worked tirelessly to dispel.

If nothing else, it will not do to let these tales cloud my perception. It is on me to rise above the fear mongering of the EMP, I cannot let myself be swayed by it, Orangecloak told herself, as she often did.

At the very least, her words had sated Myles enough to make him stop pacing. Though steady, he was still anxious and fidgeting and he idly picked a bit of sawdust that had fallen into Orangecloak's long red hair that tumbled well past her shoulders. For a moment, Myles looked as though he was going to break his brief silence, but just as he opened his mouth, a scarcely audible knock came on the door.

There was not as much as a breath while the three of them waited. Coquarro raised a hand with three fingers raised and counted them down wordlessly until he was at a fist. The person without knocked again, this time in a pattern of rap-a-tap-rap-a-tap tap-tap-tap, repeating it over again twice more.

Myles exhaled with relief and went to the old door, peeking through a knothole in the wood for added security before finally unlatching it. "It's Ellarie and her ladies," he declared as he stepped back, door in hand and gave entry to four cloaked figures, hoods drawn and heads down.

Only when Myles closed the door behind them did the four reveal their faces. They were young and fair, near Orangecloak's age but all younger by a few years, save for one.

"You're the first to return, Ellarie," Orangecloak told her first lieutenant and dear friend. "Have you crossed paths with the other lieutenants?"

Ellarie shook out the dark, wavy hair that fell just past her ears before she answered. "I haven't seen Merion, Joyce, or Lazlo since we split up this morning. I just came across Edwin and Garlan not far from here. They were coming to report that they had spotted the Master of Blades. When we found one another, they gave their report to me and returned from whence they came to keep an eye on him."

"Well, where was he? What was he doing?" Myles asked eagerly.

"He was in the market square," Ellarie began to answer.

"See, Orangecloak?" Myles said, rudely cutting Ellarie off. "I told you that's where he'd be, he knows you're coming-"

Ellarie returned the gesture and stepped in. "The Master of Blades was buying an expensive bottle of liquor. He left the market as soon as he had it and seemed content to wile his morning away in a small inn several streets away, drinking mead and eating mutton in the common room."

"See, Myles?" Orangecloak mimicked him jokingly. "I told you that you were working yourself up over nothing. I think you owe Ellarie an apology."

He grumbled and turned to the first lieutenant of the Thieves. "Sorry, El, I shouldn't have cut you off like that. Still though, we should keep Edwin and Garlan in position to track Tryst Reine, if he's still at the inn."

With an overdue stretch, Orangecloak slid from the woodpile to stand up. "Indeed, Myles. I intend for Edwin and Garlan to stay on him. What of your own scouting trip, Ellarie?"

"Outside of the Master of Blades' presence, there's nothing unusual to report," Ellarie went on. "This is Breakday, so the markets are bustling and you should have a large audience. We counted six guards and one overseer patrolling inside the market, all armed with swords and pistols and in groups of two." She gestured towards a fellow raven-haired woman standing beside her and to one of the two blondes. "Bernadine and Nia were sent to the rooftops and they counted just two riflemen stationed up there today. I think standard procedure should be enough to distract them all without incident."

Orangecloak considered everything she heard and looked to the last blonde. "What about you, Coramae? This is your hometown. Did you see anything out of the ordinary?"

The woman had been looking all around the shed and looked surprised to hear her name. "No, milady, I noticed nothing worth reporting."

"That settles it, then," Orangecloak decided. "Once Lazlo, Merion, and Joyce return, we will proceed." She eyed Coramae again, still glancing all about the tiny building. "Coramae, we will likely have time before everyone else arrives, if you'd like, you can go have a look around your old house."

"I think I would like that, milady, thank you," Coramae said.

Orangecloak gave her a nod. "Take Nia with you and keep an eye out for the others. Return to the shed if you see them."

The two departed and Myles latched the door behind them once again.

"That poor thing, I feel for her," Coquarro said from where he still sat on the woodpile. "It's been two years since she and her friend Alia came to us and she's still so full of longing."

"I feel badly every time we drag either of them back here," Ellarie commented sadly. "This was their home, I know, and they know this city better than anyone, but they've been through so much here."

Orangecloak pitied Coramae and her friend as much as anyone. "It was the EMP that was responsible for what happened to them. They came for Allia's father's tailoring business, tore down his building, and give him a pittance for it. As if that wasn't enough, they drafted her oldest brother into the Illiastran armed forces and arrested her father when he complained about the whole thing. He's in Biddenhurst now, as is her mother. We all know that anyone who goes to the Prison City never returns."

"You forget that Coramae's family fared just as poorly after she left," Ellarie reminded her. "Her father died at sea and her mother was not permitted to earn a wage under the laws of the Triarchy religion. Coramae doesn't even know what happened to her, or her younger siblings for that matter. Biddenhurst again, I would imagine. Although, her siblings might be holed up in a Triarchy orphanage somewhere. Though, I don't think that's necessarily any better."

Bernadine stepped forward. "With all due respect to the both of you, I don't know one of us that *haven't* come to the Thieves through tragic circumstances." Though she was the youngest of Ellarie's unit, Bernadine was wise beyond her years, unwaveringly loyal and perpetually sullen and stoic.

"That's a fair point, Bernadine," Orangecloak agreed.

From the corner of her eye, Orangecloak espied Myles taking a sudden peek through the knothole again. "Someone's coming, looks like Lazlo and he's alone."

As Ellarie before him had done, Lazlo knocked, waited and went about tapping out the same pattern three times over. He was admitted and the instant Myles closed the door behind him he had his cloak drawn back, sending long, blonde ringlets tumbling over his toned shoulders. "By Aren's beard, it's too bloody hot outside for wearing cloaks," Lazlo said to no one in particular as he wiped at the beads of sweat forming on his forehead with his cloak.

That garnered an amused scoff from Coquarro. "You know nothing of heat, my friend. Remind me to take you to Johnah someday. The desert in the interior of my country will make you beg for the ocean breezes of Aquas Bay in summer."

"Forgive me if I somehow forget to take you up on that offer, Coquarro," Lazlo said with a jovial wink to the tall, dark skinned man before turning his attention to Orangecloak. "Donnis, Etcher and I had quite the busy morning, despite the unyielding heat and humidity."

"Speaking of those two, where are they?" Ellarie asked quickly. "Also, did you happen to come across my sister and Joyce?"

Lazlo produced a canteen hanging from a leather thong around his neck and took a seat beside Coquarro before granting an answer. "Merion, Joyce and the three with them are not far behind, actually. We spaced out our arrivals to avoid suspicion. As for my own lads, I left them to investigate a potential distraction for you on the waterfront."

The mere mention of one of Lazlo's distractions caused Orangecloak's brows to furrow. "What sort of damage is this going to cause?" she asked suspiciously.

"Just some bruises, broken noses and busted lips on a bunch of sailors," Lazlo explained with a sly grin. "There's a ship in port from one of the nations from the Crescent Island's, Gallick, to be exact and this particular ship of Gallicians are looking particularly surly today. Donnis and Etcher were just going to instigate a little scuffle between them and the crew of a merchant ship from Weicaster Bay docked nearby. Both crews are drinking heartily as we speak, so it wouldn't take much to set the Gallicians on them, but it would require quite the compliment of guards to get in between the brawl."

"Your damn distractions are always more trouble than they're worth," Orangecloak said with a shake of her head, though she did not dismiss it outright. "Keep Donnis and Etcher there, but don't do anything unless we absolutely have to. It might be that our usual tactics will suffice to draw the guards out of the marketplace." She passed a hand through her red locks and sighed loudly. "At any rate, go on with your report."

Lazlo casually crossed his legs and took another sip of water. "Right then, you may be interested to hear that the Master of Blades doesn't seem to be in Aquas Bay for any official reason. It is purely pleasure... A lot of pleasure, if I do say so."

She narrowed her gaze on him. "How did you come into this information?"

"There's a certain city councillor's assistant who is willing to tell me everything he might hear just to keep me coming back to his bed," Lazlo admitted with tongue in cheek. "Although it may also be to prevent me from telling his wife and the rest of the world that he enjoys *having* me in his bed. Either way, I sought him out and he told me that Tryst hasn't been to visit Minister Polliane or any of his city councillors nor anyone else related to the EMP. However, our sellsword friend has been spending a great deal of time going between a cheap inn and an expensive brothel since arriving in the city."

Orangecloak thought that a little puzzling. "The protector and enforcer of the very same Lord Master that views prostitution as a crime worthy of public flogging and lifetime imprisonment has been seen frequenting a brothel? Are you certain of this?"

"Quite," Lazlo told her, his smug grin never fading. "As it is, I happen to know one of the workers there, so I did a little more digging around. Apparently, he's been spending all his nights with a freckled, brunette woman near our age named Sinzia."

"So he came to Aquas Bay to drink and screw," Coquarro concluded with what they were all thinking. "Not exactly my idea of scandalous. However, the good news is that he should not be a problem for us. Is there anything else you have to add, Lazlo?"

Lazlo clicked his teeth while he thought about it before ultimately giving a quick shake of his head. "That's all I've got. The other Dollen sister and Joyce went deep into the market with the other Aquas Bay girl. They'll have a better report."

All eyes were on Orangecloak then, waiting on her order. She dusted off her green leather trousers, matching bodice, and white, sleeveless tunic and took a deep breath. "We're going ahead as planned. I'll meet Joyce and Merion on the road to the market and give them their orders. Coquarro and Myles, as always, are with me. Ellarie, separate your unit into pairs as you see fit, harry the ground patrols and lead them out of the market. Lazlo, ready your men on their distraction. If I feel we need the extra help, I'll have Myles give you a signal before I start the rally. I'll stand in the market as long as I can and when the time comes I'll make my escape by rooftop. We'll meet outside the town walls in the south woods gathering point after it's all over. If you're not there by nightfall, we'll move on to the Amarosha ruins and you can find us there. Does anyone have any questions?"

When no one spoke up, Orangecloak took that as an affirmation and extended a fist, finding it soon joined in a circle with the others, everyone touching knuckle to knuckle.

"We are the Thieves," Orangecloak stated in a strong, firm voice.

They looked to her and answered as one with the three words that had come to be a mantra and rallying cry alike for their movement: "Stealing back freedom."

As they had arrived, so too did they leave: Ellarie and Bernadine went first, to collect Nia and Coramae and make for the market. After a few minutes had passed, Lazlo departed with Myles, so that they could work out a means of sending signal from the marketplace to the waterfront. Once they left, Coquarro latched the door behind them, leaving him and Orangecloak alone to wait and leave last.

He came to stand before her, his big hands on her shoulders. "Are you ready, Red?"

"As much as I ever will be," she answered firmly while reaching into the pocket of her trousers and drawing out a green ribbon to tie back her red hair into a neat tail.

Coquarro knelt and scooped up the weighty satchel that had been between his feet where he sat and slung it across a shoulder. From within he drew a brown, linen cloak and handed it over. "I have your other one tied in a neat little bundle and at the ready."

"Good," she said with a nod as she fastened the light cloak about her shoulders and drew the deep hood down to cover her face. "Let's be off."

"And may good fortune be upon us," Coquarro added as he brought his own hood up.

Outside the air was sultry hot and Orangecloak sympathised with Lazlo's disdain at wearing a cloak at all, even if it was made of linen. She and Coquarro walked side by side down a dirt road, passing a few other farmsteads. There were but a few in this one corner of the city that were permitted to keep small patches of land for livestock and produce, nestled safely beneath the walls. The family of Coramae had been one such farmstead, though when the family fell from grace, their home and land had been forfeited to the EMP. Their house and shed sat empty, waiting to be razed so the land could be sold off.

Green knolls and quaint homes soon gave way to crowded houses that were lumped together and fronting on streets bustling with activity. People passed, shoulders were bumped, but no heed was paid to the pair of cloaked strangers. As long as her face and trademark hair were covered, Orangecloak could get about fairly easily in any city. Even then, passage wasn't impossible, provided she wasn't wearing the brightly coloured cloak her name derived from.

A couple were walking in the street ahead of Orangecloak and Coquarro. The man wore a grey, velvet suit and matching wide brimmed hat and the woman was in a light blue dress and white bonnet. Their pace was tediously slow and Orangecloak nudged Coquarro to make a move to walk around them.

"There you are. I was starting to think you had second thoughts on this whole operation," the woman suddenly said to Orangecloak as they began to walk around them.

Orangecloak looked into her face to find Merion Dollen, sister of Ellarie, staring back. The younger Dollen was light complexioned and freckled like Orangecloak, with her own head of red hair falling in long, natural curls. Given those similarities and the fact that they were of near the same height and size, Merion had taken on the role of being Orangecloak's double. Whenever a protest was staged, Merion was there and dressed in raiment to match Orangecloak to serve as a diversion during the inevitable fleeing.

She eyeballed Merion and Joyce beside her, dressed in the suit. "Where did you two get these getups?" Orangecloak inquired whimsically.

Merion shrugged nonchalantly. "An untended clothesline behind a large house is a great place to find a new wardrobe."

"You know I don't approve of that," Orangecloak reminded Merion with a hard stare. "We may be known as the Thieves, but we do not steal from the people."

Joyce Keena, the lean muscled, hard hitting, blonde haired lover of Merion leaned out around Merion's bonnet to get a glimpse of Orangecloak. "The people we took these clothes from will not miss them," she argued while rolling her shoulders and looking herself over.

"Look at this suit, the man who can afford this is not in a sore need for coin."

There was little time to squabble over it and Orangecloak reluctantly pushed beyond the issue to more pressing matters. "I assume you're both wearing your own clothes beneath those outfits. We're going ahead with the plan. You might have been told by the others already: Tryst Reine is not going to be an issue for us. Where is your unit?"

"Aye, my sister came through here and told us everything," Merion replied, her voice dropping to her usual, serious tone. "I left Ami and Alia in the market with a plan to draw away the riflemen on the rooftops. Barring something unforeseen cropping up, your path should be cleared by the time you need to flee."

All while they talked, the four kept moving towards their destination. Directly ahead lay a crossroads between the poorer neighbourhood they were leaving and the more upscale homes and businesses of the upper reaches of the middle class. The streets were wider, but no less crowded, and the four turned off the main road and into a dusty alley. Orangecloak's two lieutenants ducked into a tiny, covered alcove and immediately began undressing.

With the bonnet yanked off, Merion made a single, deft move and pulled the dress over her head. Beneath was a full outfit nearly identical to Orangecloak's, right down to her worn and weathered leather boots.

"You've done great work, as usual," Orangecloak complimented them. "Merion, I want you in place on the roof of the naval recruitment building. Hide behind the spire and wait for me." She turned her attention to Joyce, who was down to her smallclothes and digging her own gear from a satchel that had been stashed in a crate. "When the guard's reinforcements arrive, I'm going to head towards the waterfront. Myles and Coquarro will be with me and we'll leave town near the lighthouse tower in the southwest corner of town. I'm leaving it to you to ensure that everyone else gets out. We'll convene at the Stone Horn in the south woods."

Joyce gave Orangecloak a confident wink while pulling a faded, short-sleeved tunic over her head and topping it with a padded leather vest. "You can count on me," Joyce assured Orangecloak as she cinched her vest tight with a matching leather belt. "I'll be sure to get all of ours out safely before evening."

Orangecloak glanced about the alley to ensure they were alone. "I have faith in you," she said, while extending a fist towards her lieutenants. "We are the Thieves."

"Stealing back freedom," they answered, touching her knuckles with their own.

That's where she left them, fastening old, faded cloaks into place and doing final inventory checks.

For her and Coquarro, it was time to go into the heart of the city and tug at its strings.

Aquas Bay was not a spacious city, by any means, but it was densely populated. The thick, stone walls that protected the denizens from the roving gangs of raiders that lay beyond had made expansion of the city limits impossible. As a result, it seemed as though everyone in the Southlands that had emigrated to the protective embrace of Aquas Bay had just piled in on top of one another. Nowhere was that more evident than in the tightly packed neighbourhoods surrounding the marketplace. Here, it was teeming with people at all hours of the day. These were the working poor, mostly and those even less fortunate than they.

It was easy for Orangecloak to blend in here, so long as she kept her head down. These were the citizens she worked to endear herself to, and her work all around Illiastra had yielded her celebrity and empathy from many. Though few among the populace dared to vocalise their support for the Thieves, Orangecloak could see who her sympathisers were when they recognised her face. Some nodded in silent understanding, while others just stared, with hope and anxiousness in their eyes. They would not alert the guards or impede her passage, but rather they would wait and see if she would speak.

If there were eyes on her this day, Orangecloak could not see them through the sea of humanity before her. The closer she and Coquarro came to the market, the closer the crowds were pressed. Soon they were beneath the archway built between two shops that stood as the entrance to the market, with neither sympathiser nor detractor aware that Lady Orangecloak was among them. Her eyes fell to the wrought iron lettering dangling from the red, brick, arching span: A Free Market for a Free People.

Except it never was free, was it? Orangecloak thought to herself. *The Elite Merchants peddle in that illusion while holding the reins in their own greedy hands.*

Another woman in a hooded cloak sidled up beside the pair and looked directly at Orangecloak. "My girls are in position," Ellarie told her in a voice that was equal parts nervousness and excitement. "Are you ready?"

"I am ready, aye," Orangecloak answered. "Joyce, Ami, and Alia are due on the roofs any moment to lead the riflemen away. That's your cue."

Ellarie gave Orangecloak a nod and disappeared back into the masses once more.

Inside the market, the air somehow seemed stuffier and it was stiflingly hot. Orangecloak scanned the rooftops, looking for the three women or Myles and finding neither of them.

Coquarro leaned down to her ear level. "Shall we go for the merchant's stall in front of Benson's Jewels again?" he asked.

"Aye, it's the best location," Orangecloak replied while still looking about worriedly. "I don't see any of ours up above yet."

"They will come, Red," he assured her. "Joyce was still readying herself when we left her. Give her a little more time."

She knew Coquarro was right, yet she remained nervous all the same. In the four years since Orangecloak's appointment to the title of Field Commander, her Thieves had grown quite efficient at planning and executing these demonstrations. There had been many before and usually her group came away unscathed. Though without fail, her stomach fluttered and a dark thought crept forward from the recesses of her mind. Each time the Thieves succeeded the thought grew louder until it practically screamed at her. *Have I pressed my luck too far? Is this the day it all comes apart at the seams and I fall from grace? So what if it is? The wheels are in motion and I can go no way but forward.*

If this is it, let them say I went out fighting.

If this is it, may the dream live on after me.

If this is it...

"We're here."

Orangecloak looked around to find that she and Coquarro were huddled between two stacks of crates beside a whitewashed brick wall and he was staring at her curiously. "Now is not the time for the mind to wander. Prepare yourself, for your moment is at hand."

Despite the doubt plaguing her, Orangecloak managed to give Coquarro a smile that she hoped displayed some measure of confidence. "Don't worry, Coquarro, I am. I was merely going over my speech to myself," she lied. "Could you go and check the skyline and let me know when Joyce and the others have begun their distractions?"

He gave her a wink and half of a smile of his own. "Of course, Red, I'd be glad to."

Once he had gone back into the fray, Orangecloak pulled her hood tighter, crouched low and took a pair of long, deep breaths to clear her mind. She heard men shouting and a collective gasp from the crowd and shortly after it Coquarro's voice, drawing her back once more. "It is done. Joyce and her pair of Thieves have sprung and Ellarie's crew have drawn the ground patrols away." He squeezed around her, put his back to the wall and cupped his hands at waist level. "Go now, so that their effort is not in vain."

"Aye, I'm ready," she said, finding her will in that instant. Her right hand went to the clasp of the brown cloak and it fell away to the ground. Repeating a move practiced a hundred times before, Orangecloak set a foot into Coquarro's hands and his strong arms vaulted her upward. As the lip of the roof of the stall came into sight, she grabbed it and clung tightly with her fingertips, feet scrabbling for purchase in the mortar lines of the bricks. With a last push she was up and looking over the whole market.

From here, she could see almost the entire square laid out before her. It gave her a good vantage point of the main access points, though she was not so high up

that she could not be heard. Her eyes fell to Coquarro, himself opening his satchel to retrieve a bundle that he threw to her above. It was snagged from the air deftly, her hands working quickly to untie the brown twine that bound the treasured garment that was her namesake.

It was a cloak that once had been orange but in time had faded to the colour of a peach. As she flung it across her shoulders and clasped it into place, Orangecloak could nearly feel the eyes of the crowd beginning to fall on her. There were whispers and even more heads turning away from the ruckus the other Thieves had incited to the woman standing high above them. *One more thing,* she remembered while reaching for the ribbon that held her ponytail, pulling it loose to let her red hair tumble across her shoulders. *Whoever hasn't noticed my presence before, most certainly will now.*

Orangecloak looked across the market and at the faces before her, raised a hand high and inhaled. "We live in a nation controlled by men who rule over us with fear," she started, speaking in a loud, powerful voice. "These men would make us believe that they are a single, unified entity bigger than any one single person and that we are each alone against them. They send out papers and criers to convince us that we can do nothing to touch them and that we survive because they allow it." She paused, looked about and made eye contact with as many as she could in that moment and spoke again. "I come before you today to tell you that is a lie."

All had turned to face her by then, poor and wealthy alike until a silence had fallen over the entire market. Far to her right, Orangecloak noticed a man in a dapper suit leaning on the railing of a second floor balcony that belonged to a bank. He was joined by others shortly after, one of which she knew to be a city councillor. Even they, the very people she opposed, stared at her in silent anticipation, waiting to hear what she might say.

She began to pace atop the roof in slow, deliberate steps. "When I look at all the men, women, and children before me, I see thousands of faces staring back, all standing side by side, together, if but for a moment. There are more people before me now than all the lords, ministers and councillors in the Elite Merchant Party together."

A man near the front who looked to be but a few years Orangecloak's senior laughed at that statement. "They have an army!" he shouted at her.

"An army comprised of your brothers, fathers, and neighbours," Orangecloak countered without missing a step. "The EMP arrives at your doors to force your own into their ranks, they give them a wage and tell them to do their bidding or rot in Biddenhurst. However, for their own worth, the EMP is but sixty men called lord and minister with five city councillors each for a total of three hundred and sixty. That's all, just three hundred and sixty flesh and blood men, no better than you or I. Just scared, frightened, little men hiding behind an army made of your own to protect themselves from you."

From over the whispering waves of the crowd, she could hear town guards yelling orders to the crowd and to one another to move aside. Out of the corner of her eye, she caught something glinting in the sunlight and looked to the rooftops to her left to see a shape she knew to be Myles. He was using a little mirror to send a signal to Lazlo to spur the brawl on the waterfront. Orangecloak knew that she was growing short of time and went on hurriedly.

"Yet, those few control almost all the wealth and resources of our country and grow fat and wealthy from our labours," she went on to explain to the crowd. "What do we, the many, get for making them, the few, into the controlling hoarders that they are? We are left to survive on the scraps and given the 'right' to serve our overlords. That's it: A mere existence, expectations of servitude and overwhelming fear. That is all we are granted under our current government. The only hope the EMP leaves to the people is that we might die before we are sent off to the prison city to be made slaves of."

There was murmuring from the crowd by now. From the voices closest to her, Orangecloak could hear supporters and detractors alike. The guards had backed off, likely to attend to the melee Lazlo's crew had started, though a few individuals remained, weaving their way through the crowd toward her.

Orangecloak spread her arms wide, in open embrace. "There is a hope, though, however small it may be. It is a hope shared by those like the Thieves and me. Do any among you know what that hope is?"

A woman's voice somewhere to Orangecloak's left spoke up above the others: "You hope that a pox will sweep through the EMP?"

"Do you hope for a quick death when they catch you?" a man japed right before Orangecloak's very feet to a chorus of laughter from other sceptics.

"You hope that we will somehow fear a band of lawless brigands?" roared a voice far to the left and she turned her head to see the same city councillor. His fists tightly gripped the wrought iron railing of the balcony and he leaned out over it.

As she was about to answer, Orangecloak spotted a man standing on the street directly in the line of sight between her and the bank's balcony. Their eyes locked and she froze where she stood. Despite the scorching heat, the man was clad head to heel in black clothing, with a long mane of straight, fiery red hair that touched his waist.

Even dressed as he is, with that head of hair I still might doubt who he was if not for those eyes, Orangecloak thought to herself.

They were a strikingly bright shade of green that she could discern despite the distance. Eyes of that shade were a rare feature and unique to a select few people from the faraway continent of Gildriad. As rare as it was among the three nations of Gildriad, to see someone with the 'Gildraddi Greens' in Illiastra was a rarity above measure and it left no doubt. *Somehow, I knew you would come, Master of Blades,* Orangecloak thought. *I tried to convince myself otherwise, but I knew you would not stay away. If this is it and you are here for me, then may you hear what I have to say, Tryst Reine.*

Orangecloak steeled her resolve, cleared her throat and answered the calls. "Our hope, our tiny, meagre little ray of hope, is that you will learn what the Thieves have all come to know: That power is but nothing but an illusion. The men we give power to are people just as ordinary as you and I, no more worthy of reverence and submission than any other. It is not we who should fear this minority of mere mortals. It is they who should fear a wakened, unified people."

There was a smattering of applause and roaring from the gathered mass, however it was clear that most were still mistrustful, apathetic, or even outright dismissive of her message.

Orangecloak tried to keep her attention on the nearing guards, though her eyes seemed intent on wandering back to the Master of Blades. He was still as stone, arms folded and staring back. On his hip, he wore a sword in a red, leather scabbard and Orangecloak knew it must be that fearsome sword made of dwarven blacksteel he was said to wield. Yet, it sat as still as he.

Have my words compelled him to stay his blade? She wondered briefly, before the councillor above him bellowed out once more.

"As you can see, no man here with any good sense will pay heed to raving woman who does not know her place," the councillor roared above the growing noise of the crowd. "You and your kind are naught but verminous, godless outlaws worthy of only continual scorn, a noose for your necks, and the eternal damnation that awaits you."

The soldiers were close enough that Orangecloak could make out brass buttons on the blue jackets of their uniforms. She turned one last time to the councillor, looking between him and the still unmoving Master of Blades below. "No, Councillor, we are none of those things. We are exactly what your party named us all those years ago."

A gloved hand reached for her ankle and Orangecloak kicked it away. She backed towards the wall of the jewellery store and looked to the roof to find Coquarro already there and waiting. He knelt and extended a hand, and Orangecloak darted up the wall to him. She grabbed at the ruts in the mortar and any outcropping bricks she could until she could make a lunge for Coquarro's outstretched arm. In a single, strong lift, she was carried to the relative safety of the upper rooftop, where she turned and faced the awestruck crowd once more. "We are the Thieves and we are stealing back freedom!" she called from the top of her lungs.

The people below erupted in a mixture of praise and derision, coming alive as she stood there, arms raised. The councillor was barking orders to the soldiers in the streets and whomever hadn't reached Orangecloak's previous position were doing anything they could to get free of the tightly packed throng. At first, she thought that the Master of Blades had would surely be advancing on her and she scanned the area to the left of the jewellery store for him. Much to Orangecloak's surprise, she followed the trail all the way back to the street where Tryst Reine had been, finding him standing in exactly the same spot.

Coquarro grabbed her by the arm and began to haul her away as soldiers began piling onto the roof of the stall below them. "Red, we must leave with haste if we are to get out of this alive and free," he advised her.

"Did you see him?" Orangecloak asked as they began running. "Tryst Reine was there."

"Then we should run even faster, Red," Coquarro cautioned, with his voice full of urgency, yet still somehow calm and measured. "I do not want to face him this day."

The guards shouted at them from below to stay put and surrender.

Given that Orangecloak and Coquarro had no intention of doing any such thing, they broke into a run.

They leapt from one roof to the next several times across the narrow gaps. The fifth roof they came to was further and lower and required a longer jump and a rolling landing. The next building was too high to leap to, but a balcony with an open door was at the same elevation as they and the two made for it. An old man was seated inside at a small table, fanning himself in the sultry heat. Orangecloak apologised for the intrusion and asked if there was another way out of the apartment. Despite his initial shock, he nodded and pointed to the right of where they came in to a long, open window.

Coquarro looked out through it and came back with a scowl on his face. "That's a one way trip to the alley below. We're not looking to die just yet."

"No, don't go out the window. Look up, young one," the man told them.

Orangecloak looked above Coquarro's head. "There's a hatch!" she pointed out to Coquarro, leaving him to open it while turning back to the old man. "I'm sorry again for barging in. Thank you for all your help."

"Least I can do. Steal back freedom, young ones!" he called out to them as they climbed the sliding ladder to the roof above. Coquarro pulled it shut behind him and they took off southward once more.

Guards were climbing onto the roofs wherever they could find ladders and were trying their best to catch up to the Thieves. "Stop at once!" one called from nearby to the left while pulling a pistol from his belt. When neither Orangecloak nor Coquarro complied, he fired his lone shot, fortunately missing them both.

For a second, she turned and looked back at him and all about, seeing only bluecoats clambering up after them. *No sign of him. If he did give pursuit he's not chasing us from up here,* Orangecloak told herself.

"Come on, Red, not too far now!" Coquarro shouted at her when he finally noticed that she wasn't beside him any longer.

They took off again, running and jumping two more roofs until they were at the catwalk that allowed the guards direct access from the recruitment centre to the rooftops.

The rickety, wooden footbridge shook unsteadily beneath their feet as they made their way, crossing over a wide, busy street filled with people, horses, and carriages below.

Behind the tall spire that stretched high enough to peek atop the city walls, they found Merion and Myles, crouched low and waiting. Along with the apparel she was already wearing to match Orangecloak, Merion had tied a linen replica of the signature cloak across her shoulders. It wasn't an exact copy of the famous orange cloak, but served more than ably to make Merion an excellent decoy.

As much as Orangecloak would have like to, there was no time to stop for a rest. As they had done many times before, Coquarro switched places with Myles without a word and the two teams bolted in opposite directions out of hiding.

The guards, having caught up with their targets, were crossing the rickety, wooden overpass one man at a time when the four Thieves burst forth from behind the spire. Orangecloak estimated there to be a dozen or so in total, some atop the same roof as the Thieves, but most waiting to cross.

As they caught sight of the two pairs of runners, every man among them seemed to have a different idea of which one to pursue. They cursed and shouted over one another and in trying to decide which redheaded, orange-cloaked woman was the real one, had stalled in their tracks.

When Orangecloak looked over her shoulder again, she saw that roughly half of the guards that had crossed the rickety catwalk were now giving chase of her and

Myles. The other half, she suspected, were hot on the trail of Merion and Coquarro.

This leg of the escape was more suited to Myles, who was far more agile and dexterous than Coquarro. The route they had mapped out led them downhill, but the jumps between buildings were longer and the drops higher than they had been.

It was no secret that this sort of risky, dangerous behaviour was commonplace for the Thieves, and to Coquarro's credit, he was passably good at the acrobatic feats. For Myles though, it was as if he was bred for it. The man saw nothing in his path as an insurmountable obstacle and for as long as Orangecloak had known him, she still found herself barely able to keep up.

Finally, after an exhausting sprint, the two of them came to the waterfront area. With a wide, open street below, the only way left to them was down. In a flash Myles had vaulted over the rear of the building, grabbing the roof's lip as he turned in mid-air and hanging from the side. Orangecloak followed suit and the two began jumping back and forth between it and the previous building they had leapt from, getting closer to the ground with every timed jump. They touched down safely and ducked inside the first unlocked door they found, leaving the door open a crack to listen for their pursuers.

"They're gone!" one guard shouted from somewhere overhead.

Another made the jump to the building facing the waterfront street and after a tense few minutes returned to his comrades. "I'm not seeing any immediate way down, but it's the only way they could have gone unless they climbed the town walls."

"The gods be damned!" a voice shouted that Orangecloak could only assume to belong to that of the highest-ranking guard among the bunch. "Hurry up and let's find a way down. There should be a ladder a few houses back we can use. Detain every red haired woman you see, no exceptions. If we've lost sight of her, she might already be in disguise."

Orangecloak exhaled at last and let her body relax. "That should give us a few minutes. Let's get out of here and make sure we put as much distance between us and them as we can." Ever so casually, she began tying back her hair into a tight tail to hide it away. For the first time since leaving the former woodshed of Coramae's family, Orangecloak actually felt calm and as she worked on the ponytail, she idly asked Myles, "Where did we end up to anyhow?"

"As to that..." Myles began to say, trailing off as he looked beyond where they had been huddled beside the door.

It was at that moment that she felt many eyes upon her, all at once. Slowly, Orangecloak turned in the direction Myles was facing and looked across a tavern full of patrons, all male and most of them at least a decade older than she and Myles. The pair of Thieves had just so happened to slip inside the rear delivery door of the establishment. Though the alcove the door rested in was darkened, it was directly beside the bar and in plain sight of everyone within.

The recognition on the faces of the men sitting shoulder to shoulder was plain to see. There was no way for Orangecloak to feasibly deny who she was, especially in light of the fact that she was still wearing the cloak she was named for. The only thing left to wonder was if these men saw her as a friend or a foe.

In an effort to gauge as much, Orangecloak took a single, careful step forward, her hands out with her palms raised upward. "Gentlemen, I apologise for disturbing you," she said as a peace offering. "We mean no trouble and we'll be leaving as quickly as we came."

Not one of them made a move to answer her, though their stares remained fixed. She glanced to Myles, who was clearly feeling every bit as nervous as she was and they began to slowly back away towards the rear door.

A big, gruff looking fellow with hairy arms, a thick beard, a fading hairline and a menacing face began to advance on them. Given that he was wearing an apron, Orangecloak guessed he was the barkeeper and she was about to apologise to him once more when he reached up high to a shelf unseen.

Myles began to work the latch on the door and Orangecloak was ready to make a bolt for it when the barkeep called out to them, "Wait just a moment, you two."

They froze in place, Orangecloak's heart beating ferociously in her chest.

The keeper's hand came away from the shelf and in it was an old, floppy, felt hat. He beat a layer of dust off it with his other hand and plopped it down on Orangecloak's head. "That should help to keep your hair covered," he said sternly, but not unkindly. "No one here wants to go to Biddenhurst on your account, miss, so I suggest you take off that cloak before you go so that no one sees it. Then scurry out that back door and make sure none of the guards see you and want to come sniffing about. Do we have a deal?"

"Yes, of course, thank you," Orangecloak answered with a bow. She undid her own cloak, rolled it quickly around an arm and stuffed it into Myles' satchel. The brown, linen cloak Myles had been wearing was then given to Orangecloak to further conceal her clothing, which the guards would most certainly be on the lookout for. With a last nod, the pair turned back to the door, checked that the alley was clear and left hastily.

The main road running along the waterfront was a hive of activity and there certainly was a heavy presence of guards about, but none seemed the slightest bit interested in Orangecloak, Myles, or the pursuit of the Thieves. The two strode amongst the townsfolk casually, trying to act as though they belonged and saw no eyes being cast their way.

As Orangecloak got a peek in the general direction that the crowd were focused she realised why the guards were so preoccupied. "I'll have to give Lazlo full credit for that distraction he devised. It worked far better than I could have imagined," she said to Myles in a low voice.

The majority of the guards had been dispatched to the pier and were still working to quell the brawl that Lazlo and his unit had instigated there. Without that, Orangecloak had no doubt that there would be far more men searching for her.

A racket to her left caught her attention and Orangecloak glanced to find the guards that had been chasing her and Myles across the rooftops were now on the ground and searching noisily through everything they saw. "Our pursuers are one street over," she informed Myles. "Just keep walking casually and they shouldn't be too interested in us."

By mid-afternoon, the two had walked unbothered along the south side of Aquas Bay. As they went, the city fell away to a smattering of modest homes. Local fishermen who docked their skiffs and dories in the

many coves that dotted this side of the naval port owned everything here. It was as ideal a location as one could get in the Southlands, Orangecloak knew. They were offered the protection of the Aquas Bay's imposing walls without the noise and bluster of the city. At the end of the long wall, the duo found the old lighthouse tower. There was always a keeper on duty and no less than two guards to keep watch, but passing beyond them unnoticed was nothing Orangecloak was ever bothered by.

The tower was built centuries before, atop a cliff overlooking the ocean. In that long time, those cliffs had been eaten away by the rough seas that roared through in the early autumn nearly every year. It had been told to Orangecloak that from the sea, the tower looked like it might well tumble to the rocks below at a moment's notice. The former basement was left open and exposed to the elements and was quite nearly rotted away, but enough remained that it made for a fairly dangerous, albeit traversable passageway to the other side of the wall.

For Orangecloak and Myles, it was a relatively easy descent over the rock face. Far below lay jagged rocks and crashing waves, but Orangecloak knew better than to look at them and she kept her focus solely on her own climbing. Finally, her foot touched lumber and she dared to look below for the first time, finding herself on a support beam of the tower's ruined cellar. She put her stomach to the rock wall and began shimmying along the beam until she came to an alcove that allowed for a little more room to manoeuvre. Myles was following close behind and they continued along the wall, stomachs against its smooth surface, feet shuffling along another beam. The climb out to the gulch was far easier than the descent and within no time they were on the other side of the city walls once more.

Ahead lay the old forest far away from the city centre that had been allowed to creep its way right into the shadow of the ancient lighthouse.

Myles waited until they were beneath the canopy of the trees before he asked the burning question: "How did the protest go?"

At first, she deigned to answer, letting herself breathe deep of the forest air and relax. Overhead the songbirds chirped and sang sweetly and gave Orangecloak an overwhelming sense of calm. Her stride slowed to a saunter and she undid both her hair ribbon and Myles' cloak. It was then she remembered the hat and took it off as well, opting to carry it in both hands and use it as a fan. "It went well, I thought," she answered Myles just as he was growing even more impatient. "A councillor happened to be in the market, I think it was Councillor Havellan. He got riled up by the things I said and I think I answered his jeering quite well."

"That's not all, is it?" Myles asked concernedly. "I had to take off and get to Merion's location midway through, I missed much of your speech. Pray tell, what happened?"

"You were right, Myles. Tryst Reine did show up," Orangecloak finally admitted.

His eyes went wide in surprise and he began glancing over his shoulder, as if he was expecting to be followed. "By the gods, I had no idea that the Master of Blades saw you. Why didn't you tell me this sooner?"

She shook her head slowly, reflecting back on the sight of him. "That's the thing, Myles. He didn't make a move to capture me. All the Master of Blades did was stand in the crowd with his arms folded, listening and watching. Even when Coquarro and I were making our escape, I looked back and there he was, still in the exact same spot."

That didn't seem to satisfy Myles and he continued to look all about. "Damn him, I bet he followed us. I should double back to the lighthouse and try to get him while he's climbing the rocks. It might be the only chance to take him unawares."

"Tryst Reine is not coming after us, Myles," Orangecloak said reassuringly. "He watched me leave and made no effort to do anything. I don't know why, but I can tell you that we're alive now for only one reason."

"And what do you think that is?" Myles asked.

Orangecloak straightened, looking him in the eye. "Tryst Reine had no desire to arrest us."

The City That Hid From Time Itself

Original publication:
***Fantasy From The Rock* (2017)**

Have you ever wondered why the two major continents of the Known World of **Gold & Steel** are bordered by massive, impassable mountain ranges, a storming southern ocean, and an inhospitable icy wasteland? If so, then follow us to three centuries before **As Fierce as Steel** and meet Arvelle and Brayda, a human and a dwarf respectively, who are out to unveil the mysteries that bind the Known World.

In **The City That Hid From Time Itself**, our intrepid explorers find themselves being hired by an elf in need of a guide to an ancient city that they discovered and had already guided his peculiar brother to. Uncover mysteries new and old in this exciting tale!

From the Author: "The characters of Arvelle and Brayda were wrote with the dual goal of giving me a playful side project to break the mood of **Gold & Steel** and to bring curious readers to the edges of the **Gold & Steel** world. I always really enjoyed the adventurer and journey tales from the stories of my youth and I really wanted to bring that to **Gold & Steel** so that I could give that style of storytelling a try for myself. In the process, Arvelle and Brayda became favourite characters of mine and I hope to have the chance to write more stories for them in the future."

The City That Hid From Time Itself

That's half of your pay," the male elf said to the two women, plunking down a hefty bag of coins. "The other half will be paid to you upon a safe return, as you promised me."

The two women eyed the bag and then one another, neither saying a word for some time. It was only after the lapse in silence broached the threshold of being uncomfortable that Arvelle spoke, brushing back the long, blonde curls of her hair from her face as she said, "Your turn or mine, Brayda?"

Across the table of the booth, the brunette dwarven woman contemplated for a moment before offering a reply: "Mine. You counted for this one's brother."

"So I did," Arvelle said, pushing the bag toward Brayda. "It's all yours, then."

The elf seemed mystified by their behaviour and slid into the booth beside Brayda in the corner of the tiny inn's common room. "Isn't it rude to count the coin of a paying person when said person is right before you?" he asked pointedly in a low voice.

"An honest person would have nothing to worry about, Mister Blackspar," Arvelle replied as she met his concerned stare. As she spoke, Brayda had already undone the drawstring on the bag and began slowly emptying large, brass coins from the Elven Forest out onto the lacquered surface of the stained table.

"Did my brother leave you short on payment?" Blackspar asked in an annoyed voice before continuing, "He is admittedly quite crass, but that would be entirely unlike him. Regardless, if that is the case I will gladly pay what he did not. I assure you that I want to see these ancient ruins as desperately as he did and you two are the only ones who know where they are."

It dawned on Arvelle that the two were being perhaps too curt with their new client and she gave him a reassuring smile. "Oh no, Mister Blackspar, Antitus paid us in full, I swear it on my life. It is just policy based on other experiences. By our method, we can confirm in your presence that the correct amount is there and neither party can later claim to be wronged."

"That is sound policy, my apologies," the elf stated, relaxing enough to motion the barkeep over while still speaking to the women. "I may be stating the obvious here, but I am not accustomed to hiring mercenaries."

"It's all there," Brayda declared. "Nine hundred and fifty Elven Brasses now and the same amount upon your safe return, as agreed. Also, I should point out that Arvelle and I are not mercenaries, ser, we're adventurers."

"Right, of course, I have no idea how I might have made such a mistake," he added sarcastically. "Though it might be on account of the fact that I am soliciting guiding and protective services from not just any graduate of the University of Combative Arts, but a Master of Blades."

"*The* Master of Blades and only the third to be named so in five hundred years," Brayda said

defensively of her dear, human friend while replacing the coins in their bag. "You would do well to remember that, Mister Blackspar."

"Please, no need to call me Mister Blackspar. I prefer Zahnthiel, or better yet, call me Zahn, as my friends do."

The two women exchanged a glance and Arvelle said what she knew they were both thinking, "For us to call you Zahn would imply we were even acquaintances."

The elf sighed loudly at their defensiveness. "Whatever did my brother do to make you think so poorly of me by association?"

"Beyond being generally rude and ignorant, you mean?" Brayda jumped in before Arvelle could. "He refused to share in his research, called us disparaging names, kept us well beyond our anticipated return date and then cast us off when we tried to convince him to leave. In short, he was an arsehole."

"I wish I could say that was out of character for him, but if I did, I would be named a liar," Zahn admitted despondently. "At any rate, tell me about these ruins you two discovered all the way out here in the far western reaches of the Gildriad Midlands. Do you have any notion of what my brother sought there?"

Arvelle leaned forward to give him the answer that the two of them had already puzzled out from their recent ordeal. "Indeed, we both know what he sought and it was what we and all adventurers before and after us seek: to push beyond the boundaries of the world as we know it and escape the prison of contentedness to dwell in the freedom of the unknown."

That elicited a humming noise from the elf that bordered on sounding impressed. "That is quite the earful, I admit. Though I may not seem it myself, I too am an adventurer. In fact, as unbelievable as it may be, my brother and I made for an incredible team. Not unlike you two, now that I think about it. Certainly, there is no mystery as to what he sought in the grand scheme of things, for it's as you said. What I am interested to know is what drew him to *these* ruins in particular."

"Order the stew," Brayda advised him.

He raised a single brow in confusion. "I beg your pardon?"

"The barkeep is approaching and will ask if you want stew or soup, as it is all they offer. I'm telling you to go with the stew and pair it with the ale."

As forecasted, the barkeeper was standing before the booth within seconds, hands buried in the pocket of his apron and a weary look on his bearded face. "What'll it be, mate?" he asked in a particularly disinterested voice.

"I shall have the stew and ale, I suppose, with much thanks," Zahn replied with a shrug.

"One stew and brew it is, then," the barman answered, turning back to the bar as quickly as he came from it.

The elf turned to face Brayda, still slightly puzzled. "What reason did you have for advising me on the stew over the soup?"

"The stew and the soup are one in the same. He merely adds more water to the former to make the latter," she explained with a nonchalant shrug.

"Oh. Well then in that case, I thank you for the suggestion," he stated while looking only mildly put off by that revelation.

The barkeep was back once more with the food and drink, placing bowl and horn before Zahnthiel with a simultaneous 'thunk'. "You paying for that with brasses, my Elven friend?" he asked, not waiting for a reply. "It'll be one each for the stew and the ale in that case."

"Why yes," Zahn responded while digging into the pocket of the long, dark blue overcoat he wore. "And I'll give you one more for your trouble, thank you."

With a grunt and a nod for thanks, the bartender left them in private once more and the elf turned his attention squarely back on the women. "Alright, now that everything is settled, I'll hear it: what did Antitus want in those ruins?"

"We don't know," Arvelle stated bluntly. "Your brother was an impenetrable fortress as far as his intentions and emotions went. He would not share in his research whatsoever, and while touring the city he never so much as gave a hint of consideration for anything we showed him. After taking him all the way there, he might have at least given us the courtesy of an explanation, but no. We were given only silence on the matter at first."

"At first?" Zahn queried, hanging on those two words above all after he took a spoonful of the stew to taste. "So you're saying that his demeanour changed at some point during the expedition?"

"It's difficult to explain, to be honest," Arvelle began of her recollection. "Brayda and I have been on many expeditions with all sorts of characters over the last few years, but neither of us can think of a similar case to Antitus. You see, he kept up that icy façade we had come to know until we came across a particular building. It was not extraordinary, by any means. In fact, it was one of dozens of tall, round buildings that all looked unremarkably similar. Yet, after taking a gander throughout it, your brother became entirely fixated on the place."

Zahn hummed aloud at that while working a mouthful of stew down. The elf's gaze had fallen away from his company and a look of contemplation had come over his face. When his food was swallowed, he turned to Arvelle. "What sort of building was it? What do you think the ancient people might have used it for?"

"It was a large building, one that is commonly found among ruins found across the known world," Brayda said, stepping into the conversation. "We have seen the size and general layout before and those same buildings are found throughout the same ruins, looking nearly identical to one another. It wasn't the first Antitus had seen either, nor even the last, but it was that one above the rest that became the object of his obsession. As far as Arvelle and I were concerned, they were simply marketplaces or public meeting areas or perhaps even storage spaces. So common they were that neither one of us thought much of them."

Upon Brayda describing the building, the elf had dug into his long overcoat and produced a leather-bound journal bound by a matching thong. It was hastily untied and Zahn was soon flipping pages madly until he found what has was looking for, whereupon he laid the book on the table for both women to see. "Did you see anything carved into the walls that might resemble these sketches here?"

His finger tapped back and forth between two pages worth of large, detailed, spiralling symbols drawn out with a graphite stick.

Both women were familiar with the carvings and Arvelle was the first to point out as much. "Glyphs, aye, there were three on the one wall. They're usually found in the bigger buildings. Brayda and I have figured them to be the words of the ancients, used in this context to describe the building itself. Much like how there is a sign above the door of this building that says 'Inn'."

"Oh no, these glyphs are not as ordinary as to say common things like 'inn' or 'market' or something so plain as that," Zahn declared incredulously, his eyes going wide at the very notion of such.

Unabated, he went on, "When my brother still worked beside me, we had found smaller, more simplistic markings to indicate single words. A large glyph such as these can say more in a single drawing than a hundred of our own written words, even when compared to the old Elven language. Look at how intricate the designs are and recall, if you will, how much space one carving takes upon a structure's wall. Three is practically the entirety of a whole, wide stone wall of a building that you thought might house a marketplace."

"Do you know what these glyphs say, then?" Brayda inquired excitedly, sharing her excitement with Arvelle in a glance as the two leaned in even closer to study the drawings.

Zahn sighed ruefully at the question before replying, "I'm afraid not, and it was in the trying that Antitus and I regretfully went our separate ways. The one thing we did glean from it all is that each 'piece', as we called them, starts in the centre." He continued to explain, aiding with words with a tap of a knotty shape in the very middle of the circular shape. "From there it spirals outward, with each aberration in the rounding curvature being its own word and the offshoot, erratic looking lines representing whole sentences and paragraphs. It was thought that when the ancients first wrote these glyphs, they would have looked much more unwieldy and wild. My brother and I both subscribed to the notion that what we find carved into stone walls are not original pieces, but finished versions. It would be similar to writing a story on loose paper and having it edited into a book later.

"The other thing to take note of is that these pieces are carved into stone. That alone is a process that takes great time and effort, especially given their size and intricacy. That would indicate that the pieces are at least of great cultural significance."

Brayda had a hand bent beneath her chin, her dark brown eyes scanning the pages intently. "This is all incredibly intriguing, Mister Blackspar. Were you able to translate *any* of these glyphs?"

"No, not at all, I'm sad to say. My proposal for learning more of the glyphs was to return home to the Elven Forest. I thought we could learn more by poring over the old scrolls of our own people stored in the depths of the great sentinel tree called Lanadorgh. Antitus, impetuous and impatient as he is, was of the mind that we should be spending our days traveling to every last site that can be attributed to the ancients. He felt more inclined to study the glyphs directly, with no further direction on the subject but our own intuition. I won the debate, or so I thought I had.

"One night, while I was deep below the surface in the Elven Hall of Records wing of Lanadorgh, Antitus left without warning. He even told his wife that he was only going nearby to visit a friend. By the time I emerged, I found our family in a frantic search, though I knew by then that he was returning to adventuring and that it was too late to stop him. I've been chasing him from site to site ever since, but he's far enough ahead and keeps going at such a pace that I might follow him for an Elven lifetime and never catch up with him. It's like an old

Elven phrase, 'the person who does not want to be found can never truly be called lost, for they are merely hiding from eyes that they do not want upon them'. That is the life my brother has chosen and my own guilt propels me to keep running after him, no matter how vain my search quite often feels."

"That chase has led you from the far, northeast reaches of Illiastra all the way into the western forest of the Midlands of Gildriad," Arvelle said in amazement.

"Indeed, and now I desire for you two to take me a little further west, as far as one can go without pressing yourself against the bare stone of the Gildraddi Mountain Range." He pushed his little journal even closer to the women, his voice taking on a pleading tone, "I am not my brother, I can promise you that. However, I get a sense that all three of us are invested in finding him, or at least discovering his fate after being left alone in those ruins. Furthermore, you should know that, unlike my brother, I am more than happy to tell you whatever I possibly can about the ancient people and their settlements."

The two women exchanged a telling look between one another and Arvelle could see the curiosity piquing on Brayda's face.

This wasn't a journey Arvelle had been interested in completing again. The road to the ruins was particularly dangerous, taking them through dense forest and a boggy marshland, both of which were home to quite a plethora of dangerous animals. Her friend wanted this, though, and the pay promised to be quite generous. *If this elf is true to his word, there is no telling what Brayda and I might learn from him along the way...*

"We leave at first light, Mister Blackspar," Arvelle decided, unsure if it was the elf or the dwarf that looked more excited in that moment. "You will want to be sure that you have everything in order by then. This is perhaps the most difficult trek we have ever done in a moderate climate, so I suggest you prepare yourself accordingly. There are a great deal of animals out there who would love to make a meal of you. Furthermore, the forest is dense and there are no discernible paths to speak of. If we make it to the ruins, you may well beg for death rather than make the return trip."

The two watched the elf for a moment, with his gaze off in the distance and horn of ale held just before his face, as if he were pondering the implications of Arvelle's warnings. After a time he tipped the last of his drink past his lips, swished it around his mouth audibly, and plunked the empty horn onto the table. "Oh, how I do love a good adventure," Zahn answered with sarcastic enthusiasm. "I will see you both in the morning, ladies."

The trip was everything Arvelle had promised Zahn it would be, but it was the elf who surprised both women with his energy and zest. For the journey, he had donned tan trousers and tunic, an olive green cloak and brown boots and atop it all he somehow managed to carry a weighty knapsack with remarkable ease. The women first led the elf through a dense forest of evergreen trees, the going slowed by the thick shrubbery that seemed to grow every which way. As they trekked, Zahn filled the time by sharing his vast knowledge of the fauna and florae of the forest.

After two days in the woods, they exited into a marshland so treacherous and muddy that it took them another full day of sunlight to cross. It seemed to Arvelle as though every dozen steps brought them to a new pool or bog hole to contend with and none among the three were able to avoid getting wet before it was over. The sky was turning dark as they reached the edge of the marshes and they spent the evening around a campfire, their boots and stockings hung above to dry out.

From there the path tilted upward, leading into the foothills of the Gildraddi Mountain Range. Another forest, tiny compared to the first, gave way after half a day's trek to a stony slope spotted here and there with wild grass and scattered shrubs.

Upon cresting the treeline, Zahn turned about and gazed out across the vast expanse of the Midlands of Gildriad that lay before their view. "My word, what a simply splendid sight to behold!" he exclaimed with his arms spread out, as if to embrace the horizon. "No matter where my journeys take me, I find the beauty and splendour of the world on display in all its glory and this moment shall be no exception."

"It is most certainly astounding," Brayda commented while approaching Zahn's side. She turned her focus to the mountain, drawing the elf's attention as well. "It is even more impressive from up there."

The elf craned his head to the sheer, stone wall that lay before them, and Arvelle could see his eyes scanning upward, until they came to a particularly flat plateau. "My word! Is that a vertical climb?"

Arvelle found his surprise amusing and chuckled. "Not quite, but it is still daunting. Come now, follow us."

The trio continued their ascent, coming to another halt at the point where the angle of the slope turned sharply vertical. Without prompt, Brayda dropped to her knees and began rooting through the shrubbery, a curious Zahn looking over her shoulder to see what she was doing. After a short time of digging, Brayda came away with a slab of slate rock that she carefully rolled to a place that would not allow it to slide down the hill.

"There we are," she said while brushing her hands clean on her light brown trousers. "The way is open. Now, who wants to go through first?"

With eyebrows raised high, Zahn looked from Brayda to Arvelle. "What are we going through, exactly?"

"A small hole in the rock face, practically buried behind the foliage here." Arvelle explained, amused by the elf's wonderment. *At the very least, he's far more entertaining than his brother. Antitus didn't seem to react to anything until he came across that one particular building.*

"I suppose I'll go first, just as I have every other time," Brayda said with a sigh when neither Arvelle nor Zahn volunteered. She removed her satchel and dark blue, waist-length leather coat and pushed them both through to the other side. With her things pushed beyond, she then dropped onto her stomach for a crawl that took her out of sight of the remaining two.

"You're next, Mister Blackspar." Arvelle instructed while removing her satchel, sword belt, and calf-length black leather jacket.

"It looks like a tight fit, but I'm guessing my brother fit through there and he's slightly larger than I am." Zahn responded while humming aloud and rubbing his chin.

Arvelle could feel the cool, crisp air nipping at her bare arms and she urged the elf on. "He did and he did so without a second word about it," she said while wrapping the belt tightly about the pair of scimitars she preferred to arm herself with.

"He also hummed quite a bit, like you do," Brayda called, impatiently beckoning them from within the hole. "So you two have that much in common. He didn't like to waste daylight though, and neither do I. So, if you would please hurry and crawl in here with me, we can get moving."

"Very well," Zahn relented, disrobing of his cloak and pack, sending them through first, just as Brayda had done before him. His crawl took longer than Brayda's, as the fit was tighter, though he made it through without issue.

"Fascinating!" Arvelle heard him declare when he had reached the other side, the declaration indicating well enough that he had gotten through unscathed.

The scramble was an easy one for her and she joined her companions in short order, dusting herself off hurriedly so that she could gather her things and put on her coat again. When she was on her feet and her bearings were gained, she found Brayda and Zahn fully dressed as well. Her dwarven friend stood with folded arms beside the hole, her attention on Zahn, now standing above on the landing of a narrow, stone staircase.

With his feet set precariously on outcroppings from the walls on either side of him, Zahn was leaning out over the tall structure to look out at the hillside below. He hopped down when he caught sight of the women approaching, his excited facial expression speaking quite audibly of his amazement. "This is nothing short of incredible! A staircase built right into the side of the mountain! Hidden within a carved trench, no less! What a marvellous architectural feat! Tell me, ladies, how high does it go?"

"Twenty-two flights of stairs, twelve steps apiece for two hundred and sixty-four steps," Brayda replied, her enthusiasm at a more subtle level than Zahn's. Two previous journeys up and down the stairwell had given both women more than enough time to count steps, but Brayda was undoubtedly the more astute of the two when it came to such details.

"Now I see why daylight was so important to you," Zahn said while tapping his nose intuitively. "This ascent might take a while."

Arvelle slid around the elf so that she might take the lead in the climb, adding to that thought with, "Aye and we've only conquered the first twelve. There are two hundred and fifty-two left to go and in many places, the rock is worn down considerably or entirely missing. Don't get too rhythmic in your stepping and pay attention to your surroundings, lest you find yourself flat on your face by the third flight."

There was a moment of hesitation from Zahn as he looked all about, his eyes darting to and fro in a confused manner. "Right, then. What are we waiting for?"

A worried glance was shared between Arvelle and Brayda. Both were recalling their last trip to the ruins with Zahn's brother, who had reacted almost identically to the stairwell. While he had been withdrawn and secretive for the entire trek, his demeanour had altered the moment he had crawled through the passageway to the stairs. It had been agreed upon by both women that this was the moment that Antitus' behaviour had taken a dark turn and now they were both concerned that his brother would follow suit.

As they took their first steps, Zahn began humming aloud curiously, which drew Arvelle's own curiosity and

she turned over her shoulder to catch sight of him. To both her relief and surprise she found him looking back to his normal self and a quick, shared look to Brayda relayed that information.

By the time they had reached the third flight, Zahn even found his voice again. "Brayda, as a dwarf who has been here several times, what do you make of this stairwell?" he asked, his tone careful in its delivery.

"I find it to be quite the perplexing mystery," the dwarven woman replied, evidently interested in discussing the matter. "I long believed that stone trenching was an architectural standard that had been created by the dwarves. It seemed to be something of an agreed upon fact by all the races and nations, going back to the earliest known recorded history of the world. Yet, I can find no trace of there ever being a dwarven civilisation in Gildriad. I even took the time to track down some Elven texts, which, as you know, go further back than human and dwarven records by thousands of years, and I still found nothing. For all of that, here we are, climbing an ancient, hidden stairwell that was meticulously carved into the stone face of a mountain in Gildriad using a method attributed to my people."

"Indeed, that was what I found most astonishing too," Zahn commented the very second that Brayda had finished, and it seemed to have taken all he could muster to not talk over her. "It leads me to wonder if these ancient folk were dwarvenkind. Certainly, they would be of a different variety from the dwarves, like you, that we know today. Why, it might be that it was from the ancient ones that dwarves evolved in the first place. What do you think, Brayda?"

Arvelle rounded the bend in the fourth landing, giving her a moment to see the two amidst their conversation. These were already conclusions Brayda had come to, and she had discussed them at length with Arvelle in nearly the exact place on their first excursion. For her part, Brayda was eager to revisit the topic and Zahnthiel, having been the one to raise it, was at the very least more pliable than Antitus had been.

"I can see all those explanations as plausible," Brayda added ponderously. "However, I posit that perhaps the dwarves learned the art of stone trenching from the ancient folk. Outside of the trenching, I have seen few other architectural traits that can tie the ancients to any one race or civilisation. At least not in any of the ruins I have visited, at any rate. Perhaps there is a place we have not yet found, just out of reach that holds the piece that will complete this puzzle at long last."

"Do you not think that piece may be here?" Zahn followed up, keeping the conversation going as the party rounded onto fifth landing.

In the turning, Arvelle witnessed Brayda shrugging out an answer. "If it is, Arvelle and I have yet to discover it, and your brother, if he found it, refused to tell us as much."

"Antitus, your staunch adherence to secrecy lingers on to taunt us all," Zahn muttered to himself.

The conversation came to a stop by the sixth landing, with the climb occupying the entirety of their focus. As Arvelle touched a foot to the tenth landing, she could hear both Brayda and Zahn breathing heavily, and by the twelfth, she had joined them in exhaustion. At the sixteenth, Zahn was practically begging for a break, but the women pushed him onward, promising rest at the top.

When the end came into view at last, Arvelle was feeling a buckle in her own legs. She was the first to step above the protective embrace of the stone wall of the stairwell and by then it felt as though her legs were ready to quit from beneath her.

Arvelle's pace slowed to a stagger and she felt Zahn bump into her. "For goodness sakes!" he exclaimed as he tumbled off his feet and onto his side.

Right on his heels was Brayda, all but crawling by that point. Arvelle could see a smile beneath her friend's exhaustion. As she reached Zahn, Brayda rolled onto her back beside him and gazed up at Arvelle, "We did it once more, old friend," she said between deep breaths.

Arvelle lowered herself down to a sitting position beside dwarf and elf, draping her arms over her knees with her head between her legs. "We're going to have to start charging much more to guide people, I can see that."

Brayda got a good chuckle from that and extended an arm so that Arvelle could help her sit up. The three sat there silently, looking out across the horizon while they caught their breaths.

"I told you the view was better from here, Mister Blackspar," Brayda stated jovially after some time, giving the elf a look to match.

That elicited a guffaw from him, and he turned to face both women, saying, "You were quite right, my dwarven friend. Please, call me Zahn. After all we have been through surely you can call me an acquaintance by now."

The two women turned to one another and when they had silently decided on the matter, Brayda answered for them. "We made this same journey with your brother and he gave us no such reason to do so, but I admit that you are a far different elf from him."

"At last a chance to step from beneath the shade he has cast over you," Zahn replied dryly after a mouthful of water from a canteen he kept in his bag. "I'll take the opportunity and thank you gladly for it."

Arvelle scrambled to her feet at that, offering a hand first to Brayda and then Zahn to get them all back to standing. "Alright, Zahn, with that settled, it's time we showed you the ruins."

"I had expected they would already be in view," Zahn commented as he took Arvelle's hand and got his feet beneath him. "Alas, they remain hidden even further, it would seem."

"Aye, but it's only a short walk," Arvelle said, leading the way once more.

The women began hiking towards the mountainside, which seemed just as far away as when they had climbed the stairwell. The plateau began to gradually descend toward the sheer rock face of the mountain, until a vast, abandoned city came into view, nestled in a hidden valley.

"My word..." Arvelle heard from beside her and turned just in time to see Zahn drop to his knees. "It is no wonder it lay undisturbed for so long. Ladies, here sits a whole city before us, unseen for thousands of years, as though it were forgotten by time itself. This is nothing short of a breakthrough discovery. Look at the condition! The only architectural artefact I have seen in better shape is Viktor's Tower in southern Johnah. This is simply astounding! This is no mere ruined city -- the air itself, the very atmosphere is different here. Do you feel it? It hit me the moment I stepped on the stairs, here we are now above that, and there is no wind, no crispness to the air, nothing. There's just this permeating feeling of total stillness. It's as though this is a world unto itself! It is no mystery why Antitus was entranced by this place. I could spend years poring over every inch of it."

The women turned to one another, their faces bearing matching expressions of suspicion and this time it was Arvelle that aired what they were thinking. "We believe your brother sensed the same thing, Zahn. As for us, outside of the lack of wind in the air and the relative mildness, neither Brayda nor I feel much different here."

"How can you be certain that Antitus felt it?" Zahn asked quickly, hopping back to his feet in the process.

"His behaviour turned strange," Brayda quickly put in. She added, "Which says quite a bit for him in the first place. It began when we led him into the stairwell and we saw you respond similarly in nearly the exact same place as he. I would be lying if I said it did not worry us."

The elf's face turned quizzical and his words were equally so. "You are both sure that you do not feel anything beyond a lack of wind and a milder temperature?"

Both shook their heads in response and Zahn began humming again, a thumb and an index finger stroking his chin. "That is most curious."

"Would you like for us to show you to the building your brother became obsessed with?" Brayda asked in an excited tone that Arvelle had not seen since their first trip to the ruins.

"Aye, let's hurry on without delay!" he answered with equal exuberance.

As with the stairwell, Arvelle led the way down through the rocky hill into the old city. Within twenty minutes of careful decent, they were inside the old civilisation and Zahn could scarcely contain his excitement.

Arvelle could hardly blame the elf, for she had felt much the same way on her first adventure to the ruinous city. The homes and buildings themselves appeared to be in astounding condition, both structurally and aesthetically. Everything was rounded and very few edges could be found. Stone and concrete were the primary building materials and it seemed as though every building had their own intricate designs on their exteriors.

It was during that first visit that Arvelle had noted to Brayda that the city looked as though it had been abandoned fifty years prior, rather than the several thousand years that it had been in reality. While there was no sign of any humanoid life, there were also no signs of disaster, either. It seemed as though the civilians had simply packed their things and left the city behind. Of the where and why to their leaving, there was no trace to be found, at least none that either Arvelle or Brayda could decipher, and if Antitus had made any headway into that, he had not told either woman.

The city looked to have been laid out in two halves that were divided between the two sides of the small valley with a main road running between. On the side that was built into the mountain range there looked to be row after row of homes until they came directly against the near-vertical rock face above. To the lower, foothill side of the valley was what looked to be the larger, commercial and warehouse type buildings, all of it culminating into a town square in the center of the valley floor.

With Arvelle maintaining point, the trio walked down into the main road, their every step echoing throughout the silent streets.

It seemed as though barely a few meters were walked at a time without Zahn pointing out something that interested him. After a time, he had even taken to walking with his journal in one hand and his slender piece of writing graphite in the other. When he wasn't talking, he was taking notes and pointing, nudging Brayda and Arvelle with the book hand to get their attention or insight, as each situation warranted.

He seemed to favour Brayda for such discussion, as she was far more interested in carrying a conversation. Arvelle, for her own part, was focused on keeping her attention on their surroundings. Though she had never seen anyone or anything living in the ruins, she refused to lower her guard. As a Master of Blades, she could not allow herself to.

She turned away from the main road and the other two followed, their discussion veering into their new surroundings as they did. They climbed the lower hillside to another street and turned again, and Arvelle began to count the buildings on this street off until they came to the eighth.

"This is the place," she declared, stopping in her tracks as she did.

Like the other structures, it was rounded and at least six storeys tall, with a domed roof and a circular staircase leading to the wide, arched front doorway.

Arvelle followed Zahn's gaze as he examined the exterior of the building. "Hmmm...I have seen similar to this. Or I should say that I saw the remnants of what were almost certainly similar buildings. The first was in a set of ruins in the interior of Johnah and the other just north of the Amaroshan half of the Varras River in Illiastra. Nothing, I repeat nothing I have ever encountered has been as intact as this city, but the architecture itself is not foreign to me."

"Would you like to go inside?" Brayda asked, her eagerness to glean any knowledge she could from Zahn bubbling over into her voice.

The elf was decidedly less eager. "In a moment, but I must ask: do either of you feel anything at all now or am I still alone in this sensation?"

"I'm sorry, but I don't feel a thing," Arvelle answered with a shrug.

For her part, Brayda rolled her arms and shoulders, as if she were trying to pick up on whatever it was that Zahn was sensing, but at last, she shook her head. "No, not me either. How do you feel, Zahn? We could move away from this building for now if you need to."

"It feels like warm waves are passing over me one after the other, without end and in quick succession. The closer we got to this place, the stronger it has grown. Antitus most certainly felt it too. That neither of you two can relate tells me that whatever this is, it likely only afflicts Elvenkind."

"Is it tolerable for you? If your brother experienced it as well, do you think he will still be here?" Arvelle queried in an effort to gauge what might be awaiting them inside.

Zahn answered first with a shake of his head, elaborating further with, "The sensation is almost pleasant. From a distance, it might even be enjoyable. However, to be this close to it, enduring it with such frequency... It would be enough to drive an elf to sheer madness within a day."

That reply did little to sate Arvelle and out of habit she loosened both scimitars in their scabbards, producing a rattling noise that got Zahn's attention.

"You have no worries, Arvelle, my brother isn't here," he said quite assuredly.

A single eyebrow of Brayda's rose at that. "How can you be so certain?"

Zahn gazed all about and took a deep breath. "Call it a brother's intuition." After a pause, he clapped his hands together and took a step forward, spinning about on his heel to face both women at once. "I am ready, let us go inside."

Together the three climbed the wide, stone steps to the front entrance. The doorway was a solid slab of stone with a wooden beam through the center that extended into both the ceiling and floor. Arvelle and Brayda approached the left hand side and began to push, causing the door and beam to rotate noisily until the way was open.

For once, Zahn had no comment, though his facial expression looked impressed enough.

Inside they went, with Arvelle leading the way, her right hand wrapped around the hilt of the sword on her left hip as a precaution.

"The floors... The walls... It's all so clean..." Zahn gasped, stepping forward ahead of Arvelle. "How is this possible? There should be some level of decay! There should be dust and cobwebs! How can thousand-year ruins look as though the occupants casually left yesterday?"

Indeed the building did look well kept. Arvelle noted a small layer of dust here and there on the stone surfaces, but otherwise, like the rest of the city, it looked miraculously maintained. Everything was made of stone, from structural elements right down to the furnishings and all of it done with incredible workmanship.

Immediately inside the door, they found what looked like a waiting area, complete with a counter backed by a wall that ran to the ceiling and obscured the interior of the building from view.

Arvelle and Brayda led Zahn around it and down a short corridor to the heart of the place.

Brayda walked ahead of them and into the middle of the tall, wide, round room, empty save for a collection of benches and seats lining the perimeter. "Here we are, Zahn, what do you make of it?" she said with her arms outstretched before the three carvings at the back.

"My word..." he gasped, taking a few slow steps forward as he did. Suddenly he opened the journal still held to hand, flipping pages in haste.

"How are you feeling?" Arvelle asked cautiously as she followed behind, eyeing the elf for any signs of distress.

He turned to face her. "Oh I am under a great deal of duress at the moment. The waves are even more intense here. I would not be able to stay here for more than a few hours at most. It is a wonder my brother lasted as long as he did. Do both of you still feel nothing at all?"

"I feel quite fine," Brayda said with a shrug. "How about you, Arvelle?"

She was anxious and a little uneasy, given Zahn's state, but otherwise, Arvelle felt no different than she did before entering the trenched stairwell. "I'm perfectly alright," she told them nonchalantly.

That baffled Zahn and he quite nearly dropped his journal. "Unbelievable," he exclaimed as he recovered it mid-air. "If what I am feeling was caused by the ancients, I think we can safely say that they were not elves. This would be unpleasant to tolerate, let alone create. Still... I must get closer."

"Is that a wise idea, Zahn?" Brayda pondered aloud as the elf strode past her.

He declined to answer and went directly before the three glyphs, looking them over and inspecting the carving of the leftmost one closely.

A look of concern was shared between Brayda and Arvelle and they hesitantly decided to join him.

The journal lay open in the palm of his right hand and the left was touching a lower line segment in the circular glyph. Suddenly he stopped and stepped back and the book fell to floor. "What in the world?" he asked no one in particular.

"Is everything alright?" Arvelle queried, her right hand held mere centimetres from the left scimitar.

"It's warm... The wall is warm..." Zahn mused, leaving Arvelle momentarily unsure if that was an answer to her question or not. Both of his hands went to the center piece, sliding over it as much as he could reach. "This one too!"

The elf turned about. "Ladies, quickly, come here and touch the wall. I need you to tell me if you can feel the warmth of it."

They walked together, side by side until they were immediately beside Zahn. A single hand of each of them was placed on the center glyph, and much to Arvelle's shock, it did indeed feel quite warm to the touch. The heat even seemed to pulse forth, as if the wall itself was the source.

"Aye, it is almost hot to the touch," Brayda said, with her eyes wide and her voice full of incredulity. "How is this possible?"

Zahn scooped up his book from where it had fallen and flipped back through the pages. "That I do not know. It is the strangest thing I have ever observed." His attention turned to Arvelle alone. "What is behind this place? You've looked, surely."

"This is an exterior wall. Behind these buildings you will merely find the roadway between this building and the next," she answered, a little puzzled by the question.

"That would mean..." Zahn started, sounding more and more confused with every word. "Then this heat... It's the wall itself that's generating it... But how?"

"Perhaps there is something embedded into the mortar of the wall?" Brayda offered in suggestion.

That gave Arvelle a thought. "It might be that the answer is written in the glyphs. If only there was a way to decipher them."

"No..." Zahn uttered, a hand of his feeling the warmth emanating from the wall again. "I think the answer is the glyph itself."

"What do you mean?" Brayda probed, her face showing both concern and intrigue.

He faced them both again, showing them the page of his journal with the sketching of the glyphs he had showed them at the inn. "Antitus and I had been too focused on deciphering the glyphs as written language. All the wavy and jagged lines, we thought they were words and sentences and we set about trying to read them, when they were never meant for such."

"What are they meant for, then?" Arvelle put to him, as eager to the answer as Brayda.

"They are a language of sorts, but not one meant for communicating with people, be they Elven, human, dwarven or any other. These glyphs... Look at the center of the spirals: each one is a particular symbol," he

stated, pointing first at the wall, then to the drawings in his journal. "We found different ones, though barely legible, in the decayed ruins scattered here and there in more central locations of our known world. Nothing was ever this well preserved except for one other location."

Brayda's eyes lit up and she gasped, "The Tower of Viktor."

"Just the one I'm thinking of," Zahn concurred, tapping a finger against his nose. "Think about it, ladies: our known world is surrounded on all sides by barriers that prevent travel. In the south, there is the Sea of Perpetual Storms and in the very southern tip of Johnah, on the lone peninsula that extends into that sea is the Tower of Viktor: a tower without entrance from the ancient era that, despite being battered by constant storms, never erodes. In the eastern reaches of Illiastra and the western reaches of Gildriad, we are surrounded by nearly vertical mountain ranges that extend high into the clouds. It is here, in the Gildraddi chain, that we found an ancient city untouched by time itself. Lastly, to the north is what we elves call the Gimault Tundra, as inhospitable and impassable as the Storming Sea in the south."

"You need not remind me," Brayda spoke up. "I am a Snowy Dwarf, born and raised in Gondarrius on the very edge of that tundra. If the city was not underground, it would be completely uninhabitable."

"That is exactly my point, Brayda," the elf declared excitedly. "All of the furthest reaches in any of the four compass direction of our known world prevent us from exploring further. I wager that if we climbed through the Illiastran Mountain Chain or somehow explored the Gimault Tundra, we would find similarly unscarred ruins, hidden away from sight. Furthermore, something tells me that if a way were found to get inside that citadel tower in Johnah, that we would find sigils, as large and as warm the ones behind us."

"Do you think Antitus went to Johnah, then?" Arvelle asked him.

Zahn shook his head at that notion. "Most likely not, as we have been there already. It has no door and the storms make climbing the tower impossible. It would be a waste of his time. As sure as I am standing here, my brother is in one of the other two points by now, looking for more ruins."

"There is still the matter of what causes these glyphs to be warm to the touch," Brayda reminded them. "Not to mention the effect they seem to have on elves."

"As to that, ladies, the answer is clear to me: it is pure energy. I hypothesise that these symbols communicate with the planet. The sigils in the center would be the focal point, in such a case. They draw specific energies and the twisting, spiralling line segments emerging from them dictate what those energies do."

"I'm afraid I don't understand any of this, Zahn," Arvelle said, shaking her head. "What do you mean by energies? How are a bunch of carvings on the walls capable of speaking to the planet?"

The elf gave a shrug. "That much I do not know myself and I am beginning to think that the ancient folk intended for us to never know. I believe they hid these ruins away, or made them inaccessible, like the Tower of Viktor. I theorise that the glyphs within here preserve the ruins and keep the mountain chain in place so that we remain sealed away in our part of the world. It was made so that we could not follow. I would imagine that my brother reached a similar conclusion."

"What you are saying is that the ruins are the keys to unlocking the world beyond our own," Brayda uttered in amazement.

"Precisely, my dwarven friend. What we have yet to know is why the ancient peoples sealed us in and took their secrets with them. It might be to protect us, or protect themselves, or something even more sinister than that. Antitus desires to answer that question, however terrible it might be and he did not trust that either of you could handle that answer if he did find it. That is why he drove you away and it is why we must follow him. My brother alone should not be the arbiter of our world's fate."

"You want us to go with you to find him?" Arvelle said with a scoff.

"Who better?" Zahn countered. "I could use the help of seasoned explorers to find him and I feel it wise to tell no one else of our potential discovery. If there is indeed some terrible fate awaiting our world beyond the barriers of the ancient folk, we cannot risk that knowledge reaching the wrong ears. We need to contain this knowledge, lest we have every careless or unscrupulous explorer and power-hungry ruler scrambling to the barriers to try and tear them down."

"When you say it like that, it seems as though we have no choice," Arvelle decided, before turning to her friend. "What say you, Brayda?"

The dwarven woman took a deep breath and glanced at the glyphs once more. "We very well can't let such knowledge fall into the wrong hands, if what you say is true. Besides, we've gone too far into this mystery. I would like to see it through to the end."

"We will have to leave at first light in the morning," Zahn said, clapping his hand together excitedly again. "Antitus will either be in Gondarrius or one of the eastern human cities nearest to the mountain range. Either way, our course will take us across the Casparian Sea to Illiastra."

The two women glanced to one another tellingly and Arvelle said what they were both thinking. "I think we'll have to renegotiate our rate. Two world-class adventurers don't come cheaply, after all."

In Defence of Our Home
Part I
Original publication:
***Fantasy From The Rock* (2017)**

The third heir of an unhinged, ruthless religious fanatic family unleashes his devoted cult army on the entire continent, hoping to seize power by domination. Having already run through the west coast of Illiastra, the followers of Valdarrow set their sights on the stronghold city of the Dwarves: Dhalla. With a brutal horde headed their way, the Chieftain clans of Goldenhair and Snowbeard must ready soldier and citizen alike for what may come. Most of all, they must prepare themselves to risk all to save dwarvenkind itself.

From the Author: "I reference the history of the dwarven folk in **Gold & Steel**, particularly this event and ever since I originally drafted it so I could lay the reference, I knew that this was a story I wanted to write in long form. With part one, the objective was to set the scene, introduce the characters and show the reader what they were up against. When it came to part two, I gave myself much more freedom. This was an all-out test for myself to write a large-scale battle that unfolds across multiple areas and is told through the eyes of scattered characters. There are quite a few moving parts and I wanted to see if I could juggle them all and still have the whole thing make sense. Did I succeed? Well, that's for you to decide."

In Defence of Our Home
Part I

The old dwarf stood like a statue atop the bailey wall in armour that looked as old as he was. It was speckled with rust here and there on the edges, but had otherwise been well maintained for all the battles it had seen. Despite its age, the armour was not yet ready to be retired. In this way, it was much like its wearer. However, unlike his armour, the old dwarf's patience was wearing thin.

"Where are your scouts, Axel?" he asked with an audible grumble. "They are long overdue."

Axel gave the old dwarf a glance from the corner of his eye. "They are not overdue. In your old age, you have lost all sense of time."

"I'm not so old that I could not best a Goldenhair in a fight. Shall I draw my sword so that I might teach you some respect?"

"I wouldn't want you to strain your shoulder, old man."

That got a grunt out of him. "That's not even your real hair flowing from the plume of your helm, is it? A pony's tail, I reckon. Clan Goldenhair always cut their manes to adorn their helms, with enough left to leave it

hanging long. You would eschew your family's tradition so easily?"

"We haven't done that in a thousand years," Axel Goldenhair said with a wry smile crossing his lips. "Though, I suspect you were here to witness that, old as you are."

Snow crunched between the boots of Axel's companion as he turned to face him. "I was here for many a-battle, youngster, though at this rate I will die of old age waiting for your scouts to return." He turned completely about, to a lad armoured in chainmail and boiled leather, standing at the ready by the stairway. "Squire Chinton, I grow thirsty. Bring me a horn of ale to quench it."

"None for me, Chinton," Axel added. "I may be younger than Snowbeard, yet I know better than to get drunk before a battle."

"I will not get drunk if your scouts return before sunset. Any longer and I give you no guarantees," Snowbeard replied.

"Since they are my scouts, it is safe to say that they will be at the gates before Chinton is back with your ale. You won't have time to so much as wet your lips."

"Is that a wager, Goldenhair?"

"Not with you. I know better."

"Then your father taught you well."

Without breaking his long gaze on the southbound highway, Axel gave the old dwarf a reply: "Of course he did. He merely recited the words that are practically the motto of Clan Goldenhair: 'Never wager with a Snowbeard, Aren would hold it against us for making such fools of them.'"

At that, the Snowbeard went quiet and combed his beard with a gauntlet-covered hand. Axel waited for what he knew what was to eventually come, but feigned notice and refused to so much as glance at him.

To the old dwarf's credit, he held out for what seemed to Axel like half a minute before he heard the Snowbeard fighting a losing battle. It came to an end with a great guffaw and a rapid reddening of Snowbeard's weather-beaten face.

Axel broke into laughter with him and there they stood, amid a stone wall capped with snow, chuckling as only two old friends could after such an exchange.

When the laughter had ebbed, they lapsed into comfortable silence, their eyes fixated on the Southern Pass. It was a long, winding gravel road, bordered by the Casparian Sea to one side and a tall retaining wall of stone to the other. The purpose of the road had been to connect the realm of the dwarves with that of the human and half-elf nations of Phaleayna and Amarosha. For centuries, it had served as just that, situated along the rugged northwest coast of the continent of Illiastra.

In the best seasons it was a difficult and remote road to make use of and, in an effort to better facilitate trade, Axel and the Snowbeard were overseeing the planning of a new passage. Though construction had yet to begin, this replacement road was to run southeast, taking it directly through Mount Montagen itself and stretching across plains, marshlands, and forests until it reached the human settlement of Obalen.

That may no longer be a wise idea, Axel noted to himself. *Not until Phaleayna can get its affairs in order and put down the menace that is the Valdarrow city-state.*

The Valdarrows were a family of humans that numbered into their third generation, having been founded by a religious fanatic whose offspring had continued to echo his beliefs.

They were devout followers of Ios, the god of man, who was one part of the Triarchy of the Gods. Alongside him in equal parts was Iia, goddess of the elves and their ilk, and Aren, god of the dwarves. Most believers whom Axel knew subscribed to the ideology that the three deities were equals. Those who followed this path believed that each god and their creations only functioned when they could all live in harmony in the same space. By these tenets, dwarf, elf, and human alike must break bread together and work as one to maintain the Triarchy for peace to bloom.

It was when, in great numbers, people picked one god above the others that problems arose. In those cases, it became all about greed and dominance for the followers of the chosen deity, who tried their hand at pushing the followers of the other gods into either submission or extinction. For their part, Axel could not recall the gods ever picking sides in the wars fought in their name.

The Valdarrow brood and their fanatics were merely another to interpret the scriptures to fit their warmongering, albeit with more success than most. By their skewered view, followers of Aren and Iia were scum worthy of death and the Valdarrow clan intended to deliver on that.

The first of the name had taken his agenda to the Amaroshan people, or the half-elves, as they were also known. The majority of the population of the hybrid of elves and humans lived in the city they were named for to the south of the mighty Varras River. The entire western half of what was known as the Southlands was their nation and they had lived there in peace for centuries.

After silently declaring war on the Amaroshans, the Valdarrow followers had ambushed roaming caravans of the half-elves and pillaged the smallest and most remote of their villages. The stories Axel had heard spoke of unconscionable bloodshed of any who could fight and enslavement for those who did not.

Using this indentured work force, Valdarrow erected himself a palace in the heart of the continent and declared himself King of the World and Grand Patriarch and Prophet of Ios, beholden to no government.

Elf, dwarf, Amaroshan, and human alike had done battle with the first Valdarrow, yet despite their efforts, he survived that war long enough to begat a son to continue the legacy of terror.

This second Valdarrow, in only his teenage years, was the first to try his hand at sacking Dhalla. The attempt was repelled at the gates by the Army of Dhalla, led by the Four Chieftains, which included Snowbeard himself and Axel's father, Raymus Goldenhair. A counterattack was launched by the dwarves on the Valdarrow City and during that siege, the dwarves claimed the life of the second Valdarrow. Though it was ruled a victory for the dwarves, they had paid dearly for it with the loss of thousands. Of the Four Chieftains to go south, only Snowbeard had lived to see Dhalla again.

A third Valdarrow came along in the years following. His claim, although dubious, had been accepted by the fanatics and they rallied around their new leader as they had the previous two. This Valdarrow, while lacking the sheer cunning of his predecessors, more than made up for it with a charismatic veneer atop a brutally violent methodology.

As it were, Phaleayna had decided to end the threat by sending their highest-ranking Knight's General, Ser Haize Corran, known as the Golden Knight, sending with him a sizeable force of soldiers. Though Phaleayna anticipated a decisive victory, what resulted instead was the bloodiest and most tragic battle fought against any Valdarrow. Ser Haize Corran was slain in battle and the five knights who served him retreated in shame.

Killing the greatest knight of the Phaleaynan King had only emboldened the newest Valdarrow and his minions. In the wake of his victory and now undaunted by Phaleayna, the third Valdarrow began to increase his lands, starting with the annexation of the vulnerable west coast. Town after town, all inhabited by Phaleaynan humans, surrendered or were overrun, with no one along the way spared from death or slavery.

With the northwest coast conquered, the first major goal for the third Valdarrow was now at hand: eliminate the dwarves, the creations of Aren.

Axel had prepared for this day. As long as a Valdarrow lived and drew fanatics to their cause, safety was but a dream for the dwarves. The grim spectre of it had loomed above Axel's head his entire life and he had trained for it as a boy under the tutelage of his now-late father. The suit of steel plate he currently wore, enamelled in the colours of cobalt blue and gold, had been crafted to protect Axel when that day came. Upon his back was a bastard sword and circular, spiked shield, forged just for his hands, so that he might fight the very foe that now marched for the gates of Dhalla.

"There," Snowbeard said with a nod to the top of the rugged, uninviting cliffs that rose to their left. "I see two of ours. Might they be your scouts or are these aging eyes tricking me once again?"

"Aye, they're riding in on their mules in a hurry. I suspect we won't like the news they bring," Axel confirmed before turning his gaze towards the guards nearby. "Open the postern gate and ready the stones to seal it tight!"

From below, Axel could hear his commands being ordered from dwarf to dwarf, and he turned to his squire, now returning with ale for his companion. "Lad, hand me the ale and go summon Parias with as much haste as you can muster."

Chinton shoved the horn into Axel's hand and the brew sloshed out and onto his gauntlet, though the lad was gone from sight before the first drip could fall to the ground.

Before giving it to Snowbeard, Axel took a drink of the yeasty brew, exhaling audibly as it rolled down his throat. The act raised his old friend's eyebrows so fast that Axel thought they might come right off his forehead.

"Taking a swallow of the good stuff after all, are we?" he asked Axel jokingly.

"Today may be the last time I ever get a taste," Axel answered, trying to match the tone of the older dwarf.

Axel could feel Snowbeard analysing every facet of his body language as only he could, his voice falling stern as he put his findings to words. "You're nervous, but you should know there is no shame in that, especially among friends. Your father was nervous too, when it was us marching to Valdarrow's gates. I would take ten of his kind over an army of reckless youths drunk on pith and vinegar. He is proud of you, Axel of Clan Goldenhair. I feel it within me as sure as I am standing here. Honour his name and his legacy this day, in actions and words alike."

"I shall do everything I can so that I may, Adlan of Clan Snowbeard. You have my word on that."

"Ser Axel!" a voice called from behind, causing them to both turn and come face to face with a broad shouldered dwarf in grey, mottled leathers and a matching cloak.

"Well met. Ser Parias and I thank you for joining us so quickly," Snowbeard said, speaking for both captains.

The dwarven man, with his hazel eyes and similarly light brown hair and beard, shook their hands in turn while responding, "My archers heard your command to open the postern gate and assumed it meant your scouts had returned. I met your squire on my way here with the same message. With hopes that neither of you would object, I took the liberty of dispatching the requested unit of archers into the hillside -- you can see them if you look hard enough. At your leave, you may barricade the postern, sers. My people are at the ready."

While Parias spoke, the three were joined by Chinton and the two scouts, looking exasperated, but not worse for wear. The squire was open-mouthed and about to speak, but Axel found his words more quickly: "Chinton, give the order to bar the postern gate. Parias has already dispatched his archers into the hillside."

The boy was gone in a flash, leaving behind the two masked soldiers in the same grey outfits of Parias in his haste.

Old Snowbeard took the liberty of burrowing to the bedrock of the matter. "Scouts, what tidings do you bring? Your urgent manner says it is nothing good."

One among them stepped forward and unfurled the scarf used to conceal their face, revealing that it was a dwarven woman. "Sers, it would seem that Lord Tusker's information was entirely correct. An army marches for our gates and have crept to within a kilometre. They will be before our eyes by high noon, by our estimates."

"Lord Tusker's timely warning may well have saved our hides," Snowbeard mused aloud. "It is unfortunate that he did not have the forces to repel the Valdarrow fiends himself. If he had, we could have joined Tusker and the other humans in their cove with its sheer, high cliffs and fought off the enemy together."

"We would not be so lucky as that, ser," Parias commented, his eyes on his archers crawling about the hills nearby.

Axel followed Parias' line of sight to see them for himself, spotting them moving here and there along the natural crenulations provided by the tall boulders. Their grey suits helped them blend so well that Axel was sure that if he had not been told to look for them he would not have seen them at all.

"I only hope that we don't become so desperate that we start praying for blind luck, gentlemen," Axel said to that, turning his attention back to the scouts. "What of their numbers? How many? How were they armed and armoured?"

"We estimate them to be seven thousand strong at most, ser," the second scout answered, his voice giving him away for a male, though he opted to keep his mask in place. "As for armour, they were clothed in fur pelts to ward against the cold. Some wore shabby mail atop the pelts, though most didn't, and there is no telling what they are wearing beneath. However, I can say that those without pelts didn't look to be wearing more than odd bits of mail and boiled leathers."

The female jumped in again. "Everything they have to fight with looks like it was scavenged, or at least not well maintained. We spotted old, stolen shields painted with the sigils of a dozen or more different houses and clans of Phaleayna and Amarosha. The soldiers kept no formation in their marching either, and there were only a few ahorse. It seems that the horses are reserved for the officers, as the men in the saddles are all armoured in good platemail."

"They are little more than a large clump of men swarming down the road like locusts," Snowbeard said with a scoff and a spit. "I take a little comfort in that, for there we have the advantage." His eyes went to the other side of the wall, where three thousand men and women stood waiting for a command. Every last one among them wore shining steel and thick chainmail, with all manner of steel weaponry on their hips and across their backs. To each who wanted it, there was also a round, wooden shield, ringed in iron and emblazoned with family or personal sigils. Some preferred to fight without, opting for dual weapons or two-handed weapons, such as a broadsword, greathammer, or greataxe.

Axel's gaze followed Snowbeard's for a moment before falling back upon his two compatriots and the scouts. "We lack the numbers, but we have disciplined soldiers, strong walls, and a few other tricks at our disposal. This day may yet be ours to savour," he stated plainly enough, trying not to instil a false confidence at this early stage.

"There's more, sers," the female scout put in when a few seconds of silence passed, giving credit to the cautiousness of Axel's optimism.

"We'll hear it, then," Snowbeard said with a reluctant sigh.

She cast her eyes downward, looking sorry to have to deliver what was coming. "They have a ram and two catapults."

"By Aren's beard..." the old dwarf muttered through gritted teeth. "The ram we can deal with -- it's the damn catapults that are the real threat. If they can launch their quarry any considerable distance, we have no chance of stopping them."

"Then we must hope that the catapults' range is as narrow as Valdarrow's mind," a new voice said, having added itself to the mix.

All eyes turned to the concrete steps leading to the top of the wall, falling on a woman with light blonde hair, clad in armour made of steel scales over boiled leathers. A deep blue cloak streaked with sunburst lines of gold flowed across her back, billowing with every graceful step she took.

Hers was a presence that always drew a smile to Axel's face and now would be no exception. "Egrid, I am glad you are here. I take it that you too heard the call of the horn?"

"I have, Husband. Are the enemy upon us yet?" she asked while still striding across the rampart.

"Not yet, love. How fare your own preparations?"

"The loading of the ships has long begun," she said, taking time to look at the entire group in turn as she relayed the information. "The children, infirm, and elderly have all begun boarding at the docks. As the ships fill, they move to the mouth of the harbour to await further instructions. The contingent of archers that Ser Parias has lent me is now stationed on every accessible rooftop within a half a kilometre radius with as many arrows as they can manage. Furthermore, the soldiers of mine that aren't assisting the civilians have begun erecting a barricade that I pray we will not have use for.”

“Excellent work as always, Lady Egrid,” said Ser Parias when she came close enough for him to give a friendly pat on the back. “You are just in time, I should say.”

A stern look came over her at that and she looked first to her husband. “Then the time is immediately upon us?”

“Aye, the enemy are just out of sight and should be turning the corner into the southern pass at any moment,” Axel answered her, meeting her eyes as he delivered the hard truth.

Her attention was quickly cast to Adlan, himself staring south for some sight of the human invasion. “Ser Snowbeard, have you sent for Dorrhen? He would want to be here right now.”

“My son is likely deep in the mines,” the old dwarf gave in reply, breaking his line of sight to look at Egrid. “He won’t hear the horn right away, but he has ears outside waiting to run to him as soon as they hear the call. Dorrhen won’t be far behind.”

“Then we’ll wait,” Ser Parias declared and the silence between them echoed in agreement.

All eyes slowly turned south once more, looking for any sign of Valdarrow’s army. Minutes rolled by quietly, disturbed only by scattered coughs of the soldiers and the sound of the iron greaves of the pacing patrolmen tapping and scraping on the stone surface of the battlements.

At his side, Axel felt a gloved hand reaching for his own and glanced to find Egrid at his left shoulder, so close that he could smell the tea on her breath. “How are you faring?" he asked while removing his helm so that he might see her better.

"I am facing the gale bravely, my love," Egrid answered with a smile, her blue-green eyes locked upon his. "We have prepared ourselves as well as we might against it and I am confident in our chances. I can fight today with a clear conscience and no regrets. There is little else that I might ask for under such circumstances."

Axel leaned in for a quick kiss to the fair cheek of his wife before saying, "I am most glad to hear that, Egrid. A clear mind is as sharp as any sword. I feel that we will do well today, my love. It is far easier to defend a wall than it is to attack it, after all. They have the numbers, that is true, but we have our defences."

"I trust you, Axel. You have not led me astray before," she answered after a kiss of her own.

A guard called out from the tower above and after him came a sharp blast of the horn. Axel and Egrid turned their eyes to the south together, but the captain of the archers was the first to see the enemy. "Look there! The horde approaches!" Parias bellowed in nervous excitement. "By Aren's beard, they number so many that they are shaking the ground!"

"The time is at hand," declared old Snowbeard. "Ser Parias, arm yourself and call your archers to the wall. It is time you took your stations."

Ser Parias was gone before the command had fully left Snowbeard's lips, and as Axel turned to watch him leave, another dwarf met him on the steps. "Sers!" he called out to the remaining three. "I apologise for my delay."

"Dorrhen, my boy, you have arrived with not a moment to spare," Snowbeard greeted his eldest

offspring, who joined the party with his sights already set on the approaching army.

Dorrhen was a young dwarf of only twenty and already a warrior in his own right. He stood nearly the height of a human, thick muscled with fearsome strength and a constantly dour demeanour that lent his face a perpetually stoic expression. Even as a small boy, Dorrhen was never one to show any merriment, as if the world and all its issues were one giant weight he had been made to carry since birth. He stood before them now in boiled leather, a breastplate, lobstered gauntlets, and greaves made of plain steel. The only embellishment he had allowed himself was the white cloak of his family, cut into the shape of a long, white beard that tailed behind him as he closed the gap between himself and the others. His long, straight hair flowed to his shoulders and was such a light shade of blond that it seemed to meld into the cloak. As for a beard, Dorrhen had shaven the entirety of his face, save for the vicinity of his chin, which was left long, and styled into what looked like the blade of a scythe.

"So it would seem, Father," Dorrhen commented with a long look at the approaching forces. "Has either of you given a speech to our army yet?"

"Not yet," answered Egrid for the group. "We were waiting on your arrival, Ser Dorrhen, so that we might hear your report from the mining tunnels and make any final preparations that must be made."

He nodded at that, his eyes still fixed on the distant army. "Understood, Lady Egrid, I shall waste no further time," Dorrhen said sternly, finally turning to face the other three. "The long trek has begun and I have been directing those who are able to endure such a walk into the passages beneath Mount Montagen. Furthermore, three of my soldiers have been dispatched to Gethos Village on the northern exit, to explain what is happening to their chieftain. It will be an unexpected influx of people, but Gethos should be able to take most of them in for the time being. We will erect tents for the rest. My builders have also assured me that the Iron Seal is fully functioning and ready to be engaged if the worst shall come to pass."

The older Snowbeard exhaled grimly at the mention of the Iron Seal and when his son was finished with his report, Adlan spoke up. "The Iron Seal... It was on account of the first Valdarrow that we had that thing built at all. We have never needed it before, and today should be no different, Son."

"It is merely precautionary on my part to ensure that it is in working order, Father," stated Dorrhen, his voice reflecting his own reluctance in even acknowledging the existence of the device.

Egrid took the momentary lapse to push the conversation forward. "I should mention that my own precautions are in place, Ser Dorrhen, as you had not been briefed on that front yet. Every ship in the harbour that can make for the open sea has been pressed into service to ferry those who cannot fight. As with your own work, mine is merely a failsafe. I have every bit of faith in my husband, your father, and our army. We will not fail Dhalla."

"Your confidence is admirable, Lady Egrid. I pray that your faith is not dashed this day," Dorrhen put back as amiably as Axel had ever known him to be.

"Sers..." Axel heard from nearby, following the voice to the panicked face of his squire standing nearby. "I mean not to alarm you, but I see... By Aren's beard... I see the catapults."

The first impression Axel had of the ugly wooden weapons rolling at the rear of the marching force was that they looked unwieldy and non-functional. *A bluff tactic, nothing more,* he told himself, until one of the two released its load.

"Everybody down!" one of the soldiers upon the tower battlements cried out, his warning heeded by all but Adlan Snowbeard.

Axel and Egrid crouched as one, each pulling the other down in unison. A thunderous blast filled the air, but it seemed distant to Axel and he looked up to find the wall unscathed. "Egrid, we're untouched for the nonce," he whispered to her while gently drawing her back to her feet. They looked beyond the embrasures at a growing cloud of dust and smoke that plumed from a newly formed crater on the road. The impact had been nowhere near the wall, but had done a fearsome amount of damage. In its wake, Axel sighted impressively large, busted barrels with a sudden abundance of crushed stone around them indicating their former contents.

"I recognise those ghastly things," Adlan commented from where he had stood unflinching. "The other three chieftains and I dealt with those very two monstrosities at Valdarrow's own gates. It seems that they have been made mobile, though barely, and have been pushed all the way here. They won't reach us yet, but when they do, and if heavy enough stones can be loaded into them, our wall won't stand for long. Should they keep firing barrels of stone, the wall will stand, but anyone foolish enough to stay atop it will perish."

The arm of the launched catapult was in the beginning stages of being drawn back as Adlan spoke. The other, situated further back, was still being pushed forward, prepared to fire a volley at a moment's notice. Axel had little doubt of the veracity of Adlan's testimony and it made his next command, as dire as its implications were, surprisingly easy. "Chinton, summon Torgus and Vargas of Clan Spearsmasher, tell them to bring Montagen's Hammer."

"Ser, are you certain?" Chinton asked in an astonished voice.

"Aye, it must be done, lad," Adlan added for Axel, knowing full well the implications of what Axel had ordered. "Now get a move on, they will need all the time we can buy them. Montagen's Hammer is bloody heavy."

A hand came to rest on Axel's shoulder and the soft voice of Egrid was in his ear. "Now may well be the time to speak to the soldiers, my love," she suggested.

"You're right. At the rate that Valdarrow's men are approaching, I may not have another chance," Axel replied, putting his back to the enemy for the moment and walking across the parapet to look upon the city of Dhalla and the gathered masses below. They looked back at him as one, and in their eyes Axel saw the determination and drive that the dwarves were long known for. These were his people and they were every bit as prepared to defend their home as he was.

It is to me to lead them and so I shall, he thought to himself as he cleared his throat and raised a hand for silence. When the voices came to a complete halt, Axel took a breath and began: "Brothers and sisters, if you have ears, then surely you just heard the commotion on the other side of the gates. The enemy has come knocking and they beg for us to answer like meek little sheep ready for slaughtering. They believe that Ios commands them to erase us from existence, but we are no sheep and we shall not be herded to our deaths this day. We are the dwarves of Dhalla, the children of Aren! The men outside our doors wish to steal our homes and put each and every last one of us to the sword for the crime of daring to exist. I say we show them no quarter in return and drive them back from whence they came! Are you with me?"

The dwarves cheered loudly at that and Axel looked to either side to see Egrid and the two Snowbeards standing proudly with him.

"The men out there see in us a short statured people," Axel continued when the cheering ebbed. "They think us to be an easy target for their aggression and expect their siege to be an easy victory. If they want to make that mistake, I am only glad to let them! Let us show them what it is to provoke the proud and mighty dwarves of Dhalla!"

"Make way for Ser Parias!" a voice called out repeatedly above the clamour and Axel spotted the captain of the archers marching the bulk of his unit up the main road of the town. Their tall longbows poked through the throng, like a line of transparent fins cutting through the sea of iron, steel and chainmail. The gathered crowd of soldier and citizen applauded and cheered for the dwarven knight and his warriors and the proud, beaming smile on Parias' face was visible to Axel from atop the wall.

Behind the stream of bows came squires pulling mules weighted down with enough arrows for a whole army of archers. Further back in the procession, Axel laid eyes on his own squire and following him were two brawny lads lugging a covered cart.

The archers had climbed the stairs to the ramparts before the crowd begun to quieten down to where Axel might hear himself above them again. From his side,

Axel heard the sound of a sword scraping loose from a scabbard and turned to see Ser Adlan with the shining steel sword of Clan Snowbeard raised high.

He propped a single foot on the edge of the wall and declared, "Dwarves of Dhalla, if you have a bow, find a rooftop near the gates and await my signal! The rest, be prepared to defend your homes, your families and your lives! Dhalla shall not be lost!"

Axel turned to Egrid and rested both hands on her shoulders. "You should go back to the docks, my love. Ensure that our work continues and prepare your soldiers to defend the barricade there should the worst come to pass. I will see you soon."

"May Aren guide your heart and your blade, Axel. I hope to see you soon," she answered, her face so close that he could see the fleck of brown in her blue-green eyes. Their lips met and it was with great longing that they did part. She turned and left him there, making her way down the steps and through the armoured throng.

Axel watched Egrid leave for a moment longer, the crowd parting enough for her to make a path toward the docks without delay.

"It is past time that I returned to my post as well," the younger Snowbeard declared. "I hope with all my might that neither the Iron Seal nor Montagen's Hammer will need be used this day, but know that I am prepared to use the former."

The father looked to the son and gave him a clap on the shoulder, his face showing the gravity of what it meant to use either device. "We are the dwarves of Dhalla, my son. We will do what we must to hold our home and if we no longer can, then it will fall to you and Lady Egrid to protect our people and lead them to safety."

"If such circumstances fall to me, I will do what must be done to ensure that we dwarves endure, Father," Dorrhen responded with a single nod, leaving his father and the others without further comment.

At the bottom of the steps, Dorrhen passed and exchanged brief words with Torgus and Vargas. After what Axel could only fathom to be well wishes and pleasantries, Dorrhen moved past them and disappeared into the crowd, leaving the smiths to their climb.

Axel watched as the pair wrestled a large, cylindrical chunk of red painted iron from the wagon, placing it carefully in the arms of four waiting soldiers. The twin brothers were scarily strong and what looked like a hefty load to them was nearly dropped by the four soldiers immediately. They recovered, and their ascent to the ramparts above soon commenced. The brothers themselves bore a massive, steel greathammer painted in swirls of gold and onyx. One brother took the head across his shoulder and the other lifted the handle, bearing in his free hand a canvas bag of tools.

The three at the top stood back for the approaching entourage, giving them plenty of room to pass by with their heavy burdens uninterrupted.

"Sers!" called one of the soldiers watching the approaching horde. "The arm of the catapult in the forefront has been winched back into place and the enemy is loading another volley!"

Axel, Adlan, and Parias all turned their attention about to the ugly, wooden machines lumbering toward their city. The closest catapult had indeed been readied and the second was near the point where the first had unleashed its volley not long ago.

"They won't fire on us again until they know they can hit the wall," Adlan surmised, a hand running through his beard all the while. "The first volley was to test the range of the catapults against the wind and give us a fright. We have a little time, though none to waste at this point."

The old man's gaze fell to Axel then, leaving the decision in his hands.

"Very well," Axel said with a sigh as he looked to the soldiers all about the wall. "Archers, take cover until further notice! Every other soldier is to get off the wall entirely and prepare to defend the gate should it fall!"

"What of us, sers?" Axel heard from behind, turning to see the brothers Torgus and Vargas standing before him. It was Torgus speaking for the pair of identical dark haired, bearded twins. "We need approval from the leaders of all the clans before we can proceed with installing and deploying Montagen's hammer, even if there are only two of you."

"You have my approval to assemble it," Adlan answered with melancholy in his voice. "However, I cannot speak for Ser Axel."

Axel glanced at the catapults, rolling closer by the second and turned back to the smiths, his voice grave, but his mind resolute. "Make it so," he declared.

The twins bowed and strode away to where the wall merged with the sheer cliff face of Mount Montagen, where they joined the four soldiers who had carried the head of the Hammer. What stood beside them was a sealed door at the base of a tall, unmanned tower that contained a contraption of terrifying power. Axel watched as Vargas produced a key and unlocked the single entrance of the stone structure. Torgus directed the soldiers to climb the staircase that wound about the outer wall and left them to it while he and his brother stepped within and out of sight to begin the assemblage.

"Rahagas Spearsmasher, their father, oversaw construction of Montagen's Hammer," Adlan stated, his gaze firmly fixed on the doorway Torgus and Vargas had entered. "Those two were but babes at the breast back then. They've grown up in its shadow and seen their father work tirelessly to maintain it and then teach them how to do the same. All of that was done with the hopes that neither he nor they or even their sons after them would see it used. Yet, this is what it has come to, Axel."

"We must defend our people and our city," Axel answered him. "It is what Montagen's Hammer was built to do and it falls to us to make the decision to wield it, my friend."

Ser Parias, who himself had taken to the elevated, rounded portion of the battlements beside the sea, bellowed, "A lone rider approaches! Looks to be a messenger, sers!"

The two stepped to the nearest opening and looked down to see a single human riding a brown horse toward their gate at a gallop. A bright red and gold banner flowing on a tall pole was in one hand and the other on the reins. The man was well armoured in plate mail and a full helm, a letter V ornamenting the forehead of what looked to Axel like a tin bucket.

The helm was removed, to show a man with long dark hair and a matching moustache beneath. While trying to hold helm and banner in either hand, the messenger tried to reach for something he kept in a saddlebag behind himself. Clumsily, the helm fell to the dirt and rolled away down the gentle slope toward the sea, coming to rest on a stone that was larger than most.

The man in the saddle cursed audibly, but made no move to retrieve his headwear and instead used his now free hand to dig out a brass speaking trumpet that had a roll of parchment stored inside. He separated the two and put the horn to his lips. "Dwarves of Dhalla, I come before you today with a message from General Maylon of House Grantmoore, Director of the Armed Forces of King Valdarrow the Third," the messenger declared in a booming voice. "He bids you to open your gates in peace. In return he promises that you, your kin, and your kind, will be given a quick and painless death to be followed by a solemn and dignified cremation."

"How contemptible these beasts are!" Adlan Snowbeard bellowed angrily. "How dare they suggest that we should lie down and die for them?"

There was no way for the messenger to hear Snowbeard and he continued on unabated, "Foul creatures of Aren, I implore you to surrender before the might of Valdarrow, the true king of the world and the chosen prophet of Ios."

"That's how," Axel answered, leaving the fuming Adlan for a moment to join Parias at his station. He pointed to where the human's helm lay on its side. "Ser Parias, show this messenger what we think of his offer."

"I had hoped you might ask," Parias answered. He knocked an arrow to his fine, varnished yew bow and raised it to eye level, drawing and loosing the arrow in quick fashion. The arrow punched a visible dent in the helm and sent it rolling to the rocky beach further below, where it tumbled and clanged into the surf.

Adlan cupped his hands about his mouth and shouted at the human, "Go back to your General! Go back and tell him that if he wants to destroy Dhalla and the dwarves, he will have to come and fight us himself!"

The shocked rider looked to where his helm had been, then to Adlan, and back again before wheeling his horse about and retreating into the approaching horde.

With a pat on the back, Axel left Parias and returned to where Adlan stood, beckoning him to follow as he strode to the tower against the cliffs. Within the confined space of the tower's base was Torgus, his bag of tools splayed before him as he worked on a raised, circular steel plate embedded in the stone floor.

"Are we ready?" Axel asked hurriedly.

"Aye, quite nearly, ser," Torgus called back over his shoulder. "How does my brother fare? He should be at the top of the tower by now."

Axel stepped back and looked up the height of the tower, his line of sight following what looked like a full-length arrow slit to the top. At the very peak, he espied the red mass of iron, loaded into position. "I see the head of the Hammer."

Torgus was on his feet then, his bag of tools gathered up beneath an arm. "Then he is ready and so am I. Would you help me seal this door, ser? It can't be open when the Hammer falls."

As Axel stepped forward, he caught sight of Chinton from the corner of his eye, rushing down the steps of the tower, red faced and out of breath. "Sers, Vargas sent me to tell you that he's ready to deploy the Hammer!"

"Yes, yes, we know, lad," Adlan said while pointing Chinton towards the tower base. "Help us seal that door! Quickly, now!"

Axel, Adlan, and Chinton leaned their weight into the door, allowing Torgus to nail it shut with iron spikes.

Once finished, Axel released his hold on the door and nearly turned directly into Ser Parias, who had covered the distance from one side of the wall to the other. "Sers, if the door is sealed, does that mean you are using Montagen's Hammer for certain?"

"Aye, Parias, you'll want to signal your archers in the hillside," Axel said grimly, his eyes downcast. "I trust you warned them that this might come to pass?"

The right hand of Ser Parias went to his hip, retrieving a curved, brass horn that he held out for Axel to see. "Two blasts, that is my signal should Montagen's Hammer fall. Can we spare them the time to move out of its range?"

Adlan stepped forward beside the two of them. "Should you blow it at once, aye."

Without further discussion, the archer captain jogged to the nearest embrasure, stepped out as far as safety would allow and blew into the horn. *ARROOOOOOOO*

Axel turned to Adlan between blasts. "We should go give the order to Vargas. He'll want to hear it from us both."

After a few seconds had passed, Parias sounded the horn again, this time longer.

ARROOOOOOOOOOOOOOOOOO

By then, Adlan and Axel were already ascending the winding staircase on the outside of the tower. Axel looked southward, his eyes scanning for sight of the camouflaged archers in their grey suits amongst the hillside, trying to ignore the encroaching mass of humanity on the road below. He saw them, scrabbling upward and away from the edges and from where he stood they looked like little stones rolling the wrong way. *I pray that they all heard. I pray that I have given them enough time to get to safety.*

At the top of the staircase and beneath a canopied roof, they found a pacing Vargus of clan Spearsmasher, cracking his knuckles and eying his black and gold greathammer anxiously. Upon sight of the two leaders, he stopped in his tracks and gave a bow. "I wait only on your orders, sers. The Hammer is ready to fall."

Adlan Snowbeard walked to the smith's side and rested his hand to the young man's shoulder. "You can do this, Vargas. Your father built this tower and Montagen's Hammer for just such an occurrence. He prepared for this his whole life, as have you and Torgus. None of us wanted to ever use it, and in fact, I prayed nightly that such a day would never come. Yet, here we are, with no other recourse left to us but to drop the Hammer. We can't turn back now, so I need you to count off two minutes and swing with all your might, Vargas. Can you do that?"

"Aye, ser, if this be what you both so wish," he answered with a slow nod, looking to Axel for further approval.

He nodded back. "My wishes echo Ser Adlan's."

"Then it shall be done, sers," Vargas confirmed, lifting his impressive greathammer in both hands and turning away to the shaft in which the red, iron cylinder sat.

Adlan was back at Axel's side then, gesturing towards the stairs so that they might leave Vargas alone to his duty and return to the ramparts. "I was fighting beside Rahagas Spearsmasher when he died, Axel," the elder dwarf began once they were out of sight of Vargas. "I saw the body of Parias' uncle, Bhoden Windpiercer, and I held the hand of your father Raymus when he took his last breaths. I outlived the other three leaders of the dwarven clans of my generation and lived to be an old dwarf. My own father died fighting the first Valdarrow, as did your grandfather and thousands more. We banded together with humans, elves and half-elves and managed to slay him, but the pox keeps returning."

"Kill one Valdarrow, another springs up to take his father's mantle, and their senseless slaughter continues when he's old enough to command the bloodthirsty cult," Axel summarised with a sigh as they reached the surface atop the wall once more. "There doesn't seem to be any way to end it, Adlan. When you returned from their city, we all believed it was the end of Valdarrow's line. You yourself left their home believing he had no heirs and that their misinterpreted prophecies would die with the name. Yet, an army stands at our gates claiming to fight on behalf of a third Valdarrow."

"He's some bastard of the second Valdarrow, most likely, or perhaps not an offspring of Valdarrow at all and he's falsely claiming otherwise," the old dwarf supposed before turning his focus to the army closing in on their wall. "Those men out there, Axel, they were born and bred in Valdarrow's city, just as you were raised here in Dhalla. Unlike your upbringing, their leader kept a very tight fist on what they could and could not know, and as a result, you have an army of ignorance trying to obliterate us all. They have been raised to think that only creatures of Ios are worthy of life and anyone who believes differently, even other humans, should be put to death."

Axel scoffed. "The word of Ios, so they claim."

Snowbeard turned to him at that, a hand to his shoulder. "Listen to me, Axel: when the other Chieftains died, I vowed to Aren that I would be as much of a father to you, Torgus, Vargas and Parias as I am to

Dorrhen. I worked to guide you on the right path and ensure you were all raised to be good, decent dwarves."

"Speak quickly, Ser, for we have little time," Axel urged him. "Tell me what this is about."

"I heard what you said when the messenger listed Valdarrow's demands," Snowbeard told him, his voice turning melancholic for a moment. "I stood proudly beside men and women of all races who believed in Ios and Iia and Aren and even many who did not believe in any gods. They were good people and I was proud to stand with them and die with them, if it came to it. Aye, there are some, like the Valdarrows, who will twist the scriptures to their satisfaction, but they are not representatives of the greater whole, for the greater whole is essentially good.

"Those men out there never had a chance to experience that, and they've forced us to kill them or be killed ourselves. Even in the face of that, when I look at them, it is not hatred or even anger I feel -- it's pity, for they never had a chance to know better. I would rather find out that the gods were naught but lies than live in a world where I was not free to learn such."

As Axel was about to respond to that, he heard a loud roar from above and turned his head to see Vargas swinging his greathammer over his head and downward.

There was a loud noise that sounded to Axel like a broken bell being rung and the red piece of iron shot downward. Through the elongated slit in the tower, Axel tracked the progress of the ugly, misshapen metal, watching it fall. It struck with a clang on the metal plate and a great, ear-ringing blast sounded out so loud that Axel was sure it was heard all across Phaleayna. A sideways plume of smoke and dust blew out through an exhaust port of the outward facing side of the tower, but the real effect was along the cliff itself.

A thin trail of smoke ran along the cliff face at a blinding speed, emitting a bang and a blast at every retaining post, the first of which sat a hundred metres away. Valdarrow's forces stopped in their tracks, watching it as attentively as the dwarves on the wall. When it reached the final post, the smoke stopped. There was a final blast and for a few seconds everything was as silent as a crypt. Axel glanced to Adlan and found Snowbeard looking back, their faces sharing in their astonishment.

It started as a cracking and creaking in the beams as they resisted the fall, until one after the other they groaned their last and toppled, releasing the boulders and rocks of the cliffs onto the army below.

"The Hammer is falling! Everybody down!" Vargas called from atop the tower and this time even Adlan listened.

A deafening rumble drowned out Axel's hearing, the ground beneath him shook violently and dust blew over the wall in a great wave. Axel did not look, did not raise his head to see what was happening outside, and instead focused his thoughts on Egrid, saying a silent prayer for her safety in the process.

Dying men screamed in unison, in what Axel thought was by the thousands amid the rumbling. It seemed as though the quaking and screaming continued on for hours, until the wailing grew louder and the shaking ebbed.

A great cloud of dust hovered in the air, reducing visibility to a few hundred metres in front of the wall. Before them, it was carnage. Twisted lumber from the retaining beams and the catapults jutted up between blood-spattered boulders, and all around there were men crying out as they lay either atop or buried beneath the rubble. Even the beach below was a mess of stones, blood, and bodies, having pushed many of the humans clear off the road.

Torgus, having crawled on his hands and knees to stay below the cloud, was now between Axel and Adlan, peeking between the same merlons as they. "Is it over? Has the Hammer smashed out enough of them to send the rest running?"

Old Snowbeard's face was grim, his words even more so. "The catapults are gone, aye, and if their ram wasn't caught in that havoc, it certainly won't be able to cross the wreckage. However, how many of their men do you think we took down? A thousand? Two at most? The scouts claimed they saw seven thousand in the first place. What remains will want blood now more than ever. This battle is not over, Torgus. It has only started."

IN DEFENCE OF OUR HOME
PART II
First appearance in print

From the Author: "Here it is, as promised, the sequel to In Defence of Our Home. In between writing The Worth of Gold and the daily grind of life in general, this took a little longer than I might have liked, but I got it done and it's a long one. Enjoy!"

In Defence of Our Home
Part II

~Ser Dorrhen Snowbeard~

Youth is a bizarre thing," Adlan Snowbeard, eldest chieftain of the dwarven city-state of Dhalla and father of Dorrhen had told his son once. "It can fill a lad with feelings of invincibility and bravado that can lead him to think that he can cross swords with the whole world when he has never so much as even seen a duel. Yet, for their unearned assuredness, they will go boldly where the seasoned swordsman will fear to tread. Some commanders, like those of Valdarrow's ranks, build their armies based on that youthful ignorance. They put a sword in young hands, yell 'charge' and watch as they run blindly into the waiting arms of their maker.

"In Dhalla, we know better. We teach our soldiers to fight for life, to fight so that they and the people they swear to defend will see the next morning's light. To do that, you will be reintroduced to Fear, he who you knew as a child but abandoned in your reckless adolescence. However, you will not walk at his side apprehensively as you did as an unlearned boy. I will teach you how to work with him, how to glean his knowledge for your own and when we are done, it is Fear who will stand in your shadow forever more. His presence will be heard and seen and yet never a distraction, for you will be as accustomed to him as you are to my face."

The elder Snowbeard had lifted his son's chin then with a finger and looked him in the eyes. "I see your confusion, Dorrhen and I understand it, as I was once a young lad learning this very same lesson."

"Aye Father, I am confused. Fear is for the weak, is it not?" Dorrhen had asked his sire, every bit as nonplussed as the elder Snowbeard had claimed. "A warrior must have courage, not fear, correct?"

"*Surrendering* to Fear is for the weak." Even years on from then, he could still feel the finger of his father tapping the left temple of his head as he gave the second part of his answer. "You must come to know Fear and everything about him before he will introduce you to the true face of Courage. Together, they will never fail you, my son."

When Montagen's Hammer fell, the entire city shook beneath Dorrhen's boots and the screams of the dying men rolled over the gates. The quaking ground was something he had never felt before and the collective roar of the enemy army sounded inhuman, as though a great beast was crying out in unimaginable agony.

Dorrhen was well away during the fall, standing on a wide, stone road in the northeast corridor of the city that led into the foothills of Mount Montagen. Where he had been standing on Okin Street put Dorrhen a little less than half of the way between Dhalla's gates and his post at the entrance to Deepstone Mines, high in the mountainside. Even from his relatively low position, Dorrhen could see the rising dust and debris generated by the collapsing wave of stone barrelling over the enemy that marched toward them all. There were soldiers all about him and thrice as many civilians, all watching in complete silence as Montagen's Hammer unleashed a great calamity on the Southern Pass.

Some among the gathered flinched, more looked away or fell to a knee when the shaking beneath their boots took them by surprise. Dorrhen stood, with his stance braced against the rumbling world and at his side stood Fear and Courage.

"Was that... Was that Montagen's Hammer?" He heard a male ask from beside him, turning to find an elderly dwarf asking in awe. "All these years I had heard it existed... I never thought I would live to see it used..."

"Aye, that was it, old ser." Dorrhen answered, at a loss for much else to say in the moment.

The cloud of dust continued to rise, until it began to blot out the sky above. The wind was westerly and had already started blowing the brown curtain of dust toward the sea, yet it continued to expand ominously northward, threatening to blanket the entire city in its filth.

"Is it done, then?" Dorrhen heard, turning to see a man closer to his own age looking back at him.

From behind a woman asked, "Can we go back to our homes?"

Everywhere Dorrhen looked, there were more eyes falling to him, looking for guidance and reassurance amid a backdrop that threatened to fall forward and engulf actors and spectators alike. He tried to speak, but his mouth felt suddenly dry.

Between Father and Axel Goldenhair, there was always a superior officer with me to address the masses. I have never seen Montagen's Hammer fall before either, I do not know what is left of Valdarrow's army on the other side of the wall, how should I know what to do? He panicked internally, hoping he still looked outwardly calm. *That's Fear talking. I need to hear from Courage, they need to hear from Courage.*

"Montagen's Hammer has been dispatched," Dorrhen proclaimed loudly, "But it is too early to say if the threat has passed. We will continue with the evacuation procedure unless we are given word from the southern gates that it is safe to remain in Dhalla. Please proceed in an orderly and calm fashion to your designated evacuation point and once there, wait for further instructions from the commanding soldiers. If you have been ordered to report to the docks, your easiest route there will be Ocean Road, through the town square. Those of you with orders to report to Deepstone Mines, I advise you to follow me there."

~Ser Axel Goldenhair~

Montagen's Hammer was every bit as destructive as Chieftain Rahagas Spearsmasher swore it would be when he had engineered and built the thing. A pair of catapults and a ram, which accounted for the entirety of Valdarrow's siege units, had been eradicated in a deafening wave of stone. As the dust dissipated and Axel dared to look southward, beyond the protective merlons atop the city gates, he saw that the bulk of Valdarrow's vanguard was eliminated as well.

Sitting beside him was Adlan, Chieftain of Clan Snowbeard and between them was Torgus Spearsmasher, twin brother of Vargas, who together had unleashed their father's creation on the enemy.

A hopeful Torgus had asked if Montagen's Hammer had done enough to stop the attack on Dhalla, only to be told by Adlan that the attack was likely to be far from over.

"Well, Chieftains, what then are your orders?" Torgus asked after silence fell between them.

Axel and Adlan had been trying to survey the damage as much as the rising cloud would allow, but it was impossible to see what the untouched remainder of the enemy forces were doing.

"We have stalled them-" Adlan declared forlornly, before the dust made him break into a coughing fit. "But they will not stop, let alone retreat. Even with their siege weapons gone, they know we cannot duplicate the feat of Montagen's Hammer. The remaining forces that Valdarrow has here will be thrown at these walls, and if our scouts are correct, that number stands to be between four and six thousand strong."

Despite Adlan's grim projection, Axel found a positive aspect to remind them of, "Even if they were to resume marching this very second, the going will be slow with all the rock and debris we have strewn about the Southern Pass."

"That should also leave them quite open and vulnerable to our archers for a considerable time." Torgus added in agreement.

"They will use the larger boulders and rubble for cover, Torgus." Adlan stated with stoic certainty. "Never underestimate your foe, lads, for they are counting on that very sort of callow behaviour."

The bailey walls above the gates were outfitted with three tall obelisks: two scout towers that flanked the portcullis gates and the third near the cliff face of Mount Montagen, from which Vargas had dispatched the Hammer. It was from atop one of the gate towers that the dreaded call came: "Enemy on the move! Infantry and archers inbound by the hundreds!"

As quickly as the thought came to Axel to order Archer Captain Ser Parias Windpiercer to prepare for engagement with the enemy, Parias' voice called above the fray, "Archers, brace and ready to fire on my command!"

Adlan was on his feet then, beckoning to Torgus and Axel, "Come, we're in the way of Parias' soldiers, take cover behind the Hammer's tower with me."

The archers were quickly in their positions, with at least two taking cover to each stone merlon atop the wall. More were climbing the stairs to the ramparts and forming up in shoulder-to-shoulder lines, ready to loosen arrows in waves. From his new vantage point, Axel could see Ser Parias readying his own bow and looking to the soldiers along the wall's edge. "Knock your arrow!" Parias bellowed out, "Find your mark! Draw! LOOSE!"

After their volleys were fired, the archers took cover and as they turned their faces away from the charging force below, the arrows of the enemy started flying, most clacking and clattering uselessly off the brick of the wall and its towers, but a few made it beyond.

"Eyes to the skies! Arrows incoming!" Adlan Snowbeard bellowed through cupped hands in warning to the waiting soldiers standing on the city side of the gates.

Axel watched from his safe cover as those with shields raised them above their head, offering shelter to those without their own means of protection. Turning back to the Southern Pass, Axel saw a scrambling mass of humans that looked less like an army and more like a swarming horde.

"They're throwing their full weight at us now." Axel said to no one in particular, "The catapults and ram were to bait us into showing and wasting our best defences, and cornered as we are, we leapt at it and exposed ourselves."

While Axel had been talking, Vargas had descended the stairs of the control tower for Montagen's Hammer, the black and gold greathammer of his father held tightly in his hands. "What choice did we have? Those catapults would have obliterated the wall and everyone standing on it. The Hammer did its job and now it falls to us to do the rest."

"There are too many for my archers!" Parias shouted to Axel and Adlan, "The enemy is amassing beneath us!"

An agonised roar cut above Parias' voice. One of his archers stumbled back from position, his bow dropped, the hands that had held it now clasped tightly around an arrow extending from his chest. A swordsman caught him as he fell and Ser Parias ran to his side, ordering another archer to take his place in the process.

Axel and Adlan ran to him as well, arriving beside the wounded dwarf as he begged, "Let my boy and girl know that their Papa fought bravely, won't you, Ser? I sent them to the docks, to Lady Egrid. My sister is with them."

"You'll tell them yourself, Daggeth. The carriers are coming to bring you to the medical ships." Parias said softly. There were no carriers, and no order had gone out for them.

"How bad?" Adlan asked the infantryman still holding the fallen archer named Daggeth.

"It's... It's mortal, Ser." The sentry uttered back as quietly as he could, to keep Daggeth from hearing.

A shake of the head and a forlorn sigh came from Adlan and he walked away toward the centre of the wall.

"Ser Axel?" Daggeth asked, his voice growing faint. "I fought bravely for Dhalla, Ser. Did you see?"

Axel took the dwarf's hand in both of his and met his fading gaze. "Aye, you fought well, you truly did. I will ensure that the bards will write songs of your courage, Daggeth and that they will be sung for all to hear."

There came another scream then, and Axel looked up to see the archer that had been beside Daggeth was now struck as well. The soldier sat down sideways between the merlons and Axel saw a woman's face beneath the open steel cap on her head. She leaned back awkwardly against the same merlon that she had been crouched behind not seconds ago, her expression twisting in pain.

The archer that had replaced Daggeth reached out to grab their comrade, but was seconds too late, as the wounded dwarf slid sideways and tumbled out over the wall.

"Gods damn it, I lost another!" Parias exclaimed.

Daggeth's replacement had been peering out to where the archer had fallen seconds ago and turned to face Parias and Axel. "Sers, there's ladders beneath us!" He started. Though his mouth opened to say more, what came forth instead was a scream as his body jolted toward them with the force of an arrow puncturing his back. The dwarf fell forward and went still, dead before he touched ground.

"The fletchings on those arrows all match!" Ser Parias shouted angrily, rising from bent knees to a crouching position. "That's one archer out there doing all this damage to my soldiers and I'm going to put an end to the cur!"

The archer captain of the dwarves was gone before Axel could stop him. Parias moved with surprising grace and speed in his crouched stance and was back to the western edge of the wall where he had taken up his original position. Upon arrival, Parias' squire emerged from cover with his master's yew bow and quiver at the ready.

"Ser, Daggeth is gone." The soldier holding the wounded dwarf told Axel, taking his attention away from Parias.

Axel gave the dead archer a last look, and nodded at the soldier, ordering him, "Carry him out of the way with me."

With the deed done, Axel looked about for Adlan and found him giving orders to a greybeard dwarf in full armour.

"The enemy has ladders. They will be on the wall in no time." Axel told Adlan upon approach.

"You heard him," Adlan said to the dwarf he had been speaking to. "There's no time to lose."

The older dwarf bowed and departed for the staircase that led to the city without further word and Adlan turned to face Axel, "I anticipated as much and put together a contingency plan should it happen."

"You never told me of any plan." Axel stated, baffled by the revelation.

"And with good reason, Axel." Adlan responded while gesturing with a hand toward the stairs.

As the grey-bearded dwarf returned, he brought with him a unit of soldiers, all of them at least as old as he and Adlan. Their armour showed the marks of time and war, and their weapons and shields, though readied for battle, were as weathered as the dwarves that wielded them.

"These are the last veterans of the same army that marched to war against the second Valdarrow menace.

These were my soldiers, your father's, Rahagas', and Bhoden's too." Adlan declared with pride.

A ladder smashed down hard against the wall directly beside the tower of Montagen's Hammer.

As Axel was commanding Vargas to destroy it, he found his friend already springing forth to do so. He swung his greathammer sideways with a grunt at one of the stringers, separating it completely from the rungs. There were cries from below as the ladder broke apart and fell away, undoubtedly from the human climbers now in freefall to the ground.

One among the long line of elder warriors handed Adlan a round wooden shield crossed and banded in iron and a plain short sword that looked to have come from the armouries. After him came another that Axel knew to be named Crego. Though grey of hair, he was younger than the other veterans, having only been an adolescent when he had served as Adlan's squire for the entirety of the Second Valdarrow Conflict. In the hands of the former squire was the horned half-helm that Adlan had worn in the dozen or more battles that he had seen.

"Why are you doing this, Snowbeard?" Axel asked, unable to keep the despair from his voice any longer.

There was another commotion as a ladder fell in against the wall directly in front of where both dwarves stood. Several archers reeled back out of its way, crossing paths with a single, grizzled, old warrior swinging a battle-axe. In the span of a few seconds, he gleefully turned the top of the ladder to splinters and shoved the remnants sideways, where it slid out of sight, scraping loudly along the wall.

When Axel looked back to Adlan for an answer, he found the dwarf who had been his mentor with helm and shield at the ready. For a moment, Axel could no longer see the rust and dents in the armour and the lines in Adlan's face. He looked like the soldier of old that Axel remembered from his childhood. The same vigorous dwarf that had marched through the gates beside Raymus Goldenhair, Bhoden Windpiercer and Rahagas Spearsmasher now stood before Axel and in the reflection of Adlan's eyes, Axel saw his own father looking back.

"How often do you hear us old folks say 'I wish it were me instead' when we hear of a youngster suffering or dying, Axel?" Adlan asked calmly, "Our wishing is done. The moment to carry their burden is upon us."

Axel shook his head and looked away, his gaze falling to the rushing swarm beyond the wall. "Dhalla will not fall today, Snowbeard. Please, I beg you not to do this."

"We are going to hold the top of the wall." Adlan stated, ignoring Axel. "It will force Valdarrow's men to focus their primary energies on the gate. Even when they get it down, only so many of them can pass through it at once. In the narrow streets you should be able to keep them contained long enough to finish evacuating."

"You're not listening to me, Adlan!" Axel shouted in frustration, "We can hold against them. You often said yourself: 'ten atop a wall is as good as fifty attacking it'. We have that advantage at present."

The dwarf Axel had looked to as a father figure turned and met his stare with a face that was one of sober determination and resolve. "No Axel, it is you that is not listening. The walls are pressed with humans and the gates are being pried open as we speak. We cannot stop their egress into Dhalla, nor do we have the numbers to withhold the relentless onslaught of their offence once they are through the gate. *That* is the Valdarrow strategy: outnumber, exhaust and overwhelm. It's as brutal a tactic as any I know, but ideal when you have no concern over the life and limb of the enemy's soldiers... Or your own, for that matter."

"Then we hold until this General Grantmoore of Valdarrow's runs out of humans to hurl at us." Axel declared firmly.

Adlan was not swayed by the younger dwarf's pleading. "At what price does the holding come, Axel?" He asked rhetorically, as evidenced by his immediate continuation, "We may hold the city, aye, but almost anyone who can hold a sword or a bow will perish in the effort. All for a collection of stone, lumber, and mortar that we won't have people enough to inhabit, let alone repair. It's a reckless and grievous waste of life, Axel. We will gain more by evacuating and regrouping."

"Except for you," Axel cut in, before gesturing to Adlan's amassed unit of veterans, "And them, clearly."

Adlan was looking at the aged warriors then too, a melancholic expression on his face, "If lives are to be lost this day, let it be ones that have already lived."

"You won't be talked down from this, will you, Ser?" Axel posed the question despite knowing the answer, hoping there might be some other solution to the problem at the gates.

"Every dwarf before you readily joined me while knowing full well that if it came to such, that this would be the last day they spend in this world." Adlan stated firmly while taking a step away from Axel. "All we ask is that you not let our sacrifices be in vain. Ensure that our people get to safety, be it by ship or through the mines. Pull back our soldiers as the streets are emptied and those civilians are given a running start to either of the evacuation areas."

As he spoke, Adlan had removed his sword belt, wrapping it about the scabbard of his family's blade, which he then placed in the hands of Crego in exchange for the plain sword. "Crego, I relinquish Frost to you so that you may deliver it to my son, Dorrhen. Once the task is complete, I command you to head through the mines to Gethos Village and lend any aid you can to the wife. I have no doubt that Narra already has a list of tasks for you. Consider this your final order from me."

The former squire looked forlornly at the sword cradled in his arms and made eye contact with Adlan when he had finished issuing his commands. "Ser, I would like to stay and fight beside you, if you would allow it."

"I shall permit no such thing, Crego." Adlan responded firmly. "Frost must be brought to Dorrhen and there is no one else in Dhalla I trust as much as you to carry that out for me. Furthermore, when this day is done, my son will need counsel as he leads our people and it should be both someone he knows and someone who knew me well. Lastly, when all of this mess is done, you will likely be the last dwarf to have seen combat in the Second Valdarrow Conflict. I want, nay, I need you to write our tale in the books of history. Take your writings to Lanadorgh and speak for all of us so that those elves in the record halls get our stories right, you hear me?"

"Aye, Ser," Crego relented, "It will be as you command. I am honoured to have served as your squire, Chief Snowbeard. May Aren guide your blade today." He left then, holding Frost tight to his chest with a weight in his heart so heavy that it was almost tangible.

Axel watched Crego leave for a few seconds and turned his gaze back to the front of the wall, where he found Adlan staring back at him.

"What are you waiting for, Axel? Pull the archers off the wall first and cover their retreat with the infantry. When the archers are safely away from the battlements, my veterans will cover your infantry so that they may do the same."

"Are you certain about this?" Axel offered back, giving his old friend a last opportunity to withdraw from his plan.

That made Adlan smile as he replied, "As certain as I have ever been about anything."

"Right then," Axel said with a single nod, turning his attention to the heir of Clan Windpiercer, "Parias, draw your archers back to the rooftops!"

The archer captain spun about with an incredulous look splayed clearly across his face. Axel figured that Parias either had not heard the order or was confused by it, given that Parias was jogging to his side without issuing the order to his charges. "You want me to do what, Axel?"

"Pull them back to the rooftops immediately." Axel repeated, ensuring that the dire seriousness of the order came through clearly. "The infantry will keep the ladders at bay while you get your troops repositioned. Hurry now!"

"But Ser..." Parias had begun to say, until he took notice of the older dwarves that had taken up position all around the bailey. "What's this?"

Adlan stepped in, physically turning Parias towards the archers still crouched behind and firing between the merlons. "Make haste, Ser Parias, time is a-wasting."

He glanced at the chieftains once more worriedly, but made no further protest. "Archers! Fall back to the rooftops! Take the positions to support both the top of the wall and the gate below!"

"Infantry!" Axel shouted on Parias' heels, "Cover the wall for the archers! Beat back the ladders!"

"You know what you are doing, I trust?" Parias asked both chieftains as archers rushed past the three of them.

"I know what I am doing, aye," Adlan answered flatly, "Be well, Ser Parias, know that your parents and your uncle smile proudly at the dwarf you have become."

"I don't understand..." Parias stammered back, cut off by Vargas as he and Torgus approached.

"Plans have changed, I would guess, Sers?"

Axel spoke up quickly, "Aye, they have. Head to the street below and form up the lines behind the Steel Barrier: pikes front and centre, spears and heavy shields in direct support, the rest of the infantry in rear support. Everyone is to be ready for when the gate opens."

The twins shared a look and Torgus asked what they were clearly both thinking, "Did you say 'when', Ser?"

"That he did, Torgus." Adlan jumped in again. "Go now and follow his orders. You have all done splendidly today, may you do no less until the battling is done."

It was down to the Goldenhair and the Snowbeard then, and of the two, it was Adlan who spoke first. "Alright Axel, call your infantry back. It's time."

However, Axel was not yet ready to leave, "Adlan, I want to thank you for all you have done for myself, Parias, the Spearsmasher twins, and Egrid too, for all of Dhalla, for that matter. You will never be forgotten. *This* will never be forgotten."

"The people of this city are in yours and Dorrhen's hands now." Adlan calmly intoned. "It falls to you two and Egrid and Parias and the Spearsmasher lads to ensure that they live to see tomorrow. Preserving the memory of my fellow greyhairs and me will come naturally, so long as there are dwarves enough to remember."

For the moment, Axel's words failed him but his instincts did not. His left hand curled into a fist and he brought it to rest on his right shoulder, making the salute that had been with the dwarves since the warriors of ancient times.

Adlan saluted back quickly, "Go now, lad." He intoned as softly as the ruckus would allow, putting his back to Axel so that he might face his aged warriors and the approaching army beyond the wall. "Brothers and sisters, stand with me now! Fight to your last breath on this day! Fight not for bricks and mortar, for the city will be lost before days end. Fight instead for your sons and daughters, for your grandchildren, fight for the survival of all dwarven kind!"

A cheer rose from the gathered force atop the wall, weaponry rising in unison. Adlan was walking among them then, his own sword held high. "Tonight we shall feast as the guests of honour in Aren's Palace, where Cygas himself will tap his best kegs of ale and casks of the finest wine from Laural's vineyards shall be brought forward for us. Waiting there, at Aren's side, will be Rahagas Spearsmasher, Bhoden Windpiercer, Raymus Goldenhair and all the dwarven warriors to have gone before us. I will see you there, my friends, and together we will toast to the survivors, that they did not let our sacrifice be for naught."

That was Axel's cue to leave, he knew and he faced the stairs to do such, stopping for the briefest of moments to see his oldest friend just once more.

Below the wall, Axel found the armed and armoured waiting for him. The first to greet him was Chinton, his ever-faithful squire, who approached hurriedly as Axel touched the bottom step. "Ser Axel, the Steel Barrier has assembled, ready for command. The infantry stand behind them in direct support, Ser Parias' archers are nearly in position on the rooftops and a small contingent of Ser Arber Wyldmare's cavalry holds the rear, led by Ser Wyldmare himself."

"You have done excellent work, Chinton." Axel complimented the young man, "Fetch for me a pike so that I may join the front line."

"Is that wise, Ser?" He asked cautiously.

"Of course it is," Axel affirmed without doubt. "Anything less would be cowardice. I cannot ask my army to die for me if I am not willing to die for them."

The squire bowed his head without further query. "Very well Ser, I shall see to that pike right away."

He left the lad to it, taking the time to look over the mass of dwarvenkind standing at arms before him. The Steel Barrier, as it was colloquially known, was a defensive infantry division, defined primarily by the large, cumbersome, rectangular shields they brought to battle. It took two dwarves to carry and hold a single shield and they required the constant support of pike and spear units when in direct combat. Alone, the shields provided great protection for infantry, but it was as a single entity that the Steel Barrier could truly shine. Each shield had a tongue and a groove on the left and right edges, allowing them to lock in to one another easily while holding tightly. A line of these shields made for a mobile barrier that could hold back an army double its size. Combining the Steel Barrier with pole weaponry and archery units made for as effective a fighting force as Axel had ever seen.

As he stood there on the steps in wait of his squire, a small gathering formed below Axel, knight captains and clan leaders mostly, with a scattered armed civilian here and there. Torgus and Vargas stood among them, having taken the time to don the finely made chain mail and plate armour each twin had made for the other. The former bore a pike of his own to hand while the latter leaned on his late father's greathammer. They were who he looked to first and his dear friends returned the gaze, imbuing him with confidence when one of the captains asked for their orders.

"Montagen's Hammer failed to adequately destroy the Valdarrow force and now the brunt of their infantry and archery units are amassing at the wall. At this rate, the wall surely will be scaled and our gates will soon fall. This is now an evacuation and our goal is to grant the citizens of Dhalla as much time as possible in which to do so. We will hold the humans here as long as we can, backing ourselves slowly to the southern square, where we will divide our forces into two. One unit will continue to retreat down Okin Street at a gradual pace, stalling as long as can be afforded on Pickaxe Hill. The higher ground will give you a considerable advantage in height and time that the second unit simply will not have."

Axel looked to a single knight captain in particular, a seasoned ranger six years his senior from Clan Belsword. The clan's colours were violet, and this one wore the hue in the form of feather plumage that poked high from his steel helm. "Ser Entmer Belsword, command of the infantry is yours."

"What of the second unit?" Torgus asked, seemingly for everyone that were assigned to it, judging by the nodding and looks of concern. "You said they would have less time."

"They will be led by me. We will provide a guard along Ocean Road. The way is downhill, and the humans both outnumber and outsize us. In fact, I anticipate that they will see the advantage and a heavier force will press us there. Time will not be ours to waste. Those of you overseeing the evacuation of the civilians, I encourage you to put as many dwarves as you can spare on the Ocean Road route and tell them to make haste. Lady Egrid and her soldiers and staff will direct the civilians and the evacuators to the ships once they reach the waterfront.

"Our formation will remain as defensive as possible." Axel continued. "The Steel Barrier will hold the front line, the pikes, spears and archers will support directly. As pikes and spears are broken, the infantry will pass more forward and stand ready to answer should the Barrier break. Those with wooden and iron-band shields will fill in the Barrier's gaps, if any should appear. At the square, the Barrier will divide into two and continue to provide frontal defence until the order to disband and evacuate is given, or, Aren forbidding, they are reduced to such numbers as to be no longer effective."

Axel looked for and found the cavalry captain next, "Ser Wyldmare, you and your pony riders will chase down any humans who can break through our forces and assist the evacuation as much as you can. When we divide at the square, you are to go with the Okin Street unit. I'm afraid the ships will have no room to spare for your mounts."

By the time the briefing had started, Chinton had returned, standing quietly at the back until Axel had finished, by which point he began shimmying through the knights and leaders with the tall pike held tight. "Thank you, Chinton." Axel said with gratitude, unslinging his shield from where it sat on his back and taking it into his right hand. "Go now to my wife, inform her of where the battle stands and assist her in any way you can from here on out."

"But Ser, my place as your squire is with you!" Chinton protested.

It was entirely uncharacteristic of the lad, who had only ever been obedient and demure before. What further struck Axel as atypical was that while Chinton had taken a knee and titled Axel correctly, his delivery lacked in the usual militaristic formality that was expected of the squire. Before such an audience of ranking military and clan leaders, Axel would be expected to reprimand Chinton for having defied his orders. However, he could not bring himself to.

"I understand how you feel Chinton, but my orders are final." Axel declared firmly. "You will go to Lady Egrid, deliver her the latest information and wait upon her command."

Before the squire could open his mouth again, Torgus stepped forward and clapped him on the shoulder. "Worry not, Chinton, for I'll be standing right beside Ser Axel. Valdarrow's humans shall not so much as slice a single strand of that long golden mane he treasures so long as I live."

"What are you waiting for, Chinton? You heard Ser Torgus. Go, quickly now." Vargas jovially added from beside his brother. "We will keep Ser Axel safe."

"Yes, Sers, of course. Please, forgive me for my insolence." He stammered out while pushing into Axel's left hand the pike he had asked for. "I shall take my leave of you, Ser."

Axel was on the verge of calling out to Chinton, but he had gone as fast as his legs could take him and Axel lost him amongst the armed dwarves in a matter of seconds.

"I understand his disappointment all too well, but there's no room for him on the front line, Axel," Vargas said, showing pity for Chinton. "You did the right thing."

"Not much else to be done about it right now." Axel stated calmly, taking the few remaining steps to the street while he did. "I merely hope he does not hold it against me."

He took a deep breath, cleared his mind of his squire's woes and directed his attention at the leaders before him, "To your positions! Make no further delays!"

~Lady Egrid Goldenhair~

"What is all this?" Egrid asked while striding up the ladder of the hold of the most recent ship to have moored itself at the waterfront. The frigate-sized merchant ship named *The Wave Glider* had docked while she was at the briefing atop the city walls and her staff had already begun the process of loading residents on it when she returned. She had expected that by now, the ship should be readying to leave. Leeda, Egrid's second-in-command, was standing on the deck of the ship, a sheaf of papers in one hand, the other pointing angrily at a member of the nobility who was engaging her in a shouting match.

The male dwarf, clad in fine robes and carrying no visible belongings, spun on his heel at the sound of Egrid's voice and marched up to her as she stepped onto the topside of the ship. "I shall tell you what this is: your feckless subordinate is condemning me to die by refusing me passage on this ship. I waited all morning for a ship this fine to dock and when it does, I'm denied a place on it!"

"I apologise, Mister..." Egrid began, trailing off purposefully so that he might give her his name.

"That's *Lord*, actually, Lord Thigmourd III of the Sapphire Clan, if you please." He declared haughtily, looking insulted all the while, likely due to Egrid not knowing him on sight.

It took all her strength to keep her eyes from rolling at him, "Right, *Lord* Sapphire, you will pardon me for not calling you as such from the outset. I would like to hear from Ser Leeda if you would be so kind as to let her speak."

Her lieutenant took her cue to step forward, curled dark hair flowing over strong shoulders covered in the chainmail of her armouring. "My lady, Mister Sapphire here-" Leeda began, until Thigmourd cut her off.

"That's *Lord* Sapphire, Ser!"

"There are no lordships amongst the dwarves." Leeda retorted bitingly, "Some human might have bestowed that title on you, but it is honorary at best, and regardless, it has utterly no meaning here."

"Ser Leeda!" Egrid interjected, her patience growing thin. "Conduct yourself with a little more decorum than that and get on with telling me your side of this dispute."

With an audible huff and a pivot towards Egrid, Leeda seemed to compose herself. "Yes, my lady, please forgive me. Mister Sapphire here wished to board the ship and just as every other citizen before him had, he was given full permission to do so. The difference in this case was his insistence that he do so with four servants carrying two large chests of gold and jewels between them. That is what the *delay*, not the *denial*, is all about."

She knew her lieutenant to be no liar, yet Thigmourd had gasped indignantly as soon as Leeda mentioned his intended cargo and would doubtlessly be seeking rebuttal.

Egrid jumped in before that could happen. "I have neither the time nor the patience to officiate this squabbling, Lord Sapphire, so I ask that you save your breath so that you might answer me one question: did you intend to board a ship with two chests of gold and jewels?"

"Lady Egrid, I-

A raised hand and a loud 'ahem' stopped Thigmourd from elucidating further. "You may answer with 'yes' or 'no', as I have no time for appeals or bargains."

The lips of Thigmourd pursed in frustration, and where Egrid expected another burst of outrage instead came a meek, "Yes, My Lady, I did."

"Lord Sapphire, the rules on personal belongings, as repeated loudly and often by my soldiers and posted on no less than three different bulletin boards in just the immediate vicinity alone state that: 'One may carry aboard a ship only what one can carry on oneself without being a weighted burden or an obstruction to oneself or other passengers.' Are you not aware of this?" Egrid stated in direct terms.

"I am," An increasingly flustered Thigmourd stammered in reply. "However, I did hope in this circumstance that you would make an exception, given that I have much more to carry than the average dwarf. Surely, someone of my financial means would be of benefit once our motley flotilla lands on the Drakian piers in search of refuge."

Egrid was aware that Thigmourd had a point about the gold and jewels, to be certain, but there was a more pressing concern for the rules being as unbending as they were in this circumstance: "I can make no such exceptions, Lord Sapphire. The ships are loaded with space and weight taken into consideration and we aim to fit every person possible, within safety, onto each ship. Two heavy, wide chests would mean that no less than three dwarves, perhaps even as many as five or six would have to be left off the ship in exchange and I will not measure dwarven lives in gold and jewels."

The noble dwarf pinched the bridge of his nose with his thumb and index finger as Egrid had been talking and threw his arms in the air when he was given chance to speak once more. "What then, would you have me do with this fortune? Let it fall into Valdarrow hands? I simply refuse to allow my hard-earned wealth to fund the enemy's war efforts."

"Drop the chests into the sea." Egrid responded calmly.

Thigmourd's eyes widened at the notion of it. "I beg your pardon?"

"I will lend you two of my soldiers and a coil of rope to aid your servants. Together, the six of them should be enough to lower your chests into the waters, preferably under the pier, where it will be out of sight. If we have to evacuate, your valuables will be recovered once Valdarrow's forces abandon the city."

"The very suggestion is preposterous!" Thigmourd exclaimed.

"It is not a suggestion, Lord Sapphire. You have before you one of only two options. The other is to leave it on the docks."

Following a few grunted expletives, Thigmourd resigned himself to the fates presented to him. "If you insist, Lady Egrid, I will obey your commands and accept the offer of aid in the form of soldiers and rope. Might I at least take a pocketful or two of gold and gems?"

"You may take whatever does not encumber you, Lord Sapphire." Egrid reiterated, relieved to have the commotion resolved.

"Lady Egrid," A new voice added to the air, one she recognised as that of her head of staff, Lewin. He was striding up the gangway of the ship with another familiar, albeit winded, face in tow. "Your husband's squire, Mister Chinton, calls upon you with urgent news."

Lewin eyed the lad for moment as he bent over, hands on his knees in an attempt to catch his breath, asking him, "Erm... Perhaps it is best if I tell the lady?" Chinton nodded rapidly in response and Lewin returned his gaze to Egrid. "As I was saying, Lady Egrid, Chinton has a message from your husband: Montagen's Hammer destroyed the siege weaponry, but barely scraped the numbers of their armed forces. The gates are expected to fall and the walls scaled. Ser Axel has called for a full evacuation and he, along with the Spearsmasher twins and Ser Parias, have joined the defensive effort to give the evacuators as much time as possible."

"You make no mention of Ser Adlan, Lewin." Egrid posed worriedly. "What of the old Snowbeard?"

Chinton was standing erect again and popped his hand into the air silently, waiting until Egrid gave him leave to provide the answer to her query. "He marshalled a force made up of his fellow elders that could still fight and they positioned themselves upon the ramparts to hold off the climbers of the city wall. They all expect they will die, Lady Egrid."

"Then we should ensure that their sacrifice is honoured." Egrid said to all before her. "Finish the boarding of this ship immediately, no delays. Put it, and all other uncovered vessels to sail and have them join the flotilla already at sea. Summon the turtle ships to the docks and have them ferry the remaining citizens to the convoy." She squared her gaze on Thigmourd alone. "If you can dump your chests before this ship leaves, you may board it, but I will not hold it for you. Consider the consequences of your actions and make a choice, Lord Sapphire."

~Ser Dorrhen Snowbeard~

"I am not worthy to bear Frost, Crego." Dorrhen explained to his father's old squire. "It is the weapon of a blooded warrior and I am but the son of such. Please, take it with you to Gethos Village and keep it safe."

The faithful servant was on bended knee, the sheathed sword of the Snowbeard clan held out to Dorrhen hilt first. "Ser Dorrhen, with all due respect, his orders were to bequeath it to you and no one else." Crego told him with as much defiance in his voice as he might dare. "I never disobeyed your father in all my time in his service and shall not do so with his final orders."

"Final orders..." Dorrhen repeated, the words tumbling from his lips in equal parts shock and sorrow.

"Ser Adlan and the other veterans of the Second Conflict stand upon the wall with the knowledge that there will be no survivors among them. I was entrusted with Frost by Ser Adlan with orders to give it only to you, so that it would not be lost to Valdarrow. He judged you worthy, Ser Dorrhen. In what judgement would you trust above your father's?"

"How did he look when last you saw him, Crego?" Dorrhen asked solemnly.

"Fearless." Crego replied back, his voice beaming with pride.

No Crego, Fear was with Father, standing in his shadow and doing as father commanded him. Dorrhen thought to himself. *What can I say of myself?*

"If the gate and the wall fall today as Crego says, you will be blooded before this day is done, Dorrhen. All of you will be."

Troysan of the Lost-Sword Clan had been the speaker, a dwarf just a few years older than Dorrhen, who had seen and survived a bandit ambush just north of the human settlement of Barnam. He was of a size with Dorrhen, dark of hair and bearing two long, deep scars across his face on the right cheek and jawline that he had been given in the aforementioned ordeal. The elders had declared him to be blooded after the skirmish, and among those guarding the entrance to Deepstone Mine, Dorrhen believed Troysan might be the only one.

"It is not something to aspire to, nor something to be particularly proud of." Troysan continued, "That sword is not to be given as a reward, Dorrhen. Your father entrusts it to you to increase your odds of living long enough to know that you have been blooded. Wield it."

By all the rights and laws of Dhalla, Dorrhen was Troysan's superior, but he had never, nor could he ever, treat Troysan like a subordinate. Rebuking Troysan for omitting Ser from Dorrhen's name would have felt wrong under any circumstances. As stern and strong an image as Dorrhen felt he showed the world, Troysan was the real thing, made of stuff so strong that Dorrhen would not be the least bit surprised if molten steel ran through his veins.

Sitting beside him on part the burlap bags of sand that had been stacked at chest height around the perimeter of the mine in layers and rows was Tinnia. The auburn haired dwarven woman was Dorrhen's closest friend and confidant and the one other person besides Troysan that he could not bring himself to correct for dropping the 'Ser' from his name.

"Tinnia, you have been quiet since Crego arrived. I would welcome your input." Dorrhen said, giving her invitation to speak up.

"You know what I am going to tell you, Dorrhen: take the sword." She told him. Though he was not one to admit as much, Tinnia did indeed know him well. "We have trained for a day like this since we were old enough to hold a practice sword. After all the lessons and practice, Ser Adlan felt confident that you were ready to face the danger with Frost and emerge on the other side with it still safely in your hands. Take it, Dorrhen."

As far back as Dorrhen could remember, Tinnia had been there and somehow, she always had the right of things. The smile on her face was what won him. It was certain and her eyes thoughtful and analytical. Tinnia had been dwelling on the matter as the three men had been talking, Dorrhen surmised, and was sure of her words.

Stand aside, Fear. Today you will be but my shadow.

Dorrhen reached out and put his left hand about the hilt, gripping firmly enough that the leather wrapped about it groaned. He took a deep breath, exhaled, and drew Frost from the scabbard in a single, deft motion.

The blade glimmered brightly, almost shinning in the daylight as he turned it in his hand. At two centuries old, the sight of it never failed to leave him in amazement, given that it always looked so flawless as to have been forged yesterday. The bright, white shimmer that so caught the eye of every beholder was an affectation of the particular alloy of steel used in Frost, he had been told, and one not easily replicated. It held an edge well, and much like the blacksteel found in newer dwarven weapons, it needed little sharpening.

"Blacksteel may be a lighter material than the dwarven steels of old, but Frost is as deadly as anything created in the Montagen's Belly Forge." His father had told him as a boy. "A member of the Snowbeard Clan trains to be a swordsman so that they might one day wield *this* sword alone. What need do we have of lighter steel, when we have the strength within to swing a blade bearing two centuries' worth of Snowbeard history? You will be its owner someday, Dorrhen, when you are strong yourself."

"Frost certainly suits you." Dorrhen heard Tinnia say, her voice suddenly sounding distant.

He retreated from the memory back to reality and saw her standing now, arms folded across the steel plating of her armour's breastplate.

"Do you think so?" Dorrhen offered in response. The sword looked strange in his hand, almost foreign, as though he had no business seeing it from this vantage. He had held it as his father's swordbearer at feasts and other important functions, but it was always by the sheath and with both hands. Now he looked upon it from behind the pommel, to his own fingers wrapped about the hilt and down across the exposed steel. It was a view he never envisioned having if for no other reason than he could not picture his father without Frost.

A weight came crashing upon Dorrhen then. Not from the heft of the sword, or any other tangible force, but from a wave of realisation that washed over him so strongly that it nearly put a buckle in his knees.

I am holding Frost because Father is gone.

"Dorrhen, how are you feeling?"

That sounds like Tinnia.

"Hey now, Dorrhen, come on back to us."

I have not gone anywhere, Troysan.

Tinnia shook his right shoulder and he looked at her, then down, to where he had lowered the sword to his side.

"My father is gone." Dorrhen muttered to her.

"And Dhalla will forever be darker without him." Troysan added, "But now it falls to you to ensure its people find their way to safety. To do that, you must set aside your grief, just for now, and be a warrior worthy of Frost and of the name Snowbeard."

Dorrhen leaned back on the smooth rock of Montagen's base, looking at both his friends and Crego in turn. "I am not half the man my father was."

"You will be." Crego told him. "Your father has been readying you for this very day since you could walk on two feet. You had the direct tutelage of one of the finest soldiers and leaders in Dhalla's written history guiding you personally, Dorrhen and you were an astute pupil in your own right.

"There is one aspect you seem to be overlooking, young Dorrhen: Ser Adlan was not born with his accomplishments already written. Just as you now, he too had to begin somewhere. Put his wisdom into action and let this be the day your record begins."

Above him on scaffolds moored to the mountainside stood a small unit of archers, their eyes focused on the streets below for signs of the enemy. Soldiers armoured in mail wielding steel weaponry and wooden shields paced nervously behind and just in front of the sandbag barrier. Metres away, at the entrance to Deepstone mine, a steady stream of dwarven civilians passed beneath the iron archway bearing the mine's name. As they came to the threshold, each stopped just long enough to give their name, age and address to one of the several soldiers keeping records.

This is war. Dorrhen reminded himself. *It is not a glorious affair as the singers and storytellers so often like to make it seem, nor has it yet devolved into a maddening melee like the battles of the Second Conflict that father survived, but it is war. I remember Father showing me an entry from the journal that Grandfather kept during the strife with the first Valdarrow. Grandfather had written the passage after the original tyrant was finally destroyed. It read, "War is the Ultimate Failing of the intelligent beings. That is all war represents: failure. It is a failure to negotiate, a failure of understanding, a failure of communication and a failure to show even the most basic of decencies towards one another. It is the failure of the peoples of the nations and lands to choose proper leadership and then the further failure of those leaders, myself included, to maintain peace amongst us all.*

Many creatures of the wilds and the oceans that we believe to be lesser than us may eat one another, but they do not know war. The tall oaks south of the Varras and the colourful wildflowers of Long Bend Valley know nothing of wanton bloodshed until our blood spills upon their leaves and petals. It is our *Ultimate Failing alone, yet it is one we inflict upon all life, both intelligent and otherwise, without consent."*

Dorrhen saw his grandfather's words etched on the faces of the dwarves passing into Deepstone. They were being torn from their homes and facing annihilation if they did not. The four chieftain families for centuries had taken measures to protect the dwarves of Dhalla from the Ultimate Failing. Montagen's Hammer, the Iron Seal, the turtle ships and the standing flotilla of seaworthy ships, all of it were careful measures taken by leaders who sought to keep the Ultimate Failing from touching their people.

Even I am one of those measures, as are Axel, and Parias and the Spearsmasher twins too. We were raised to be the next in line to prevent the descent into war and if we cannot halt the descent, we must be prepared to face the abyss ourselves, to bear that burden so that our people will not.

"Send word to the evacuators to double their efforts." Dorrhen commanded, the suddenness of it turning the heads of Troysan, Tinnia and Crego alike. "Let them know that should the enemy pass the southern wall, the Iron Seal will be engaged not long afterward. Tell them that I will give them time, but only as much as my unit can give until they are fatigued. Give the orders and remind them that we are beyond saving the city itself now. This is about saving as many lives as we can."

"It shall be as you command, Dorrhen." Tinnia stated with a salute, "Let's go, Troysan, we have work to do."

Crego was looking at him again and Dorrhen gave him leave to speak. "Ser Adlan's other command was for me to go through the mine to Gethos Village, to lend aid to your mother and the others overseeing the refuge situation that is most certainly unfolding there. I would not like to break the final orders of my liege, but if you so command it, I shall, Dorrhen."

"I will command no such thing, Crego." Dorrhen uttered with a slow shake of his head. "Please, go to Gethos, inform my mother of what has transpired and lend her all the help you can."

"As you wish, *Ser* Dorrhen," Crego replied, emphasising the word 'Ser' with great pride. "And may Aren guide your blade."

~Ser Axel Goldenhair~

Despite a concerted effort of the enemy, the southern gate remained closed. They pounded as one, simultaneously and timed seconds apart, so that each crash they made against the timber doors sounded forebodingly loud. Above it, Ser Adlan and his fellow veterans were battling upon the ramparts against the ladder climbers. The clanging of steel and the screams and shouts of those fighting and dying overhead rang eerily over the waiting army on the street below.

"We should be up *there*." Torgus said in Axel's ear, just as the gate absorbed another blow.

"The gate will not hold forever, Torgus. We are exactly where we should be." Axel answered him.

Ser Parias began shouting from up on the rooftops, distracting Axel and Torgus from their conversation. The archer captain was pointing and commanding for a select few of his archers to draw and loose on the top of the stairs leading to the ramparts and Axel looked to see why.

Standing there was a single human, tall, even for them, spattered in blood and wielding a longsword. He shouted something inaudible, followed it with a deep, guttural, menacing laugh that would have curdled a weaker person's will, and took his first step.

It would also prove to be his last.

Arrows pierced the human's chest in quick succession and he tumbled off the stairs onto the stone street. If he survived the fall, the quick work of the spear carriers nearest to where he landed ensured it was not for long.

"No armour beneath those ragged pelts, not even mail, judging by the way those arrows punched him." Torgus postulated to Axel, a twinkle of hope in his eye. "If that is their army, we might yet win."

Regardless of Torgus' optimism, Axel remained grounded. "He was just one, there will be many more coming and we do not have archers enough to stop them all. Be ready, Torgus."

The pounding on the gate ceased and the fighting atop the wall became the only source of noise for what seemed like two to three long minutes.

"Perhaps they have pulled back?" A soldier standing near Axel queried anxiously.

"I sincerely doubt that." Axel began to reply, being cut off by a loud crash that shook the entire timber gate and its iron fittings. "Dwarves, take positions!" He bellowed out while lowering his pike to the shield in front of him. "Pikes forward! Spears ready for their cue!"

Another crash sent splinters flying inward and bent the iron support bars along the impact zone. It struck again, showing the first sign of the destruction of the wooden gate and a third time gave a glimpse of the southern pass beyond. The forth crash brought through what Axel had been expecting: the head of the battering ram.

"A ram!" One of the soldiers bearing the shields of the Steel Barrier cried out from directly in front of him. "They have a ram!"

It was a demonic looking thing, like something from one of the horror fables come to life. The head was black, whether it was made of wood or iron was yet to be seen, but someone had painted large red eyes on it and carved a mouth of jagged, crooked teeth. On the fifth crash, which sent a horizontal iron support bar tearing away, Axel even saw that the ram was affixed with horns modelled after those of a wild goat.

"They won't be long before they are through our gate!" Axel bellowed out, hearing his words being reverberated throughout by the other leaders. "Dwarves, brace yourselves!"

Then they came.

First, there was just one or two of them, what could fit through the relatively small hole that the ram had made thus far, on what was either the seventh or the eighth crash, the gate gave up its fight and the double doors swung inward with a loud and terrible whine.

A screaming horde of humanity charged in, running with all their speed toward where Axel and his fellow dwarves had made their stand.

Axel cleared his throat and let roar as loud as his lungs could bear, "Pikes and shields, brace for impact!"

The meeting of man and dwarf proved to be a sickening clamour of screams and colliding metals that echoed deafeningly in Axel's ears. During the collision, several humans became impaled on the pikes, the steel points ripping through flesh and bone in a disgusting orgy of splattering, gushing blood and squishing noises overlaid with screams of terror and agony. Those that managed to evade the pikes pressed themselves against the Steel Barrier, with all of them trying to climb over it or hack at the dwarves on the other side.

His own pike was still clean, though humans stood to either side of it, trying to reach him and his soldiers standing opposite of the wall of shields.

"Pikes, spread!" Axel called while moving to the left, sliding his pike hard until it could move no more against the humans. The action served to push the humans close together, immobilising them to a degree, with nowhere for them to retreat behind the growing mass of their own still piling through the destroyed gate.

Axel kept the pressure applied, grunting out his next order through the strain as loudly as he could, "Spears, thrust!"

From behind and beside him, the spear fighters stepped forward, driving their weapons into the enemy lines.

Blood rained down and the screaming grew.

Mere metres away, a human had jumped the Steel Barrier, swinging an axe downward as he did. A single cry echoed in Axel's ears and he knew in that moment that dwarven blood was being shed before him.

The soldiers nearest to the human responded in a flurry of steel and the threat cried out in defeat and death. Axel turned his head for visual confirmation and received a crimson spray.

He had meant to call for a shift in the pikes, to give the spears another chance to attack, instead he began to spit almost involuntarily as the blood hit his lips.

It was a mistake to look at his feet to spit the enemy blood, he knew it even as he heaved it out, and when he looked up a human was plunging over the shields at him.

His arms rose defensively, the human roared in his face and the red tide showered over him.

What? How am I not...?

"Push him back, Axel! Help me before he crushes us both!"

Torgus had saved him, his pike bending beneath the weight of the skewered human he was trying to keep aloft above them.

Axel grabbed the dying man, others came forward to help, and with a great heave and a loud crack from Torgus' breaking pike, they threw the enemy back among his own.

The humans were pressing hard and the pikes that remained among the dwarves seemed useless in their efforts to hold back or repel what now pushed against the steel shields. Axel looked to the rooftops for Ser Parias and his archers and found them trying to contain the enemy units on the ramparts and those in the streets simultaneously. They lacked the numbers to handle both of those tasks and it was clear that the direct threat to Parias' unit were the men on the ramparts that were slowly overwhelming Ser Adlan's elder fighters, but the Archer Knight was trying to direct as many of his bows as he could afford toward the invaders below him too.

The sight made Axel's next decision an easy one to make.

"Retreat fifteen paces!" Axel commanded as loudly as he could.

Once the order had worked its way from end to end of the shields, the dwarves holding them let out a harmonic grunt. The shields lifted as one and their carriers began walking backwards with their armed comrades trying to keep ahead of them.

The humans followed, ensuring that every centimetre of the retreat was ground lost, keeping up their attack as much as they could.

"Get back, you accursed brutes!" Torgus bellowed while driving a fresh spear he had obtained from the back lines into the nearest enemy.

One of the two shield carriers operating the shield directly to Torgus' right stumbled, creating a visible gap in the Steel Barrier. Before Axel could blink, a burly human kicked his way through the space. Pikes and spears made for him, but his own wooden shield sufficed to keep them away.

"I told you to get back!" Torgus shouted again, this time specifically at the human on the dwarven side of the shield wall. The spear of Torgus found its home in the human's right leg, tearing through the flesh just below the hip. The man dropped a rusted sword from his right hand and grabbed the shaft of the spear that pierced him, pulling it free with a great grunt and a gush of blood. The human's shield deflected a blow from up high, but more blades began to land on his lower torso and legs and he slipped from sight beneath the dwarven soldiers.

"Lift that shield! Get it back in place!" Axel ordered quickly, before looking about to take in the rest of the scene unfolding along the shield line. There were more gaps in the Steel Barrier now, more humans breaking through their defences and worst of all, more bloodshed from both sides. Amid that chaos, the futility of fighting the humans further became starkly clear. "Pikes and spears push the enemy back, and everybody retreats to the city square! Divide at the fountain!"

It is what the old man would do. What he ordered us *to do.*

The retreat went quickly, with the shield-bearers moving fast enough that the pike and spear-carriers had to trot to keep from being trampled by their kin. The speed made for a small space between the opposing armies, but there was no room to waste and soon the city square was under their feet.

Axel took a breath so that his next command would carry loud and clear. "Steel Barrier, divide in two!"

What remained of those holding the shields separated at the midway point and kept retreating east and west until the square was on the other side of the steel defences and the narrow streets leading to the evacuation points were to their backs. Axel, with Torgus beside him, went west to Ocean Road, leading to the docks where Egrid and her unit were overseeing the evacuations.

Over his shoulder, Axel saw their efforts, as her soldiers were few and far to be seen and civilians rarer still. It gave him hope that the efforts and sacrifices of the defenders would not be in vain.

"Brace for impact!" He heard a dwarven voice say, turning in time to see the humans crashing upon the remnants of the steel shields. This time, Axel found a human to plunge his pike into, sending a bloody mist into the air as it sheaved clean through the man's body.

As the human lunged back, it took Axel's weapon with him, which left him temporarily unarmed and vulnerable, save for his shield. Another enemy filled the wounded's place, and with no time to get a pike or spear from the soldiers behind him, Axel drew his sword.

Overwhelmed once again, Axel had time enough just to call for a further retreat. His words went almost unheard beneath the clanging of iron arrowheads bouncing off the steel shields.

"Archers from above!" Another dwarf cried out.

Axel looked to where Ser Parias and his unit had been. The rooftops were now lined with dead dwarves and attacking humans, carrying bows and arrows of their own, and Ser Parias nowhere to be seen.

What remains of Parias' archers are likely beating a retreat of their own. This can only mean that Ser Adlan's crew are completely depleted.

On the ground there seemed to be more attackers by the heartbeat, throwing themselves recklessly against the steel shields, caring not if they lived or died.

Such is the minds of those consumed by fanaticism. They want us dead, even if they have to pay the ultimate price themselves. Not for any personal gain, but to appease the will of their master, who himself claims to be the voice of their god.

Arrows continued to rain in the direction of Axel's unit, hitting dwarf and human alike. He lifted his own shield over his head, ordering the same from those who could.

The human archers have no care if they hit their own and their own have no care if they are hit. Just so long as we are destroyed. How do we fight an enemy with such complete disregard for itself?

The sheer number of attackers both ranged and near made defending, let alone fighting back, practically impossible. The only recourse Axel had was to retreat, and so he ordered it.

"Fall back by twenty paces!" He shouted, until a heart-wrenching scream from directly to his right stuck the words in his throat.

An arrow had taken Torgus just north of the lip of his breastplate, skirting the steel to penetrate chainmail, boiled leather and tunic where it buried in his collar. Blood began to ooze immediately and his balance failed, sending him backward into the dwarves behind him.

"Torgus!" Axel cried out to his friend, looking instead to those who had caught him as he fell, "Get him help! Bring him to the back of the lines! Go!"

He called again for the retreat and this time, the unit listened. They ran together, far beyond the twenty paces, trying to outrun the bowmen and screaming attackers, and there was no relenting until Axel saw civilians and Egrid's unit assisting them.

"Yield here, soldiers!" Axel told them. "Turn toward the enemy, plant your steel shields, and hold your ground!"

They did as told and the hateful wave of humanity crashed upon the steel once more. Axel stepped forward, laying his wooden shield atop the steel one directly in front of him, giving protection to himself and the steel carriers from the arrows. From this position, he could thrust his sword forward and he did so with haste, bringing up on flesh on the very first stab, which was met with a yell. The sword was drawn back, returning to sight bathed in red, and he sent it forth again. Something violently slammed down on his shield repeatedly, sending shocks through his right arm. Axel blindly stabbed around his shield, the sword finding purchase in something fleshy again. After the third or fourth stab in this direction, the thrashing ceased and he withdrew the shield with a new and vicious pain that now radiated down his shoulder.

There was no reprieve for his sword arm, though it too grew heavier as the minutes passed until every new swing burned deep in his muscles. Still, the enemy kept coming. It seemed as though every centimetre of his sword and left forearm were coloured red and dripping with the sticky substance of life.

His brothers and sisters in arms were tiring also, those that remained unharmed. Their own blood was being shed too and with each blink of his eyes, the redness grew, spreading across their faces and armour.

Where are they all coming from? How can there be so many?

The pair of dwarves holding the steel shield directly in front of Axel began to look at him with concern etched on their faces, though he could scarcely fathom why until he realised he was standing still, both arms slumped at his side. He tried to raise them, but the weight of shield, sword and armour kept them fumbling uselessly from where they slumped.

"Are you alright, Ser Axel?" One of the shield-carriers called out to him.

He was not. Every milligram of energy that Axel had was spent and even his feet felt anchored to the road beneath them.

Several hands began to pull Axel backward, creating a space filled with fresh dwarves ready to put their swords and axes to use. Try as a he might to resist, Axel found himself further at the rear of his defences, until he came clear of the amassed dwarven fighting force entirely.

Another dwarf's squire had grabbed him by the shoulders, a young woman he did not recognise, and he breathed in the cool, fresh air around them deeply.

"Ser Axel, are you wounded? Shall I get you some water?" She asked with a voice full of concern.

"Not hurt... Just drained," Axel stammered back, before another thought came to him. He turned in either direction as much the squire's grasp would allow, looking all around for a friend who had been injured in the chaos. "Where is Ser Torgus?"

The squire hesitated, her facial expression going from concern to dread. Axel asked again, this time firmly, and she finally relented, stepping to one side and turning her gaze to the wall of a stone building nearby.

What Axel saw when he looked to where the squire pointed was not Torgus, but Vargas, having taken a knee with his back to them. Axel gently pushed the squire aside and shuffled toward his friend. At Vargas' side was his father's greathammer, the gold filigree painted upon it glimmering in the daylight. Before him sat Torgus, his back against the wall, the arrow that had struck him broken off at the shaft, and his forehead tilted forward against Vargas'.

"Vargas, tell me, is Torgus..."

Without moving so much as a hair, Vargas gave him answer: "He's gone, Axel."

Axel dropped to his knees beside Vargas, "By Aren... This can't be happening."

A young male dwarf on a pony came barrelling through a nearby alley, but Axel paid him no mind. There was bellowing and shouting from the front line of the fighting, and yet Axel had little regard for it in those few seconds. Torgus, who had been raised beside him as a brother, was gone, taken by a single arrow. It seemed impossible to believe, even with Torgus' body before him. They were fighting side by side not moments ago, protecting one another, and just as fast, he was dealt a mortal blow.

"Ser Axel?" He heard from somewhere near at hand, the 'Ser' part of it reminding him of his position and the expectations placed upon him.

Axel glanced over his shoulder at the female squire who had helped him, now standing beside the young man in the pony's saddle. "Yes? What is it?" He asked them.

"The humans, Ser," the fellow began, and as Axel looked upon his young face he saw panic streaked across it. "They brought their ram to bear on the Steel Barrier holding Okin Street. It fell, Ser, the Barrier fell! The enemy are through and heading toward Deepstone, pillaging as they go."

The female squire took on a look of terror to match the rider's, her eyes falling on Axel with desperation. "What do we do, Ser?"

His gaze went to the dwarves still trying to hold Ocean Road, their rear guard vulnerable to the same alley the pony-rider had used and others that opened onto their route. Further off in the opposite direction he saw the sea, the streets leading to it largely empty, save for a scant few civilians still attempting to flee.

"We won't be able to hold this position for much longer at present as it is." Axel surmised firmly. "The humans will soon be upon us via the alleyways and if we are taken from the rear, they will have us surrounded in a pincer attack. There will be no saving us then. It is high time that we pull back to the pier.

Once there, we can form a semi-circle around it with the combined numbers of Egrid's and my units to allow for a final defence and evacuation of civilians and soldiers alike. We must help those still evacuating and leave none behind. Carry them if need be, for we have no time to dawdle with the slow and infirm, but do not abandon them. Go now, Squire, spread my command!"

She left with a 'Yes, Ser' and Axel pushed himself back to a standing position, squaring his attention on the dwarf in the pony's saddle as he did. "Lad, did anyone send a rider to the mines to warn the garrison there of what happened?"

"Yes, Ser, they sent a pony-rider like me, Ser." The fellow answered diligently.

"At least there is that." Axel said with a sigh. "I pray to Aren that Ser Dorrhen can handle what is dealt to him."

~Ser Dorrhen Snowbeard~

The sound of hurried hooves on stone heralded the arrival of a pony-rider delivering ill tidings. "Make way, for I have urgent news for Ser Dorrhen!" The cavalry soldier called as he closed the distance to the barricade at the entrance to the Deepstone Mines.

"Let him through." Dorrhen commanded his soldiers that were maintaining order among the civilians passing through for the safety of Gethos Village on the other side of the mining tunnels.

"Ser Dorrhen, I am a lieutenant of Ser Wyldmare, Captain of the Cavalry." The soldier started with a little bow from the saddle. "I was sent to inform you that the Steel Barrier that was defending Okin Street has been irreparably breached by a ram and that all units are falling back to the mines."

"Well, shit." Troysan uttered with a weary exhalation, his eyes skyward.

Dorrhen's own gaze fell to Tinnia, her face showing the weight of what the rider's words meant. She looked back, and he read the words on her face plain enough.

"We have but minutes before the wave of enemies and allies alike hits us." He heard himself say aloud. "I have archers on the rooftops ahead and two dozen on the scaffolds behind me."

Troysan shook his head, rattling his sword loose in his scabbard as he did. "They are all completely useless now, Dorrhen."

"Gods be damned Troysan, I know that perfectly well." Dorrhen returned, cutting him a stern look before finishing his thought. "I'm not going to have them loosen arrows at an enemy surrounded by our own. I want them called back, immediately, and sent through the mine before the horde comes. Leave me two on the scaffolds to serve as scouts. For those among Ser Parias' ranks that are capable of direct combat, give to them a sword if they are without and reposition them on the barricade with us. We will have need of every able hand."

For once, Dorrhen thought Troysan might be a little ashamed of his impetuousness. "Right... My apologies, Dorrhen... Ser." He said while slipping a half-helm on his head, departing within seconds of that to deliver Dorrhen's order.

"Rider," Dorrhen addressed the dwarf in the saddle. "What were you commanded to do once you had delivered this most unfortunate message?"

"There were no other commands, Ser." He answered morosely. "Normally, I would be expected to return to Ser Wyldmare, but I am unsure if that is wise now, or even possible."

From beside Dorrhen, Tinnia spoke up, "The horde is not yet here. Perhaps you should ride out and take the first civilian you see, a child preferably, and carry them back here. Keep doing so until the enemy is upon us."

"An excellent suggestion, Tinnia," Dorrhen commented, glancing back long enough to nod affirmatively at the pony-rider.

"Aye, Sers, leave it to me!" The rider said with a salute. He wheeled his stead about, shook the reigns and galloped off down Okin Street until he was out of sight beyond the sloping road.

"The humans will crest that same hill soon, driving what remains of our soldiers and the unarmed." Tinnia stated dryly, her breathing growing rapid.

"It is not how anyone planned it, that's for certain." Dorrhen responded with a single, sad nod.

His hand wrapped tightly around the hilt of his father's sword, its scabbard now belted on his waist. He felt the ridges of Frost's crossguard beneath his forefinger, running digit gently across the steel for luck. With a final exhale, he drew the blade out in a single motion, holding it high for all to see while stepping up onto the sandbags to elevate him above the others.

"Soldiers, hear me!" Dorrhen began, all eyes falling on him as he did. "The enemy are soon to be before us. The Steel Barrier is broken and soldier and civilian alike are making for Deepstone as I speak. Draw your weapons and ready yourself for what is to come, as it falls to us alone to hold back the scourge long enough to let our folk into the mine. There will be blood, there will be pain, but we will prevail, for who are we?"

Arms wrapped in gauntlets, bracers and chainmail rose into the air below Dorrhen, with all forms of weaponry to bear. "The Dwarves of Dhalla!" The gathered replied in unison.

Dorrhen felt a surge go through him, part pride, and part raw energy. He had heard his father say similar words several times to trainee recruits and on each occasion, he felt that same surge, reverberating through his veins. There was more to it, this mantra of the fighting dwarves, and he knew those listening wanted to hear the phrase as much as he wished to say it.

"We stand strong, we stand proud..." Dorrhen started the chant.

"And we do not yield!" His soldiers replied.

The steps of the returning pony and its rider reached Dorrhen's ears, turning in time to see his own soldiers rushing to help a boy down from the saddle.

"How near are the humans?" Dorrhen asked the member of Ser Wyldmare's unit.

"Not far, Ser." He answered hurriedly. "No more than twenty paces beneath the top of the hill. There are still several civilians trying to flee, I'm going to make one more run down Okin Street to see if I can save one more."

"May Aren be with you." Dorrhen told the rider as he left once again.

He put his attention back on the scene unfolding at the entrance of the mine. Residents of Dhalla stood in line, waiting their turn to have their names written down before entering Deepstone. Some looked to him, others kept their gaze focused ahead or at their feet, but worry and fear were worn as plain as daylight on their faces. The archers of Ser Parias that had been sent to aid Dorrhen were now approaching from their positions along the top of the hill, their pace at a jog. Their comrades on the scaffolds behind the barricade joined them at the mine entrance for a brief reunification.

There was little time for further measures, Dorrhen knew. Names could be taken later. "Clerks at the entrance, your job is at an end for now. Make your way through to Gethos Village and guide those who need help. You will have time to worry about taking names when this is over. Hurry on now, go!"

That got the line moving, just as the pony rider returned to the barricade once more. It was a young dwarven woman sharing the saddle and in her arms was a swaddled infant.

"Dorrhen, I have the last of the archers with me." He heard Troysan say, finding him standing on the outside of the barricade, his sword drawn, but his wooden shield still slung over shoulder.

"Ser, the enemy are just coming over the hill!" The rider called out above Troysan, sliding to the ground as he did and taking the bridle of his pony in hand.

Above both voices, Dorrhen heard it, the roar of the roaming battle barrelling down on them all.

His commands came easily then. "Archers, if you can fight in the melee, take a position beside the other soldiers. If not, then assist the civilians making their way through the mine. Pony-rider, take your mount and go with the others to Gethos."

"Ser, with all due respect, I can fight and I will stay if you will let me." The rider replied.

Dorrhen was not about to turn away a fighter when needed most and took him on the offer. "Fine by me, give your pony to the first person you see that can take it through the mines. What is your name, my friend?"

"It's Raygo, Ser Dorrhen. Lieutenant Raygo of the Crestfell Clan." He told him.

"Lieutenant Raygo, Dhalla thanks you for your service." Dorrhen said with a hasty salute. "You have my leave to take a position when you can."

There was just time enough for a hastily formed defensive position to be put together, as chaos came at them quickly. The first wave was civilians running for their lives, followed closely behind by the remaining soldiers that had been holding the enemy at the Steel Barrier. Tough battered and exhausted, the remnant soldiers were still trying to fend off the human assault.

"Troysan, Tinnia, I need you two with me." Dorrhen stated rapidly, his throat tightening and the words nearly stammering out.

Fear is still here too, I see.

He swallowed hard to bury the creeping feeling, carrying on with his preparations by picking a single archer from within the crowd waiting to enter the mines and pointing at them directly. "You there, archer, tell the builders to have the Iron Seal ready to deploy at a second's notice. There will be no time for delays once I give the order."

"Aye, Ser Dorrhen! I shall see to it immediately! The archer called back.

The action not only served to give warning to the operators of the seal, but to take Dorrhen's mind off the fear looming in the back of his mind. He continued with his duties, pointing Adlan's sword at the front line that was defending the sandbag barricade around the entrance to Deepstone, "Shields, establish a perimeter in front of the access through our sand barrier. Permit only dwarves beyond. Expect no quarter from the humans and give none in return.

"Archer scouts, you are our eyes." Dorrhen told the remaining pair still perched on the scaffolds behind him. "When you see no more dwarves on the street, signal us and we will begin the final retreat into Deepstone."

He followed the shields, and Tinnia and Troysan followed him. The latter had a wooden kite shield, banded in iron and further enhanced with a single spike on a plate in the centre, both made from iron. Meanwhile, the former eschewed shields entirely, preferring a double-headed greataxe that took both hands and looked almost as big as she.

The defensive shields were positioned into a 'V' pattern, starting on either side of the barricade and coming to a point several metres out from the entry area that led to Deepstone's opening. It was at that apex in the 'V' that the three planted themselves, with Troysan and his shield standing foremost.

"Here they come!" One of the archers shouted from atop the scaffolding.

What few civilians remained in the district seemed to all be running towards the barricade, with dwarven soldiers here and there among them. The gap between the runners and the shields narrowed far quicker than Dorrhen could have imagined.

"Open the shields!" Dorrhen commanded, following the movement so that he could stay clear of the panicked people.

"Humans inbound!" The same archer relayed out at the top of his lungs.

Dorrhen could see them, being held back by the last of the Okin Street defenders trying vainly to keep the savagery at bay. For every two fighting dwarves there seemed to be a gap that the enemy could get through to either chase down civilians or further tear at the depleted remainders of the Steel Barrier.

"We have to help!" Tinnia shouted in Dorrhen's ear in an effort to be heard above the growing wall of noise.

"If we fan out, the humans will take us and overrun the barricade in no time." He told her, hoping he sounded certain of himself in his delivery. "We have to stay together to be effective, or we will all perish."

A woman's scream pierced the clamour, and Troysan was gone in an instant and without so much as a word. Tinnia was shoving by Dorrhen then too, her axe held overhead to keep the sharp blades away from the others.

I cannot let them go it alone. He reasoned with Fear. *What kind of friend would I be? How could I look another dwarf in the eye, or even my own reflection if something happened to either of them while I stood here?*

"Hold this position until the humans close in." Dorrhen commanded the shield-bearers, "Close formation to a 'V' and keep permitting dwarves at the point until the archers give the signal to fall back to Deepstone."

With his orders given, Dorrhen waded out into the chaos, holding Frost aloft as he searched for his friends. Carefully winding his way through the living river of dwarvenkind, Dorrhen felt his search was to be fruitless, until he heard the cursing and hollering of a wounded human nearby. With a quick look upward, he spotted the brute and soon after, he came upon a terrible scene.

A woman lay on her hands and knees, her back a bloody mess and her clothing shredded and beneath her

Dorrhen saw a crying child that she had been trying to protect. Ahead of her stood Troysan, his shield running red starting at the spike and trickling downward, having clearly impaled the human responsible for the heinousness upon it before Dorrhen's arrival. The liable human, a boorishly large one by even their standards, lightly swung a spiked mace with one hand while the other covered the wound caused by the thrust of the shield's spike. It grunted at Troysan, wincing away whenever the dwarf drove sword or shield at him, and looked frantically about, as if hoping for reinforcements.

Tinnia swung her axe at the human's midsection, narrowly missing as he jumped backward. In his effort to dodge, the human crashed into fleeing dwarves behind him, sending them tumbling further into others. The opponent lunged forward again, grabbing for the lip of Troysan's shield while swinging the mace at his head.

Dorrhen was there first. The human was paying him no mind, allowing Dorrhen to slide in directly alongside it, his sword swinging downward at the back of a right leg that was protected solely by a flimsy boot made of animal hide. Adlan Snowbeard's sword cut clear through to the flesh and Dorrhen slid it upward in one swift, turning motion, unleashing a spray of blood and buckling the foot underneath the human.

The man went sideways towards Dorrhen, narrowly missing his frame. For a second it tried to stand, falling on its face in an attempt that landed him at Tinnia's feet. Her axe went overhead and then down in a flash, putting an end to the human as it severed muscle and tendon from the neck to the collarbone.

"That woman's hurt badly." Troysan told Dorrhen while flicking the human's blood from his sword.

"I'll carry her." Dorrhen stated, looking to Tinnia in the process. "You take the child. Troysan, protect our backs. We make for the barricade!"

The woman fought back at first, trying to keep the young boy she held from being ripped away. It took a great deal of reassuring from both Tinnia and Dorrhen before the woman would allow the separation of the two and a moment further for Dorrhen to take her over his shoulder.

"We just have to make it to that mine up ahead." Tinnia told the woman. "Let Ser Dorrhen carry you, I'll take the boy. It's not far. We promise to get you there. We solemnly swear it to you as knighted dwarves of Dhalla."

The three hurried along with the pace of the others, reaching the shield formation quicker than they had left it. Dorrhen set the woman down before two soldiers standing inside the barricade, instructing them to take both her and the boy.

"Ser, what boy might that be?" One soldier asked, the words giving Dorrhen a sudden pause.

"The humans are at the shields!" An archer scout called out immediately after, his observations only adding to the dread creeping over Dorrhen.

A look back over his shoulder revealed to Dorrhen that Tinnia and Troysan had both fallen behind, their progress slowed by the shield-bearers having suddenly closed in to reform their 'V' shape. Both of his friends were outside the protective embrace of the armoured dwarves, with civilians ahead of them trying to get through the point of the formation. Among the dwarves stood three humans, all armed and swinging violently into the running crowd. Troysan's shield was up, in an effort to protect those nearest to him. However, Tinnia had only the armour on her back for defence, her arms wrapped tightly around the boy she held in them.

Dorrhen ran back toward his friends, bumping into civilians with every step and fearing he would not make it at all before the humans did. Two of the attackers had cudgel-type weapons, clearing a path with them for a third that bore a large spear tipped with an ostentatiously long piece of sharp steel.

Troysan kept his shield in the trajectory of one of the clubbers, its wood splintering with every blow landing upon it. No more than a metre away, Tinnia pushed closer to the entry point between the shield-carriers, nearing it at an achingly slow pace now. A single, adolescent female dwarf stood between Tinnia and the relative safety behind the shields. Dorrhen bridged the space just as the female dwarf stumbled and fell, and he caught her before she hit the ground. With a quick lift, he got her back to standing and sent her on her way, turning to see Tinnia almost at an arm's length away now.

He reached out for her and the boy and Tinnia passed the lad into Dorrhen's arms, though she did not follow. Despite his plea for her to follow, Tinnia had gone still and her face showed a mix of disbelief and terror.

Behind Tinnia was the human Dorrhen had identified as the spear-carrier, his hands wrapped tightly around the shaft of ugly weapon that was now driven into her back.

With the boy in his arms, Dorrhen was helpless to do anything.

Say something.

"Somebody kill that human!" Dorrhen yelled as loud as his lungs could handle. "I want him as dead as dead gets!"

His words were heard and heeded by the shields and as they closed in on the enemy trio, the spearman put a foot into Tinnia's back, plucking the spear free and sending her downward and out of sight into the crowd.

As his feet found life beneath him, Dorrhen ran to the barricade, nearly colliding with the remaining soldier of the pair he had handed the woman off to minutes before. "*This* is the boy, get him to his mother." He shot out while pushing the child into the soldier's grasp.

Frost was drawn once more, and Dorrhen charged back into the fray.

Dorrhen found the spear-wielding human still alive upon his return, jabbing and prodding with his spear at the shields closing in on both him and the two with the cudgels. Of Troysan, Dorrhen saw nothing, until he caught the glint of the daylight on a sword being raised overhead. As it swung downward it took a human hand clean off at the wrist, fist and cudgel separating in a red river at the end of his arm.

Screams of the dwarves caught in the ghastly spray combined with that of the maimed human, and Troysan closed in for the kill, stabbing at him until the human collapsed from view.

Two dwarves came rushing toward Dorrhen with Tinnia's arms slung over their shoulders, her limp frame staggering between them.

"Get her inside Deepstone!" Dorrhen commanded them as he brushed past quickly on his way to contend with the two humans still standing.

I should be with her.

There was no way he could though, not yet at least, and his will held him fast to his duty in what was almost a moment of weakness.

The human that had wounded Tinnia had lost his spear since Dorrhen's last sight of him, and looked to be bleeding from a dozen wounds or more inflicted by the shield line. The numbers of those taking flight had dwindled noticeably, a notion that struck Dorrhen as odd, yet one he tried not to dwell on. Instead, he focused on the two attacking humans and the ease of which he had in reaching them.

The lone cudgel-swinger lunged in Dorrhen's direction, whether Dorrhen was his target would go unknown, as the human was tripped by the spear of a shield-bearer and sent sprawling metres away. His back was plunged with a further two spears and he had stopped moving altogether by the time Dorrhen stepped around him.

"Even should you stupid dwarves kill me, Ios shall dispatch you back to Aren's Lair before the sun sets." The human ranted at no one dwarf in particular. "You are vermin before the eyes of my creator. Abominations thrust upon this world by an inferior god that shall be cast down by the one true king, he whose bloodline was chosen and blessed by Ios himself. Bow down, scum! Bow down and surrender before the anointed army of the Holiest of the Holy: Valdarrow the Third!"

Every muscle in Dorrhen's body tensed with pure rage as the human had spoken and as each word was uttered fourth, Dorrhen grew closer to him. By the time that the human invoked the name of his master, Dorrhen was reaching with his right hand for the shaggy pelts that the human had garbed himself in, pulling the man down to his height. In Dorrhen's left hand was his father's sword and he slashed it across the human's throat and pushed him to the ground.

"Fall back to the barricade!" Dorrhen ordered when the grisly deed was done. His gaze went to Troysan, soaked in the blood of humans but looking unharmed and then beyond him, to what was but a scant few soldiers fighting to keep the bulk of the humans at bay. "Troysan, we need to tell those dwarves to fall back too!"

"It shall be done!" Troysan said with a nod, darting off to give the order.

Once at the barricade, Dorrhen began dispatching soldiers into Deepstone in pairs, doing so in such small groupings to allow as much time as he could for any remaining civilians.

An engineer emerged from the mine to find Troysan, asking him pointedly, "Are we dropping the Iron Seal soon?"

"Aye, as soon as Troysan and the last soldiers retreat to us." Dorrhen confirmed, "Are we ready? When the defenders of Okin Street are here, so too will be the humans. There will be no time to-

"Here they come!" A voice from upon the scaffolds shouted, rendering anything else Dorrhen had to say as moot.

Dorrhen walked out of the mine far enough to see the scaffolds above and the two archers still upon it. "Get down from there or you'll be left behind! Hurry!"

A number of exhausted, blood-covered Dwarven soldiers came rushing past Dorrhen, led by Troysan, his shield now reduced to little more than the few slats of broken lumber that still clung to the iron banding. While the other soldiers began their march into the safety of Deepstone, Troysan came to stand at Dorrhen's side, throwing down his destroyed shield and flexing the arm that had held it with great struggle.

"Is that the last of the Okin Street defenders?" Dorrhen asked, though he already felt he knew the answer.

"Aye, Dorrhen, that's it." Troysan grimaced through his pain. "When I got to them, they were blocking the street with a pair of burning wagons, hoping it might keep the bulk of the humans back for a little bit. Bloody fools, they could well burn the whole city down with that stunt."

Dorrhen looked Troysan over, taking notice then that his helm was askew and a gash had opened over his right eye, bleeding heavily over a face already reddened with the blood of their enemies. If Troysan was aware of that wound, he was ignoring it in favour of his right arm, which seemed to be giving him a great deal of grief at the elbow.

"Anything broken?" Dorrhen asked Troysan, gesturing with an open hand at the arm.

Troysan shook his head quickly, "Not broken, or at least I don't think so. The pricks just smashed my shield so much that I think I'll be bruised from wrist to shoulder and all the way through to the bone."

"You have served enough for this day, Troysan." Dorrhen told his friend, "Head on through to Gethos with the Okin Street soldiers. I would like at least one of us to be there with Tinnia, I fear the worst might have happened to her."

That seemed to resonate poorly with Troysan, judging from the angered look on his face. "I'm not done yet, Dorrhen. I still have my sword arm."

"Your right arm is battered and you are bleeding above the eye, which will no doubt reduce your vision." Dorrhen had begun to counter.

"Piss on that, I can still fight, Dorrhen. Don't you do this to me." Troysan cut in, a fury growing in his voice.

Dorrhen was not about to yield, not now. "Tinnia might be dying, Troysan. I don't want her to die alone. Please, for her sake, go on through and find her, see that she has someone at her side. Her father is long dead and her mother and little sister boarded the first evacuation ship this morning. She has no one in Gethos, just you and I. We both know I have to stay here until the Iron Seal closes, but I can send you. Please, Troysan."

"You'll be heading that way soon yourself. In fact, you won't be far behind me, even if I left at this very second." Troysan argued.

"We cannot say that with any certainty." Dorrhen responded quickly. "Who knows what will happen when that seal falls. Odds are we could be stuck there for hours tying up loose ends. In the meantime, Tinnia's bleeding to death in whatever is passing for a hospital on the other side of Deepstone. One of us needs to be with her, Troysan."

"What about Lady Narra or Crego?" Troysan propositioned.

Dorrhen was ready for that too. "Who would tell them? I can send someone else, aye, but they would arrive when you do and then have to find Mother or Crego, both of whom are trying to organise chaos. Even if they did find the time to go to her, they would probably be too late. Listen, Troysan, you might have noticed that I have not once said the words 'order' or 'command', because I am asking you not as your captain but as my friend and Tinnia's, to do this."

Troysan grunted loudly and sighed, "Gods damn it all, fine, alright? I'll go."

"Thank you, Troysan. I shall be with you both soon." Dorrhen said with relief, patting his friend on the back. As he was leaving, Dorrhen stopped once more. "Wait, before you go, have you seen any sign of Ser Wyldmare?"

"I never laid so much as an eye on Ser Wyldmare, or any of his cavalry for that matter." Troysan answered frankly, pointing at a soldier with a violet feather plume in his helm standing on the other side of the procession of soldiers. "Ser Belsword over there told me that he had command of Okin Street, I would ask him."

Dorrhen thanked his friend again and the two parted, Troysan heading beneath the archway of Deepstone mine and Dorrhen going to Ser Belsword.

After getting Belsword's attention, Dorrhen lightly took the knight by the arm and pulled him aside beneath the scaffolds. "Ser Belsword, I need a moment of your time." He started, watching the two archers climb down and join the march to the underground before asking his questions. "Where is Ser Wyldmare? Where are the ponies?"

The dwarf gave a slow, remorseful shake of his head as he answered, with his voice as morose as his expression, "I am fairly certain that they are gone, Ser Dorrhen."

"How could that happen?" Dorrhen queried in disbelief.

"After the Steel Barrier fell, Ser Wyldmare and his cavalry rode out to throw back the enemy so as to give our side time to reform the shields." The knight began to explain. "He told me what he was about to do, but he had told his cavalry first, and before I could forbid it, they were gone. I will say that they did wonderfully with their objective, drove a wedge right through the human forces, even. Why, they managed to cut down a great number of them, I should say. They just did not come back, Ser. I have not laid eyes on Ser Wyldmare since. He might still be out there in the city. Perhaps he made for the waterfront to help Ser Axel and Lady Egrid, or rode to the city gates to try to break the enemy leaders at the rear of their own offences. At least I hope it to be something I have described and I would rather not think of the alternative. I have seen enough of that this day to last a lifetime, Ser."

"I see..." Dorrhen said in response, feeling a sudden dryness in his throat. "Either way, I cannot hold the Iron Seal open for him any longer, so let us hope you are right and that Ser Wyldmare's unit either found an alternate means of escape or at the very least, a dignified end. For now, we have little time to dwell on it. Let's go, Ser. The time has come to leave Dhalla."

At the entrance to Deepstone there was but a few shield-bearers now, forming a shrinking semicircle around the entrance to keep the humans at bay. Standing on a rock and looking over the defenders, Dorrhen espied Ser Raygo, lieutenant of Ser Wyldmare.

"Do you see any more of our people out there?" Dorrhen asked him as they got near.

"No Ser, but that does not mean they are not there amid the humans." Raygo replied despondently. "It would be hard to see them amongst the tallfolk. What's more pressing is that I see a great deal of smoke far off to the south, Ser. I think the humans are trying to raze all of Dhalla."

"We had all suspected they might do that." Dorrhen told Raygo sombrely. "It will take more than fire to destroy Dhalla, though. You will find lumber here and there, and even thatch roofs on some of the smaller and older buildings, but Dhalla is made first and foremost of stone and fire cannot destroy stone. So I say let them light their fires, for when the humans are long gone and the last of their embers have been snuffed by the snows of winter, us dwarves will endure like the stone from which our city is built: blackened from the flames, yet unburnt."

A defender shouted out in terror, and as Dorrhen looked in the direction of the scream, he saw the soldier being pulled, shield and all, over the barricade and into the growing human mob to what was certain death. Those who had been beside the defender attempted to rescue him, though they had to relent or risk being pulled over the barricade themselves.

The sight left Dorrhen with little doubt as to what he should do. "Final retreat! Everyone inside Deepstone, at once!" He ordered, hoping to spare the tiring defenders from the same fate as their fallen friend.

Stepping inside the mine, Dorrhen came face to face with the two archers, their bows now in hand and quivers readied for use at their side.

"What is this?" He asked them while gesturing to their weaponry.

"Ser, it's not much from just two of us, but a few arrows into that mob may halt the attackers long enough to allow our defenders to escape." One spoke for both of them, the other nodding in agreement.

Dorrhen looked about the gaping maw of an entryway to Deepstone, seeing outcropping rocks and ledges on either side that might give the archers an advantage in height. "Climb up there, so you are over the heads of ours, and fire away until I say otherwise."

The two saluted and went about it, as the last defenders retreated one by one, their semicircle shrinking quickly.

"Ser, I saw no other dwarves at last look on Okin Street, but should we not hold for Ser Wyldmare and my fellow riders?" The voice came from behind Dorrhen, but he knew at the mention of 'fellow riders' that it must be Raygo and turned to face the increasingly disheartened dwarf as he continued, "They are out there yet. The ships will not have space for ponies, and we riders never abandon our mount unless it is perished. The cavalry will die if we close off Deepstone."

Dorrhen was facing him by then, looking him in the eyes and unsure of whether or not to tell him the truth. It was not in his nature to be dishonest to any degree, but he genuinely feared that Raygo might do something rash if told that he might well be the last of his unit. "I spoke with Ser Belsword just moments ago," He began, taking a last split second to decide his course. "After you were sent my way, Ser Wyldmare gave Ser Belsword command of the defences and led a charge to push back the humans and give our dwarves time to restore the Steel Barrier as best they could."

"He sacrificed our entire force?" Raygo attempted to ask, his words being lost beneath the sudden roaring of the enemy army.

"What in Aren's name?" Dorrhen asked, looking just in time to see humans rushing the entryway. "Drop the Iron Seal immediately!"

"The defenders are overrun!" An archer cried out.

"Drop the bloody Iron Seal!" Dorrhen repeated, even louder than before.

There was a deafening rattling then, one that seemed to shake the entire mountain above them and the mine that was carved into it.

Is this the Iron Seal? It could well result in a cave-in before it closes up the entryway.

As the rattling persisted, Dorrhen dropped to the ground, pulling Raygo with him and covering the dwarf with his own body.

Daring to look up, Dorrhen saw the two archers standing as tall as humans from upon their high perches on opposite sides of the entrance, silhouetted by the daylight shining in. A wall of pure black descended from the ceiling quickly, rolling down to the ground with no concern for anyone that might be in its way. Humans and dwarves went hurtling out of its path and when it hit, it was as if the sun itself had burned out in a deafening 'thud', replaced by distant torches and a cyclone of dust.

He closed his eyes as tight as he could and buried his head until the shaking ceased. The shouting, however, continued on, and Dorrhen opened his eyes to a dusty state of near-darkness. There were torchlights, but the dirt kicked up by the seal made it nearly impossible to see through it and Dorrhen could only make out the shapes of humans and dwarves still fighting with one another.

"Raygo, get up, there are still humans in the mine." Dorrhen told him loudly, extending a hand to aid in getting him back to his feet."

Raygo strained to look through the dimly lit, dust-filled passageway just as Dorrhen had, before turning to him in confusion. "What would you have me do, Ser?"

Dorrhen drew Adlan's sword forth, pointing it toward the ruthless attackers casting shadows on the wall in the torchlight. "Fight with me, with us, for our battle is not yet done."

All that Raygo had for a weapon was a dagger, yet he took it to hand and took no quarrel with Dorrhen's orders. They ran into the melee, collided with the first human they saw and drove him to the ground, their steel rising and falling in quick succession until he fought back no more. Dorrhen was on his feet again, looking for another and encountering him quick enough. This one tried to parry Dorrhen's sword with one of his own, their blades meeting on their flats, each one trying to push the other aside.

"Foolish dwarves, you cannot not match a human's strength in combat." It spat at Dorrhen through the strain.

Dorrhen lifted the human's sword, heaving heavily until he had put the weapons at the height of the human's chest.

"You mistake our small size for weakness, human." Dorrhen shouted back.

The lifting was meant for more than a show of strength, it had created an opening at the human's torso and Dorrhen levelled a kick directly into his stomach. It staggered the man, taking away the weight of his sword from Dorrhen's and creating an opening that Dorrhen seized upon. The human was still trying to protect himself above the waist, but his legs were open, and Dorrhen drove his sword deep into the unguarded flesh beside the femur.

Father told me that humans could bleed out from the legs easily enough. I shall see if he was right.

The human was writhing in agony, his sword gone and both of his hands on Frost in an attempt to wrest control of Dorrhen's blade away from him.

Dorrhen pressed his weight towards the human, and the cur pushed back just as hard. The press was a feint by Dorrhen, and he leaned in the opposite direction, now having both his own momentum and the human's behind the manoeuvre. With a mighty ripping noise, the sword came free from the human's leg. Dorrhen stepped back to find his way clear of man, nearly tripping over debris in the process. The human fell toward him face first onto the ground and with his own balance restored, Dorrhen positioned himself above the human and drove Frost downward just beneath the left shoulder.

Once the enemy stopped writhing beneath him, Dorrhen drew the sword out and staggered backward, his back bringing up on a smooth, solid surface. *The Iron Seal. It worked.*

During his battle with the human, the dust had somewhat settled and more torches had been lit. The fighting had ended, Dorrhen saw and only dwarves remained standing, much to his relief.

"Is anyone hurt?" Dorrhen asked aloud to all between quick breaths.

"Aye, Ser. We have many wounded." Someone answered back, though Dorrhen could not see whom.

"Those who are unharmed, tend to the wounded as best you can." Dorrhen ordered, his eyes scanning the mineshaft as much as the low light allowed. "If you can walk, help those who cannot."

To his left was an alcove, one of hundreds within Deepstone made by the dwarves over the centuries. This one was where the Iron Seal's controls were kept and maintained, and once Frost was sheathed, Dorrhen made for it. Following a near trip in something around his feet, Dorrhen steadied himself with a hand pressed to the slick wall that now separated him from Dhalla and continued onward.

After but a few steps his greave hit upon something and he looked down to see Raygo crouched on the ground, his left hand tucked under his right arm and against his ribs.

With bended knees, he offered his hand to the brave soldier, "You're wounded, Raygo."

"Something sharp managed to get through my chainmail," Raygo told him while accepting the help to get to his feet. "It's just through the flesh, though. It pains and bleeds, but I shall be fine, I believe."

"I hope that is so. Worry not, for we shall get it tended to in Gethos." Dorrhen offered with a gentle pat on the back. "Have you seen the archers?"

Raygo shook his head, looking about for them himself. "No Ser, everything happened so fast, I have no idea if they made it through or not."

An engineer had emerged from the control alcove, younger than the one who had been spearheading the readying of the Iron Seal. Dorrhen guessed him to be an apprentice of the older dwarf that had spoken to him earlier.

"Builder, I am looking for two archers that were standing on either side of the cave upon the high rocks. Have you seen them?" Dorrhen asked with growing worry.

The dwarf looked about, "Why no, Ser. In fact, I do not see many places on this side of the Iron Seal where the rocks could be considered high enough for what I assume was loosening arrows at the humans."

"They were on the wrong side of the Seal..." Dorrhen exclaimed, suddenly feeling week. "Gods be damned, they probably knew as much when they hatched their plan. Damn fools."

"With all due respect, Ser, I would call them brave heroes." Raygo stated between grunts of pain.

Dorrhen sighed, removed his helm and ran a hand over the top of his long, braided mane before replacing it. "You are doubtlessly right, Raygo. Who knows how many more humans would have been in here with us if not for those two archers."

Looking around, he took a quick count of the dead. "I count six of their brutes and two of our soldiers on the ground. Ensure the humans are dead and check ours for signs of life. We will leave the bodies for today and send fresh help tomorrow from Gethos to retrieve them. I hear no noise on the other side of the Iron Seal, and there is nothing for us to do about it now regardless. With that, I declare that we will move out for Gethos Village at first chance."

"You hear nothing, aye, but not for the reason you think." The young engineer put in to Dorrhen.

"What do you mean?" He propositioned tiredly.

A hand of the engineer's pressed flat to the heavy hunk of metal, gliding over the smooth surface that looked almost like glass in the torchlight. "We call it the 'Iron' Seal, but it is not entirely iron. The core is, for certain, but it is thickly coated in the blackened steel alloy found far below the surface of these mountains. The humans are still on the other side, and your archers too, but this steel has the bizarre property to dampen sound."

"I stand corrected, I suppose." Dorrhen muttered with a shrug, in no mood whatsoever for a lecture. "Is your master finished tamping things down in the control alcove?"

"As to that, I should probably return to him. The other apprentice has been tending to a wounded soldier that was left in our care by two concerned citizens. Apparently, they thought the soldier would not make it to Gethos Village unless the bleeding was stopped first and they had no means to do so. Perhaps the soldier is ready to be transported now. Could you help, Ser Dorrhen?"

Dorrhen gestured toward the alcove, "Aye, of course, lead the way, Builder."

Inside the alcove there was but a single lantern for light. Nearest to the cave's entrance sat a wood-panelled wall with levers, valves and cranks protruding all about from floor to ceiling. Standing before it the contraption was the engineer that Dorrhen had been speaking with all throughout the day, his name escaping Dorrhen as their eyes met briefly.

"Oh good, you must be here to move the wounded," Began the main engineer, before Dorrhen saw recognition flicker in his eyes. "Ser Dorrhen! I did not think the lad would bring you. Though, I am glad he did."

This was neither the time nor place for typical procedure and Dorrhen raised a hand to gesture as much. "I can help as well as anyone else. Are you ready to leave for Gethos? Is the Iron Seal locked?"

"We will soon be done and will find our way to Gethos on our own, but thank you for offering to wait." After he spoke, the head engineer pointed to the opposite side of the alcove. "That one has not the luxury of time, though."

Turning about, Dorrhen laid eyes on the second apprentice and a soldier lying on a side, their face to the wall and the apprentice's hand pressing a mound of some sort of cloth to a wound on their back. Their armour, though breached, was of good quality and a head of long, auburn hair tied in a tail caught the lantern's light.

That looks like Tinnia, but she was carried off into Deepstone.

"Tinnia!" Dorrhen exclaimed as the realisation sunk in, falling to his knees before his friend as her name left his lips. He turned her over to see her face, finding it pale and her breathing so shallow he might have thought her dead if not for her eyes still having life to them.

"Dorrhen?" She murmured, her voice barely passing for a whisper. "Are we dead? Is this Aren's Palace?"

He unbuckled his gauntlets, throwing them aside so that he might touch her face with a bare hand, the other gently squeezing hers. "No, no, you're not dead. I'm going to take you to Gethos Village so we can get you some help. Hush now and try not to talk too much. You need your energy."

"Ser, she has lost a tremendous amount of blood." The apprentice began to explain as Dorrhen gently pushed him aside and scooped Tinnia gingerly into his arms.

Dorrhen's patience was at an end as he sidestepped the young man. "Gods' damnation, I know full well she has. Thank you for tending to her, but I have to get her to Gethos Village. Now, if you do not mind: please, get out of my way."

Much to Dorrhen's annoyance, the apprentice was not done. "But Ser, it's at least two kilometres to Gethos Village. You cannot expect to carry her the whole way, can you?"

Dorrhen had navigated around the apprentice then, but took a second to glance back at him. "My friend is of no weight to me. I assure you, I will not falter."

~Ser Axel Goldenhair~

Where Axel summoned the energy to gather up his sword and shield again he would likely never know. The loose strands of his long hair had become matted to a face wet with his own sweat, and blood that he suspected was of both human and dwarven origin. His armour and helm were dinged and dented and the cobalt and gold enamelling was almost entirely covered in crimson. Every muscle in his body resisted movement, even his eyelids wanted to close. Yet, there was still work to be done, lives in need of rescue and an enemy to be fought. There was no rest for Axel Goldenhair and his soldiers, no reprieve, just battle against what felt like a ceaseless foe.

Despite his efforts, Axel's forces were unable to withdraw with enough haste to the docks and as he predicted, they were now facing assault from multiple directions. With little other option, Axel ordered his unit, comprised of all the surviving infantry, to slowly retreat toward the ships. However, the closer they edged to the waterfront, the more Axel worried.

If they can surround us on even two sides, they can try to force us into the sea. With so much heavy armour, we will sink like stones before anyone on board the ships even sees a splash.

"Which one of you pricks killed my brother, I wonder?" Axel heard Vargas ask rhetorically from beside him, following the last Spearsmasher's line of sight to the encroaching human archers firing casually at his unit from atop the roofs.

Above our heads, another direction from which the enemy are attacking. All my tactics have turned to shit. Every advantage I thought we had evaporated in the face of a ruthless, merciless enemy seven thousand strong with no regard for their own lives. It almost feels like they are cheating, bypassing all the rules of engagement and just running us through with an endless, brainwashed horde. Our army has discipline and extensive arms training. All those hours spent with the Spearsmasher brothers, Parias, Dorrhen and I studying old books written by the most brilliant minds that ever looked upon a battlefield, wasted. All our advancements in weaponry and defences, the work of the best smiths that ever struck a hammer on hot iron, amounted to nothing. We studied, trained and built, and blind idiocy and unbridled hatred bowing to a family of connivers tore us all down in our own homes.

What lunacy is all this? How do the minds of these humans become so warped beyond reason? What god would ever devise a world so cruel and unjust?

"The humans are storming down Bergen Street!" A dwarven accent called out in warning, referring to yet another road that ran east to west between Okin Street and Ocean Road.

"Swing the left side of the defensive line hard northward!" Axel commanded reflexively, trying to put his line ahead of the Bergen Street assault. "Order those at the back end to begin cutting and running in pairs for the ships! Everyone else, keep moving at a steady pace!"

Vargas was in Axel's ear then, his voice taken with rage and grief. "I don't want to run. I want to kill these humans down to their last."

"There are too many, Vargas." Axel tried to reason with him. "Stay with us, keep moving toward the ships. We will regroup to have another day to fight these vermin, with a unified army of elves, Phaleaynan humans and Amaroshan half-elves."

A ball of phlegm from Vargas' mouth landed on the ground at their feet. "Piss on all of them. Elves, humans, Amaroshans, where are they this day? The Drakian humans want an alliance with us too, yet I see not one of their warships in our harbour lending aid. It is just us, the Dwarves of Dhalla, left alone to die without a friend in the Known World."

"Archers, draw!" Axel heard a familiar voice cry out from overhead, looking in time to see Ser Parias standing on the rooftops with a unit of archers standing in two staggered lines. One stood on the building cornering Bergen Street and Ocean Road, the second was further back, on a higher roof than the first. The entirety of them, Parias included, had bows taught and fletchings against their cheeks, their arrows trained on the human archers standing on the roofs south of Bergen Street.

The humans panicked, some attempting to return fire, others running away, a few even jumping, taking their chances on the unforgiving stone below. It was too late for most though, as Parias commanded his archers to loosen their arrows, putting down the bulk of their undisciplined human counterparts. What still stood were taken with a second, smaller, directly aimed volley of arrows, and for once since Montagen's Hammer fell, Axel felt things tilt slightly toward their side.

The enemy infantry on the ground felt the strike of the arrows shortly after, while dodging the tumbling bodies of the slain archers. It was enough to force the humans to go on the defensive themselves, dodging away from corpse and arrow alike.

"Now is our chance to strike!" Vargas stated excitedly, lifting his hammer to shoulder height.

"No," Axel corrected him. "Now is the chance to retreat. We shall not waste the distraction that Parias has granted us." He took a deep breath and called out, "Everybody, fall back, double time!"

The marching picked up, though they were still moving backwards and sideways, keeping the enemy in their sights. Vargas came along grudgingly, cursing audibly over his thwarted desire for vengeance.

An armoured human, one of the few that Axel had seen since the assault started, came forward, his face hidden behind an ugly bucket of a helm with a narrow slit for his eyes. As he approached, he shifted a tall shield from his left arm to his right, raising it to guard him from arrows. In his now empty left, he placed a fearsome sword that he levelled at the retreating dwarves and bellowed out, "The cowards run! Get after them! Onward, Valdarronians! For Ios!"

Leading the charge, he caught up to the dwarves quickly, a growing collection of arrows in his shield, but otherwise undamaged. On his heels were more humans, rushing in with an assortment of weapons to harry the defending dwarves.

For a brief moment, the two were so close that Axel saw the human's eyes through the slit of his helm, full of loathing and malice.

"In the name of Torgus Spearsmasher, I strike thee down!" Vargas cried out, his hammer swinging high in a horizontal arc. The bucket helm caved in sideways, producing a mist of red from the slit and a river that poured out from beneath and down over his breastplate.

The human lurched to his left with the blow, his limp body likely dead before it touched ground.

Dispatching the leader among the group stopped the humans yet again, if for only a few fleeting seconds. Their rush resumed with a simultaneous roar, the humans crashing into the shields so that they might stab and smash at the dwarves in furious bursts.

A sharp, cold gust of salt air washed over Axel, and a quick glance to his right revealed that they had walked out and away of the row of buildings that faced the ocean. Only the quays stood between his dwarves and the frigid waters now.

As harrowing a thought as that is, it means we are ever closer to Egrid and the fleet. Axel reminded himself.

"Archers, fall back!" Parias called out, Axel looking his way to see a bevy of fresh enemy infantry and archers closing in quickly on the archery unit. While the others ran for cover, Parias stood where he was, firing a few choice arrows at particular targets, taking out at least four or five combatants before the pack got dangerously close.

The opposition infantry on the ground were becoming every bit as thick as those on the roofs, leaving Axel with no choice but to call for a similar retreat. "Shields lift! Everyone put your backs to our enemy and pick up at a jog. We make for the docks!"

Try as the dwarves might to put distance between them and the humans, the heavy shields and their shorter gaits made it quite nearly impossible. With every few steps, Axel took a glance back, finding the humans to be growing dangerously closer to them every time. There was a terrified yell, and Axel looked in time to see a hefty dwarf with a wooden shield on his back being pulled backwards and down.

"Everybody halt!" Axel beckoned, refusing to leave the fellow to his fate. "Steel shields plant in the ground!"

They did as commanded, sticking their heavy steel plates into the street so quickly that most of the humans had no time to stop, crashing into the shields and into one another as they piled on. His sword was out then, and he held it aloft for all to see. "Infantry, attack!

Though others followed him, there was no one quicker to join the fray than Vargas Spearsmasher, his greathammer in mid-swing before the words could even leave Axel's mouth. All those who had struck the shields in Vargas' reach were at his mercy and he kept his movements in a steady, almost rhythmic cadence, every swivel, turn, and landed blow feeding from the momentum of the last.

Axel was slower to enter into the battle, his exhaustion loitering about, waiting for the chance to spring on him again and turn his limbs to lead. A rust-encrusted sword was brought to rain down a flurry of blows on his shield, thudding heavily, but barely biting the wood. A hard push against his attacker gave Axel space and sent the human tumbling backward to regain his balance. Axel glanced around his shield, levelled his sword and let the attacker run himself into it, too late to realise what he was doing to himself.

Two more rushed in, trying to overwhelm Axel, and he lost sight of what had been a relatively young human. The pair came forward with but one weapon between them: a mace. One human held it, the other grabbed for his shield, trying to pull his right arm open to allow the mace-holder a chance to swing.

Though holding tight to the handle on his shield, Axel allowed the attacker to pull his arm about, not wanting to waste the energy in his arm. The attacker of the duo came in, his mace, with its wooden shaft and spherical, iron head held above his own, which forecast its downward path plainly. Axel slashed high and felt the weight of the mace hit the sword, watching as the wood split just beneath the head, the human face behind the weapon tearing open from ear to chin.

Wails of agony came out of the attacker, his hands dropping the splintered remains of its weapon to clutch at the sliced flesh that had been his cheek and jawline. The other still held Axel's shield, but was focused on his bleeding ally, and not on the sword that Axel sunk deep into his abdomen.

Axel pulled his blade loose from the human's belly in a downward manoeuvre, bringing the maimed man to his knees and at a height where Axel could easily open his throat to end the struggle.

Breathing deeply, Axel took a moment to reorient himself with the battle's layout. The human with the mangled face had been felled by a spear-wielding soldier of Axel's and the young human with the rusty sword was out of sight, likely retreating to deal with his wound.

Around Vargas, there was a great deal of open space, as the humans tripped over one another in their unsuccessful attempt to evade the path of the greathammer. The remaining Spearsmasher twin was fuelled by anguish for his slain brother, his rage bursting forth in great roars that would break even the coldest of hearts. Where the hammer landed, destruction and death were certain and every human in close proximity seemed acutely aware of that.

Halting his attack when there were no targets in his orbit to strike, Vargas raised his hammer overhead with both hands, his armour and face drenched in the crimson tide that had been flowing wherever he had struck. "You call us cowards when you have us outnumbered five or ten to one, yet every last one among you bows in fear before the Greathammer of Clan Spearsmasher!"

From the corner of his eye, Axel caught sight of a single bowman loosening an arrow and before Axel could react, it struck Vargas in the right armpit, one of the few places his armour left him vulnerable. Vargas jerked to the left off balance, his hammer's head slamming hard to the ground. Letting go of his hammer for but a second, Vargas reached beneath and pulled the arrow out with a loud grunt.

A human ran in, seconds ahead of Axel, and Vargas levelled the foe square in the stomach with the arrowhead. The attack doubled the human over, his body giving inadvertent cover to Vargas while he picked up his hammer.

Axel threw down his battered shield and reached for his friend with his now free arm, hoping to pull him back behind the shield line. Instead, he found Vargas pushing back.

"Go, Axel. Go to the ships." Vargas told him, his voice laboured, but strangely calm.

Axel shook his head, "Not without you."

"Aye, it will be without me." Vargas said with shallowing breath. "That arrow hit deep. I will not live to see any ships and if it is all the same, I would much prefer to die fighting. Farewell, Axel!" Vargas shouted the last two words, giving him a final shove backward, before charging headlong and alone into the encroaching enemy.

The dwarves behind Axel grabbed him before he could follow, and he lost sight of Vargas behind both attacking humans and the sudden mob of his own dwarves.

"Everybody, fall back! Move out!" Axel shouted to marshal the soldiers into resuming their retreat. Sheathing his sword and leaving Vargas was painful for Axel, but he would not waste the final gesture of his dear friend.

The enemy archers had taken notice of the movement and resumed firing into the assembled dwarves, much to Axel's dismay. He took the action as reason to usher his unit to move as quickly as possible, and got everyone at a jog once again, for the final stretch to the evacuation point.

As the docks came into clear sight, Axel counted five of the armoured naval vessels known as turtle ships moored and ready for boarding. All about were Egrid's soldiers, protecting a low, hastily built barricade, the loading of civilians still going on behind it. Further out in the wide, shallow bay was the flotilla comprised of every seaworthy boat and ship in Dhalla, waiting for word to make for the open sea.

It looks like Egrid moved everything to the mouth of the bay besides the turtle ships. A wise decision, my darling, Axel thought to himself proudly.

"Defenders, encircle the docks and barricade!" Axel called out, his eyes scanning for his wife as he did and seeing no trace of her. In his state of worry, he looked about to the rooftops and found Parias, he and his archers still trying to fend off the human bowmen and infantry occupying the slanted slate perches with them.

His thought was that perhaps Egrid had gone up high to help Parias, but he did not see her among the fighters. On the ground, his shields were lining up, spears and infantry of both his and Egrid's units behind them. It seemed that what civilians remained was waiting for their chance to board the ships, and he could see none beyond the defences in the open streets.

It's just a matter of getting those few out, then I can start evacuating mine, Egrid's and Parias' soldiers.

The humans were upon them hurriedly, pushing and slashing at the defences and taking every spare millimetre of ground that Axel forfeited. He slipped to the back of the lines, falling to his hands and knees as he did in absolute exhaustion.

A hand came to rest on his triceps, gently trying to pull him back to standing, all the while a voice asking, "Are you wounded, Ser? Can you stand?"

The lobstered gauntlet encasing the hand looked as though it had not seen battle yet, which led Axel to believe it was one of Egrid's units. "Have you seen Egrid?" He asked its owner while still buckled over, "Where is my wife?"

"She's commanding her unit, Ser." The gauntlet's owner answered, the voice clearly male and sounding suddenly familiar. "They are trying to get yours aboard the last of the ships. I think her fresh soldiers will give us time to do so, or at least I hope so, Ser."

"Chinton?" Axel asked, looking up into the face of his squire.

"Yes, Ser? What is it?"

"It *is* you. Why are you not gone to sea?"

The squire dragged him back to standing, sliding Axel's arm over his shoulders to help support his weight. "It is a squire's duty to serve his knight, Ser. I cannot do that at sea while you are still here."

In spite of himself, Axel did find the lad's dedication admirable, and he almost laughed. "Did Egrid give you permission to stay? If I recall correctly, my instructions were that you were to put yourself under her command."

Chinton looked nervous and averted his eyes in reply, "Lady Egrid offered me a berth on a ship, Ser and I begged her leave to remain until you arrived. She was not pleased with me, Ser."

"No, I suppose she was not." Axel commented, a laugh nearly escaping. With a sigh, Axel patted Chinton on the chest with his free hand and took his weight off him to stand freely. He was about to ask his squire if he had any water to drink when the ground beneath their feet shook and the sound of a huge slam echoed throughout the city.

Axel stumbled, being caught again by Chinton, who frantically queried, "What was that, Ser?"

His gaze went to the general direction of Deepstone mine, and above the sightlines of even the highest rooftops near there, he could see a rising cloud of dust. The sight left little doubt as he turned toward the squire, his voice grave as he replied, "I believe that was the Iron Seal, Chinton. Ser Dorrhen must have been terribly pressed if he felt the need to seal off Deepstone so soon. Like it or not, our ships are now the last means of escape from Dhalla."

Another thought came to Axel, *If Deepstone is sealed then the remaining human forces are likely to all converge on the docks. We have to get all hands to sea immediately.*

He turned to his squire once more, "Chinton, find Egrid, tell her we must commence with the shrinking semicircle, no more delays. I'll need to get word to Ser Parias on the roofs too and I have no horn with which to signal him."

With Chinton gone to carry out Axel's tasks, Axel took the precious few seconds he had to spare to survey the battle. The combined efforts of his and Egrid's units were producing results and it seemed that Axel's order to start shrinking the circle in around the ships was two steps behind hers. On the roofs, he saw no sign of Ser Parias, or any living dwarves, for that matter. The enemy was continuing to send arrows into the semicircle, though it seemed that either their physical presence had been reduced or their quivers had begun to empty. Either way, it was a slight relief to Axel. Behind him, the first of the remaining five turtle ships was pushing back with its oars from the dock, filled to capacity and ready to join the flotilla.

"Incoming!" Axel heard being shouted from somewhere to his left, pivoting on a heel as a finely armoured human mounted on the largest horse Axel had ever seen came bursting through the defences. The beast and rider barrelled through the dwarves with ease, sending soldiers sprawling in all directions. To Axel's horror, he heard the sound of splashing and screaming, telling him that his worst fear for his defences was coming to life.

The rider let slip into his right hand a long pole, on the end of which Axel saw an iron ball shaped into the head of some ugly demon. It bore down on him quickly, having likely identified Axel by the Goldenhair blazonry on his armour and cloak.

His hand went for his sword and as he drew it forth, Axel heard the sound of a broken bell clanging in his head. Everything spun, a bizarre taste formed in his mouth, and he descended into darkness.

~Lady Egrid Goldenhair~

It never occurred to Egrid just how brutal and savage Valdarrow's humans could be until she witnessed it personally. Even with her comparatively fresh soldiers added to her husband's numbers, Egrid was not sure that they would last to see the evacuation through to its conclusion.

Especially now that the Iron Seal is closed. If only Dorrhen had held out just a few minutes longer.

At present, she was staying at the very rear of the defensive line, picking dwarves in pairs to retreat for the ships. Her strategy was to remove her husband's soldiers primarily, given their already exhausted state. Within that parameter, she started with anyone who looked to be wounded. There was a streak of stubborn pride that seemed to run through the entirety of the dwarven people and unless their wounds directly inhibited their ability to work or fight, they would not yield unless commanded to. It fell to Egrid to be that commander in this instance. After the wounded, she picked those at the extremes of age, taking the youngest folks and the greying in their turn. Then would come the rest of Axel's depleted warriors and lastly, her own.

"Lady Egrid! Lady Egrid!" She heard from near at hand. Axel's squire Chinton was the source of the shouting and as he came running toward her, he quite nearly failed to stop.

"Watch where you are running, Chinton." She warned him, "What is it? Have you found Axel?"

The lad tried to tell her, getting as far as "Yes, my lady, he sent me to tell you-" Before a louder voice cut him off.

"Incoming!"

By the time she looked toward the origin of the warning, an armoured human on a fearsome, dark brown warhorse had broken through her defensive barrier. His target seemed to be Axel alone, and though she began to run to her husband's side, all she could do was watch. The rider bore an iron cudgel on a long pole, and swung it at Axel as the horse began a charge. Axel looked as though he was trying to pull his sword loose from its scabbard, but it caught on the way out. The abrupt interruption in Axel's motion was enough for the human's ugly ball to catch him in the side of the helm. He landed flat on his back, supine and frighteningly still, the sword that stalled him clanging down beside him.

"Axel!" Egrid called out, dodging a second swing of the cudgel that the human swung at her haphazardly, seeming to do so only because she was in his path and not with any predetermined measure.

Practically falling atop Axel as she got upon him, she began looking for signs of life. The horse bayed, and Egrid looked up in time to see the human in its saddle pulling hard on the reigns to rear it up for a quick turn.

He's preparing for another run.

A few dwarves charged the human, but he batted them away with his weapon, and levelled his sights on Egrid alone.

She grabbed Axel's sword, moved as far away from him as she could, stood as tall as her dwarven frame allowed and beckoned to the human with her free hand, taunting him, "Come on, you cursed fiend, let's dance!"

There was little room for the long-legged warhorse to get to more than a gallop, but it was fast enough that Egrid just had time to sidestep the cudgel and take a swing at the pole itself. The steel cracked hard against it, and as Egrid spun about, she saw the shaft fractured near the ball, the piece of iron hanging on uselessly by mere slivers.

The human cursed and threw the broken weapon aside, his now empty hand going for the hilt of a sword poking over his right shoulder. Judging from the length of the hilt alone, Egrid had to guess it to be a broadsword and the struggle with which the human had drawing the thing out confirmed as much. He kicked frantically at Egrid's soldiers who tried to approach him and the frightened bucking of the destrier further kept them at bay.

There's no way he can hope to use a broadsword while ahorse.

Egrid glanced to where Axel had been lying, finding nothing but a small bloodstain in its place. Glancing in either direction, her eyes fell on Chinton, who had taken it upon himself to drag her husband towards the relative safety of the turtle ships.

"For Aren's sake, someone help Squire Chinton with Ser Axel!" She cried out. Spotting two dwarves crouched near a stack of barrels, she pointed at them directly, "You two, I command that you get over there and help him!"

The pair she singled out stood up, revealing that they were her assistant Lewin and Thigmourd Sapphire, who had previously been worried about his chests of riches. Egrid had lost track of them and assumed they had both long gone to sea, having already ordered them to do just that. Somehow, they had missed boarding any ships prior and were hiding out of sight with ill-fitting half-helms sitting on their heads.

Though the two unarmed and practically defenceless dwarves had failed to follow her earlier orders, they complied without question now. They ran to where Chinton was struggling and each grabbed a leg of her husband, lifting him as best they could, allowing Chinton to raise Axel from beneath the arms. The three were barely enough to keep her husband off the ground, yet they managed to get him through the hatch of the nearest turtle ship, where waiting hands reached out to help them further.

The human had dismounted, slapping his destrier on the hindquarters as he touched ground, to send the beast running. His armour was chainmail overlaid with sections of plate over the most vulnerable areas and atop the outfit was an off-white tabard, upon which there was a sewn insignia.

I see a gold boar on a red and white chequered field, the sigil of House Grantmoore.

"I was not expecting you to take to the field yourself, General Grantmoore." Egrid stated dryly, giving Axel's sword a twirl in her hand. "Although, I would be lying if I said I was not looking forward to this opportunity to kill you myself."

Letting his sword gently touch ground with one hand, he used the other to flip open the visor on his shining, rounded helm. "Look around, Woman," Grantmoore said arrogantly, making a wide gesture with his sword once both hands could hold it again. "Dhalla is gone. The dwarven presence in Illiastra will be no more after this day. Our goal is achieved and King

Valdarrow has scored yet another victory. Your time is over."

"We're not dead yet, Grantmoore." Egrid shouted as she rushed in on him, sword flashing at him in hurried slashes.

Her first target was his exposed face, though his visor was closed by the time she got upon him. Instead, she went for the torso, an easier target given the height disparity. What Grantmoore did not evade, his armour bore without issue, and Egrid had little recourse but to dodge clear of his range so that she might take measure and avoid any counter attack.

A single strike from that broadsword would be enough to end me.

His return offence was a single cross slash, the sword making a deep 'whoosh' as Egrid ducked beneath it. Inside his guard, she cut and thrust at the leather buckles of his platemail and anywhere she could find the comparatively weaker chainmail in between.

There was a second swing of the broadsword, aimed lower than the first and Egrid had to tuck into a forward roll to escape it, following through with the movement so that she returned to standing on her two feet. She spun about and found following, his sword striking the hard lumber planks of the docks with a crack.

Egrid looked over Grantmoore's armour for weakness, centring in on a single clasp on the left side of his breastplate that was now barely hanging on after her last attack. He came forward for another wide cut and Egrid timed her rush for the moment he began to draw his arms back. Crouching to avoid the broadsword, she slid to his left, Axel's blade going under his arm. Once there, she dragged the sword downward, splitting the leather binding and giving her an opening in the space beneath the plate that she then stabbed at vigorously. Grantmoore winced audibly and Egrid leapt backward four paces to stand clear of his reach.

"Why you accursed little thing!" Grantmoore moaned, trying to put a hand to where her sword had just been.

She came back in a hurry, making a feint to the exposed area. Grantmoore fell for it, turning that side away from her, his stance going sloppy to do so. From there, Egrid intended to make two cuts: the first was aimed at the thigh, her sword looking for the gap between the cuisse on his legs and the tasset protecting his pelvic area. With it striking flesh directly in the meeting place of leg and groin, she pulled hard on the sword, deepening the wound further. The second blow was for the back of the knee, though the first had been enough to bring Grantmoore off balance, leaving her swinging at air.

There came the sound of steel clanking to the ground and as Egrid came to face Grantmoore, she found his sword abandoned, his hands feeling for wounds around his manhood.

"This is where it ends, General Grantmoore." Egrid told him flatly between rapid breaths, her sword pointed at him from waist height.

He lunged at her, throwing his weight fully into it so that she crashed painfully onto her back with him atop her, the breath leaving her lungs from the force of it. Her helm was pulled off with a single hand and the gorget protecting her throat ripped away savagely, leaving her terribly exposed above the collarbone.

"If I die, it won't be alone." Grantmoore scowled at her, his furious gaze visible through the visor of his helm. Leaning back, he dove forward with both gauntleted hands, wrapping the blood-covered things tightly around her neck.

Egrid still had her sword in the left hand, and she managed to slide it up into the space between them until it was against his breastplate. Through struggled gasps for air and fading consciousness, she worked it between Grantmoore's helm and gorget until she felt it nestle into a beard. With the last milligram of her ebbing strength, Egrid jabbed the blade inward, watching as Grantmoore's eyes went wide behind the visor. Almost immediately, she saw his life running thick and red down the sword where it dripped onto her face.

Her airway was free then, as Grantmoore put one hand on the ground to stabilise himself while the other gripped the steel of her sword, trying frantically to pull it out of his own throat.

The blood began to trickle through his helm's visor, indicating his mouth and nose were filling with it. Shortly after, his eyes rolled to white and his full weight fell atop Egrid.

She was pinned beneath the dying human, a heavy weight atop any dwarf, let alone with a full suit of plate armour and chainmail on him. No matter how she tried, Grantmoore could not be moved.

"Somebody, get him off me! Help!" She tried to scream, her words barely coming out due to his weight on her chest and the damage to her own throat from the near-strangulation. Somehow, she managed to roll onto her side, and from there, she got a leg out from beneath his torso, flailing it about so that she might be seen.

"Here! She's over here!" A voice cried out, and soon she felt the pressure of the dead Maylon Grantmoore being lifted from her.

"Pull the human off and get Lady Egrid up!" A woman commanded, and Egrid found herself looking up at Leeda, throwing down spear and shield as she approached. "My Lady, you're alive!" Leeda exclaimed while grabbing Egrid's arms. "Please, forgive me for not being at your side, I was caught at the front line of the defences and only got reprieve to evacuate seconds ago."

Egrid tried to answer, but her words were still not producing anything more audible than a whisper and she opted instead for nodding as her friend helped her back to standing. Groaning and tapping on Leeda to get her attention, Egrid leaned into her ear, "Pull everyone out, last haul to the ships, you give the order."

"Are you sure, My Lady?" Leeda queried back, her gaze going across the street as she did. "Ser Parias and his archers are still trapped on the rooftops."

"Yes!" Egrid croaked back. "Cannot wait forever. When we move, Parias will move. Do it!"

Deigning to ask any further questions, Leeda released her hold on Egrid and scooped up spear and shield from the ground, holding the former aloft to get attention. "All units of Ser Axel's fall back to the ships! Lady Egrid's unit, close in tight around them!"

It's a start. Egrid thought to herself while looking to the roofs to see if Ser Parias had noticed.

He had, and though she could scarce hear him, she could see he and his whole unit throwing down their bows and producing their melee weapons.

What in Aren's name is he doing?

"Archers, ready... Now!" Ser Parias shouted, before leading the entire remainder of his unit in a freefall jump from the rooftops and onto the enemy horde below.

"Parias, no!" Egrid gasped hoarsely.

After their leap of faith, Egrid lost sight of the archers, leaving her with naught she could do but hope and pray that they could cut their way through the humans to safety.

"My Lady, for you." She heard from her right, turning her gaze to a soldier of hers named Dartell holding out Axel's sword and the blood-spattered front half of Grantmoore's tabard.

Nodding deeply and mouthing a 'thank-you', she took both in hand. With no scabbard for the sword, she wrapped the blade with the piece of cloth and stuck it through her belt, to sit beside her own sword.

Egrid nearly tripped over the dead knight's body as she walked away from it and stopped to give it a last kick before moving on. An arrow struck his breastplate, denting it and ricocheting off into the waters, and Egrid looked to find the roofs overrun by enemy archers.

And here I am with no helm or gorget to protect my head.

Beyond them, Egrid saw an even more distressing sight: black smoke.

They're burning the city.

There was no telling where her helm had gone, so Egrid covered her head with her armoured arms and ran towards Leeda.

"The humans are burning Dhalla." She said as loudly as she could to her assistant, her throat burning with every word.

Leeda looked to the sky and saw for herself, her voice echoing the urgency as she said, "All of Ser Axel's unit seems to be gone to the ships, and I shall give ours the order to follow straight away, My Lady."

Though she could not talk, Egrid could still direct dwarves to the remaining boats, pointing with one hand while using the other to continue covering her head from arrow fire. The turtle ships were covered in arrows themselves, but the thick layer of lumber and sodden pelts would prevent anything from penetrating or burning through, should any arrows be lit ablaze.

Two of the ships launched almost simultaneously, their skippers evidently declaring them full to safe capacity.

That leaves one. Egrid reminded herself, noticing that the semicircle had shrunk to but a dozen defenders.

The shield carriers were so close that Egrid began tapping on them one at a time, pointing toward the turtle ship to convey her orders. During this, she felt a hand grab her shoulder, looking to find Leeda leaning in to her ear.

"My Lady, you should head for the last ship and ensure a place for yourself." She proffered, a notion that Egrid thought ludicrous.

"I go last." Egrid grunted back, brushing Leeda's hand away in doing so.

The defensive line continued to close in, until there were but five protectors, with barely room for Egrid and Leeda behind them.

I am sorry, Ser Parias, I can hold out for you no longer.

"Leeda, it's time." Egrid strained to say in Leeda's ear. "Tell the oarsmen to ready for push-off, then break the line and fall to the ship."

As Leeda went to give the order, Egrid produced her own sword and cut the hempen lines mooring the ship, taking one rope to hand in order to hold the vessel until the others could board.

The oars reached out, gently scraping the posts of the docks, readied for the push. Seconds later, Leeda called on the defenders to drop their shields and run, and they, along with Egrid and Leeda, all leapt to the roof of the covered ship together.

Her body slamming against the rigid, wooden frame, Egrid clung tight to the pelts, fingers digging in as much as possible. She dared not to move until she was sure of her grip, all the while hearing shouts and curses being hurled from the docks. There was hard splashing then, and she glanced back, seeing a number of humans thrashing about in the waters.

Are they swimming after us? She began to wonder, until something convinced her otherwise.

An upturned rowboat had come barging through the enemy, resulting in those at the front being driven into the sea. The lower height of its carriers indicated that they were dwarves, and as they flipped it over into the water and jumped in after it, she identified them as Ser Parias' archers. However, if he was among them, she could not tell.

"My Lady, you must get inside before the humans fill you with arrows!" Leeda called out, herself shimmying on her stomach towards the turtle ship's hatch.

Egrid tried to get Leeda's attention, but to no avail, as the shouting from the docks and the commands of the ship's skipper to his rowers drowned out what little voice she had. The archers clambering into the rowboat began paddling with their hands as soon as they were over the gunwale, trying vainly to catch the turtle ship. Two among them tried to fight off the thrashing humans in the water and pull more of their own aboard.

Reaching the hatch, Egrid stuck her head in, immediately hauling herself back before anyone could pull her further. Dartell and Leeda came to the hatch together to grab Egrid, and she resisted them both, getting out a "No!" and "Look there!" while pointing at the rowboat.

Finally, Leeda seemed to understand and shouted "Skipper, turn the ship about, for we have dwarves in the water!"

Until she felt the ship turning, Egrid stayed where she was, refusing to climb within the ship before being certain that there was an effort to rescue the archers. That there were arrows hitting the ship all about her was of no bother, she could not abandon those soldiers.

They were nearing the dory before Egrid attempted any movement. She slid down the roof of the ship centimetres at a time, feeling with her feet for a lip where the sides met the ship's roof. Once she found it, the slight ledge gave her room to roll to her back, so that she might better see the dory, the surrounding waters and the burning city of Dhalla beyond. As she got herself into the position, a female in the rowboat had grabbed a mooring line that still dragged from the turtle ship and was pulling the two together. By Egrid's count, there appeared to be five survivors, three women and two men, all of which were in various states of injury.

"Is that Lady Egrid atop the ship's roof?" The female with the rope asked a male beside her. He looked up, and though his face was dirty, bruised and bloody, Egrid recognised Ser Parias Windpiercer immediately.

He gave Egrid a pained smile as their eyes met and answered, "Aye Deela, that's Lady Egrid alright and by Aren, I am ever glad to see her."

With little voice and the threat of arrows still coming down upon them, there was little response Egrid could give, but she was every bit as glad to see him alive.

~Ser Dorrhen Snowbeard~

The cold winds blew from the northwest, sending the patterned white cloak on his shoulders billowing eastward as Dorrhen emerged from Deepstone to the tiny village of Gethos. Though it was located in the southerly corridor of the Snowy Lands and nestled in the protective foothills of Mount Montagen's northerly face, Gethos was given to frigid weather and frequent snows during three of the four seasons.

"The Snowy Lands are a raw and unforgiving realm, and yet, this place is more welcoming and hospitable to the dwarves than anywhere else on the continent." Dorrhen said to an unstirring Tinnia, still held tightly in his arms as he looked out across the frozen flatlands beyond, dazzlingly bright in the glow of the two full moons.

During his observation, Dorrhen made a point to keep moving, knowing that Tinnia could not afford for him to stop and admire the scenery. They were among the last to arrive from Dhalla as it was and her condition had been dire to begin with when he discovered her in an alcove beside the Iron Seal.

The few inhabited buildings of Gethos lay downhill from Deepstone, with only the smelter and mineral storage facilities near the mine. As such, Dorrhen kept walking down the winding path that led to the village, trying to discern from the mania before him where treatment for the wounded was being administered.

A dwarf in heavy, woollen clothing came clomping through the fresh snow towards Dorrhen, waving an arm at him to get his attention. "Ho there, Ser Dorrhen Snowbeard!" He called, the clean, neat nature of his garb giving Dorrhen reason to believe him to be a villager who had seen no battle. "Please, hold on just a second! I was sent here to wait for you and take you to Mister Crego and your mother." As the fellow approached, he seemed to catch notice of Tinnia. "Good gracious! That woman in your arms, is she hurt?"

"Gravely, aye," Dorrhen replied, still without stopping.

"Oh, dear! Shall I help you carry her? Or go fetch a gurney, perhaps?" The stranger asked, adding, "If you brought her here yourself you must surely be exhausted. I can help you, Ser."

Dorrhen shook his head, eyes on the potentially slippery trail ahead. "I thank you for your offer, but I need only know where the wounded are being taken."

The dwarf pointed a mitten-covered hand further below. "Aye, Ser, Gethos has no proper hospital like the city folk, so we turned the longhall into one. Take her there or into one of the two pavilion tents beside it, that's where anyone who knows how to wrap a bandage has been put to work. Oh, but what will I tell Mister Crego and Lady Narra, Ser?"

"Tell them where to find us." He shot back over his shoulder, leaving the villager behind.

As he approached the huddled, displaced masses from Dhalla, Dorrhen felt both sorrow and relief to see so many. They saw him as well, and Tinnia too, parting so that the pair might pass to where they needed to be. At first, he had steered towards the longhall, though as he neared, it became apparent by the crowds filling every stone step that getting inside was near impossible. Dorrhen instead veered for the more accessible of the two pavilion tents, ducking beneath a canvas flap that a village guard held up for him with one hand while saluting with the other.

"Right this way, Ser!" The guard shouted, adding as Dorrhen went by, "We have an incoming wounded soldier!"

"My friend needs help!" Dorrhen called out immediately after.

"Is anybody free to help young Snowbeard?" An unidentified voice asked from somewhere within the madness.

There were white linen sheets as far as the eye could see, or at least they had been at one time, as hues of pink and red seemed to stain everything that bore the injured upon it. As fast as one surface was clear of a patient, the reddened sheets were pulled off and fresh ones put down, ready to soak up the blood of the next wounded person.

"I'm scrubbed and ready for the next one, I'll take care of it!" Another voice responded. A dwarf dressed in a bloodstained, white smock came forward, holding his hands up at chest height, palms toward himself. Of the man's face, Dorrhen could see only his eyes, as he had wrapped his head, mouth and nose in white linen. "Bring the woman here, young dwarf." He instructed Dorrhen, pointing to what looked like a table with a clean white sheet still catching the air as it was being unfurled atop it.

Dorrhen hurried over and was about to set Tinnia down when a hand was turned out to stop him. "Wait now, hold on, lad." The masked dwarf said, his tone suddenly changing. Before Dorrhen could put Tinnia on the table, the dwarf in white tilted her head back and looked at her face. A pair of fingers went to her throat just beneath the chin, where they held for a few seconds.

"I'm sorry, she's too far gone." The dwarf solemnly stated. "There's nothing to be done."

An odd feeling coursed through Dorrhen's entire body, like a tingling wave. His mouth felt dry and when he tried to talk, his voice stammered.

"You are mistaken…" He said to the doctor.

"I wish I were, young Snowbeard." He replied with a slow shake of his head.

"N-no, you are mistaken." Dorrhen said, louder this time. "You have yet to even check her wound. Ha-How can you say that without having even looked at the wound?"

A second dwarf in white garb had appeared beside Dorrhen then, carrying themselves much the same as the first had. "What's the patient's status, Doctor?" A female voice asked.

"She bled out from a single wound located on her back." The first responded in a tone as soft as it was sad.

"How d-do you know that? I never…"

The first doctor lowered a hand, sweeping it across Dorrhen's lower half, "Your armour is covered in her blood, Snowbeard. There's a river starting just about at your stomach going all the way down to your shins."

While the original doctor had been talking, the other stepped in close to look Tinnia over, careful to not touch his friend with her clean hands. "Doctor Zett, she's hardly taken a breath while you were speaking."

"Face and hands as cold and pale as the driven snow, little pulse and barely breathing." Doctor Zett sighed. "She's bled too much to help, that's not taking into account the severity of the wound to cause such damage in the first place. I am terribly sorry, but there is nothing we can do and she is one among hundreds that need our attention. Please, Ser Snowbeard, you have to understand."

"How long... How long d-do you think she has left?" Dorrhen managed to say.

The female shrugged, "She could linger anywhere from a few minutes to an hour or so. It might be best if you help her make the last of her time in this world be as peaceful as possible."

Dorrhen adjusted Tinnia in his arms, his heart sinking with every step and word. "I shall do that... Thank you, both of you. I apologise if I behaved poorly. You may go back to your work."

Suddenly, his feet felt like iron, and the energy that he had thought limitless on the trek through Deepstone was now almost entirely sapped, leaving his body a depleted husk. He turned and left the doctors where they stood, walking out of the tent and back into the cold. All about him were the refugees of Dhalla, brushing against him as they walked past or tried to move from his way. He heard chatter from some, wails and cries from further away, even screams of agony and angry shouting.

Dorrhen heard them, some part of him knew he had, just as he was aware in part that he was walking out of the tent and yet, he was strangely distant from it all, floating along with Tinnia in a most peculiar way.

"My apologies, Ser Dorrhen." A voice said from at his right, Dorrhen's shoulder jerking slightly from a mild impact of some kind.

"Nothing to worry about. As you were, Soldier." He replied instinctively, his words feeling mumbled. A remote part of him thought it a queer thing to say when he did not know if the speaker was even a soldier at all. The other dwarf seemed to be befuddled by it as well, or at least Dorrhen thought so from the tone of their voice, he could cypher no words, just the puzzlement with which he spoke.

Freshly fallen snow crunched beneath Dorrhen's feet as he left the exchange without further comment. The moons still shone out over the barren lands to the north, but not directly above, where Dorrhen saw only blackness broken by falling flakes.

"Odd weather here, wouldn't you say, Tinnia?" He heard himself asking aloud. "It seems like the clouds have moved in over Gethos, but not out there on the barrens."

In the aimless venturing that had taken hold of him since leaving the tent he seemed to have found his way onto a flat clifftop that dropped off sharply. There were no others to be seen, and the torches and fires of Gethos felt far off, leaving his eyes to adjust to the soft glow cast by the moons on the distant field of white.

He looked about his feet, kicking away the snow to find their little perch to be grassy. "I think this is a good place to sit. Let's set you down."

Despite the threatening buckle in his knees, Dorrhen laid Tinnia atop the snow and grass gently. He took a second to brush the hair from her closed eyes and sat down beside her with a weary sigh.

There was peacefulness to her face as he looked upon it, as though she were blissfully sleeping and not mortally injured. He laid the back of his hand against her cheek, nearly fooling himself into believing as much.

As cold as the snows all around her. He registered somewhere within.

That same hand hovered above her mouth and nose, feeling a faint breath.

Still here, though.

There now was a shake in that same hand he held above Tinnia, Dorrhen noticed. His throat was as dry as it had been in the medical tent, and the numbness persisted, but the shaking was new. Shifting from where he originally sat, Dorrhen suddenly found himself encumbered by his armour. He stood and undid the clasp on his cloak, pulling it away to find it torn, shredded and spattered with the blood of others. It dropped unceremoniously from his open hand, thumping heavily into the snow. After that, he began undoing the buckles on his vambraces, pauldrons and revebraces that had covered his arms and shoulders, throwing them onto the pooled cloak. Next went his breastplate, which came away easily without the overlapping pauldrons. Looking at the cloak and pile of expensive steel plates on the snow, Dorrhen barely recognised any of it from when he had donned it all that morning. Where once the plates shone like mirrors, now it all looked dingy and darkened with odd splashes and streaks. The cloak had even been white once, he remembered, though beside the snow for contrast, it looked anything but.

Is it even mine?

He kept undressing, standing now to remove the cuisses and greaves that had kept his legs guarded. To top the pile, he threw down the chainmail that had been worn beneath the plates, leaving him with only his boiled leather doublet and trousers for warmth.

Plopping down beside Tinnia again, Dorrhen took her right hand in his left, using his right to check for life again and finding her to be holding on still.

"Don't worry, Tinnia, I'm still here. I won't leave you." Dorrhen said to her in a low voice. He averted his eyes away, searching for something idle to talk about.

"Look at the lovely view we have. Might well be the best in the whole of Illiastra, I think, next to the sunsets in Dhalla, of course."

Dorrhen had tried to see it for himself, but found only a wobbling blur where once he had espied the tundra of billowing, snowy dunes. With a shudder his vision partially cleared, the obstructive rivulets now winding down his face to drip from his jawline.

His eyes continued to water unbidden, and after the second or third time wiping them, he simply relented, letting the sobs come forth. "What is it all for, Tinnia? Why do you have to go? There's too much left for you to do in this life. You were supposed to be here, I was going to make you my First Commander and we were going to lead our people together to build a new city and a new army. Please, don't go, Tinnia. We only just got this far."

At a loss for further words, and left to only his tears, Dorrhen kept holding tight to Tinnia's hand and despite his pleas, she departed quietly in the night.

~Lady Egrid Goldenhair~

It had been two days since the city of Dhalla had been taken from the dwarven folk and everyone aboard *The Aurochs* were deep in their sorrows. Egrid could not deny feeling as much herself, though she took pains to hide it. Command was hers for the nonce and along with the usual responsibilities, the morale and spirits of those under her charge rested on her as well. If she were to fall into despair, then all hope would be utterly lost.

There were successes to be hailed, though, despite the carnage: every ship in the flotilla was put to full use and sailing without internal issue, throughout the civilian ranks there were no reported injuries of significance, and even the death toll among the wounded soldiers was minimal. The doctors even expected that those who had survived this long should be well enough to survive the journey westward, where they could get further treatment in Drake.

The only hindrance thus far had been the wind, which had been blowing against them for almost the entirety of the two days that they had been at sea, slowing the convoy to a crawl. Even that, Egrid admitted, had its advantages, as it allowed the smaller ships propelled by oars to serve as liaisons between the larger, sail-reliant vessels, ferrying messages, information, supplies and even passengers back and forth. Due to of the efforts of the intermediary boats, Egrid had compiled a thorough crew, passenger and soldier manifest for the entire flotilla, copies of which were steadily being made by Lewin and Thigmourd Sapphire for distribution to all.

The battle had altered Thigmourd, replacing the pompous attitude with graciousness and gratitude, at least towards Egrid. It was such to the point that when she sought for a volunteer to aid Lewin with the task, Thigmourd literally jumped from his seat in the dining hall to do so. Not that Egrid was upset by the dramatic shift. On the contrary, she was glad for it and the newfound respect the two shared for one another.

To serve their task, Egrid had commandeered the unused brig in the belly of the ship, outfitting it with desks and candles and anything else the three might need. The door was propped open and tied firmly to the wall to prevent accidental closing in the rolling of the ship and the cell itself provided more than enough space to conduct their work.

Judging by the light shining through the tiny porthole, it seemed that the midday was upon them. While the two copied the individual manifests, Egrid had been going over them personally and cross-referencing them with lists of names of those who had been reported missing by family members during the evacuations. It was tedious work, and depressing, for it seemed that for every one name she found, three more were yet unaccounted. It seemed likely to her that most of those had gone to the Deepstone evacuation point and were now in Gethos Village, yet she was troubled by the thought that some may well have been left behind in Dhalla.

When she had finished with the passenger manifest before her, Egrid set it aside and rose from the desk. "Let's break for the luncheon hour." She suggested to Lewin and Thigmourd with her nearly recovered voice, hearing their chairs grunt as they shifted in them to look up at her as she continued, "I know that no one from the galley has come to let us know that lunch is served, though I was thinking we could break a little early. You two might get to the line first, for once."

Being in the bowels of the ship meant they were usually among the last to be informed when meals were ready. As a result, scraps were usually all that was to be had. The cook had offered to whip something up for the three of them and any other latecomers at the previous mealtimes, but Egrid felt like beating the rush for once.

"That's kind of you, Lady Egrid, thank you. Come, Lewin, let's take her up on her offer." Thigmourd stated while standing.

With a stretch and a yawn, Lewin was up too, and the three left together.

The Aurochs was the largest ship ever built by the dwarves, with a name to reflect such. Given its spaciousness and stability, the vessel was pressed into service as the primary medical ship and it was where Axel was transferred to when the turtle ship carrying him reached the fleet. Once Egrid made her way to *The Aurochs* to be at his side, it became the flagship of the flotilla as well.

On her way to the galley, Egrid left her companions with a promise to meet them later, and ventured off to the stern of the ship to the captain's quarters. As she neared, she heard what sounded like Ser Parias talking, which was not odd in itself until she heard a second voice respond to him. Her heart jumped a beat in her chest and she all but ran the rest of the way to the closed door. Upon practically flinging the door open, she found Ser Parias sitting at the side of the captain's bed, Squire Chinton standing at his side with a cup of water to hand. Seated in the bed and propped up with pillows was Axel, looking awake and alert for the first time since being struck by Maylon Grantmoore.

"Oh, my dear Egrid, how good it is to see you safe." Axel said with that familiar, warm-as-a-hearth smile she treasured.

"Axel..." She stammered, as joyous tears welled in her eyes, running to his bedside to take him in a careful, tender hug as those same tears began to fall across her face. "I was worrying you might never wake. I'm so glad to see you and hear your voice."

The blow to the head from the now-dead knight had resulted in a significant amount of swelling and a nasty laceration on the side of Axel's head. The wound had been sewn shut and cool, damp cloths were applied steadily to bring the swelling down, but Axel had remained unconscious since the attack. There seemed to have been differing opinions between the doctors and nurses that spoke to Egrid on the matter as to whether or not his slumber was beneficial to his healing. However, there had been an underlying concern that he might not wake at all. Much to Egrid's delight, Axel had come through.

He managed a pained chuckle, "Of course, my darling. I cannot sleep forever, there is simply too much to be done. Parias was just telling me that you seem to have everything in hand though, so perhaps I will go back to sleep after all."

"I love you so much, Axel," Egrid told him while wiping away her tears. "I never got to say it before the battle and I thought I would never get to say it again."

A muscled arm drew her head down to Axel's chest softly, "I love you too, Egrid. I hope I get to tell you that for the rest of a long life ahead."

~Ser Dorrhen Snowbeard~

The day was clear, the wind low, and in Dorrhen's gloved left hand there was a burning torch. He wore his boiled leathers and the ragged remains of his white cloak, all of it cleaned as much as could be done after the battle. At his right side were Narra Snowbeard and Crego Lorbhen, Steward of the Snowbeard Clan. On the left of Dorrhen was Troysan of the Lost Sword Clan. His friend's arm was now in a sling and a bandage had been wrapped about his forehead and eyebrow to cover the sewn gash that would be a third scar on his face.

The three were with him, as were all of Dhalla that had come through Deepstone and were healthy enough to walk and most of Gethos Village as well. Dorrhen had stood quietly among the throng, waiting for his cue from the Clerics of Aren of both communities, who had been praying over the largest pyre he had ever seen.

Those who had succumbed to wounds sustained in battle or had died in the skirmish that followed after the closure of the Iron Seal were laid out atop the brush and timber plinth, waiting to be set free into the cosmos by the flame in Dorrhen's hand. Even if the Goldenhair Clan succeeded, Dorrhen knew there was a score more of the dead left behind in the city. This funeral was not just for those upon the pyre, but for all that perished due to the destruction waged in Dhalla.

He heard one of the clerics calling then, "Come forward, Brother Dorrhen, Son of Adlan and Successor of the Chieftain Clan of Snowbeard. We have given to you, as our new Chieftain of both your Clan and the Dwarves of Dhalla that walked beneath the Iron Seal, the honour to usher our fallen brothers and sisters onto the Stairway of Stars, so that they may ascend to Aren's Palace, and partake in his eternal feast."

From beneath him, Dorrhen's feet carried him until he came to stand at the base of the platform, his boot stopping against the tightly packed timber shavings it was built upon.

Troysan had marched a step behind as the Right Hand of the Chieftain, a title freshly bestowed upon him by Dorrhen immediately after Dorrhen himself was named Chieftain. Further back were his mother Narra and Crego, and somewhere between them was Fear, having never been too far away during everything that had happened. Dorrhen felt Fear now, creeping about, reminding him that all eyes currently in Gethos were upon him.

"She looks so calm," Troysan said from behind Dorrhen, his gaze on Tinnia lying before them, "Like she just went to sleep."

The undertakers had wrapped Tinnia carefully in the same white linen sheet they had used to lift her from the bank where Crego had found her and Dorrhen. After taking her away, they had removed her plate armour, chainmail and boiled leathers and after cleaning the body, had put her in a crisp, plain white tunic. As was the traditional pose among the dwarven deceased, her hands were folded upon the breastbone, and along with her face, were left exposed in the wrapping process.

"Aye, she does." Dorrhen said in answer, trying his utmost to stay strong before the gathered crowd, to which he now turned to face. Nudging Fear aside, he began a speech he had prepared the morning after Tinnia's passing. "Dwarves of the City of Dhalla and of Gethos Village, we are here to pay tribute and respects to the lives lost at the hands of what has been the greatest tragedy we have ever known. Before us lie brothers and sisters in arms who sacrificed all and the unarmed that they gave their lives for, all of them victims of senseless violence and empty hatred. We mourn not just those here among us, but those left behind in Dhalla."

Stopping to take a breath, Dorrhen looked about the crowd until his eyes fell on Raygo, who was standing in full armour just off to the side of the clearing. The last known member of the pony riders had volunteered as a vigil-keeper at the pyre while it was being prepared, standing at full attention in shifts with other soldiers healthy enough to do so. Their eyes met and Dorrhen saw him give a soft nod.

"We remember and pay homage today to the ultimate price paid by Ser Arber Wyldmare and his cavalry, to my father, Ser Adlan and his fellow veterans of the Second Conflict who stood with him on the town walls. To they who gave all for their beloved city and the people within it, from old clans, new clans and no clans at all, the courageous many that fought with valour against the savagery that beset us, we give our solemn and eternal thanks."

Dorrhen raised his torch high, glancing over the gathered slowly. "May the fallen rise again on the embers so that they might climb the Stairway of Stars to Aren's Palace, to be feasted and honoured until time's end."

The last line was a familiar one he had heard said at last rites for old warriors of generations gone by. The reverberation of the words throughout the crowd told him that he was far from the only one to remember them. When silence fell again, he turned back to the rows of the dead, took a knee and placed his torch beneath where Tinnia lay. With a muttered prayer beneath his breath, he closed his eyes and remained where he was until he heard the crackle of the wood shavings and dried hay beneath her as they began to burn.

From either side of the pyre came more survivors of the battle in turn, each one repeating the procession that Dorrhen had started.

"Goodbye, Tinnia of Clan Gondarra." Dorrhen said to the stars above. "I vow that your name will live for eternity. Your deeds will be etched in the books of history and your memory will be that of a warrior and a hero. Yours will be a name that dwarves will proudly give their daughters as long as there are dwarves to do so. I promise you, my dearest friend."

"*This* is what it means to be blooded, Dorrhen." Troysan said from at his side, his tone sombre. "There are no elder soldiers left to give you the distinction, so I suppose it falls to me do. The youngsters think being blooded is some title given to warriors for slaying enemies in battle, but that is far from the truth. It is not even about seeing your own blood being shed and living to talk about it. Being blooded by dwarven terms is seeing those you love and care about bleed, suffer and die. It's not an honour, or a battle scar to brag about, it's a wound that does not heal and takes with it a little part of you that will never come back."

"Blooded..." Dorrhen said with a deep breath. "My father and his friends, their faces and voices as familiar to me as yours, are all gone. Men and women we grew up with, learned and trained beside, are lying dead in the street or on this pyre in front of us. Those two archers that had been my scouts, Ser Wyldmare, so many that had been in my command, are just no more. For all I know, the Spearsmasher twins, Parias, Egrid and Axel might all be dead too. We might be all that's left. If just seeing even one person die marks a dwarf as blooded, who in their right mind would ever want such a title?"

"No one should, and knowing that is how you know that you are blooded." Troysan stated flatly. "You have to live your life ensuring that you never become so callous and empty that you forget how terrible a thing it is to be blooded. That's the only way to know you are still on the right side of things, Dorrhen."

Dorrhen's gaze was on the ground as Troysan talked, a single tear having run down his face. "How do I learn to live with this pain? How do I go on?"

Troysan wrapped his good arm about Dorrhen's shoulder, "With great difficulty, I'm afraid. But you will not have to go it alone."

THE WORTH OF GOLD
BONUS PREVIEW CHAPTER

From the Author: "It's been a long wait since I published *As Fierce as Steel* and I am regularly asked where **The Worth of Gold** is and what my timeline is to release it. The best I can say is that I want it done as much as everyone else. I'm putting every second of spare time that I can into making that happen, as I'm not fortunate enough to be a full time writer yet. As much as I would like to set a firm date, it would not be fair to the team and myself or to you, the reader, if that date comes and goes. What I can offer you though, is a chapter and it's the first one. Marigold Tullivan will tell you more."

THE WORTH OF GOLD
CHAPTER 1
MARIGOLD

On the sixty-third day of the autumn season, Marigold Tullivan, the Lady, and heir apparent to Daol Bay, rose from her warm and cosy bed and greeted the morning. At least, she assumed it was the morning. From within her guest chamber at the Parliamentary Manor of Illiastra's capital city of Atrebell, it was difficult to be certain. The lavish apartments given to the lords, ministers, and their families by the Lord Master Grenjin Howland were windowless and reliant on artificial lighting sources. The accommodations on that level of the manor were sandwiched between the servant corridors running along the outside walls, and the central hallway that was reserved for the guests. Should Marigold want to see the outside world, she would have to venture through the servant's door of her room and step into their narrow passageway to find it.

Though she was dressed in naught but a sleeveless, powder blue, silk nightshirt and her underclothes, Marigold was quite warm and comfortable in the bed of her heated guest quarters. Yet, she knew she must rise and so she stretched, yawned, and slid her legs from under the covers. A lamp beside the bed was switched on, giving her enough light to find her way to the lavatory so that she might begin her morning routine.

Marigold had barely slept, and her face showed the evidence of that as she looked upon it in the mirror. Despite her comfortable accommodations, there was a great deal weighing on the mind of Marigold that had prevented slumber from truly finding her. As she washed her face and brushed her hair, she did her utmost to divert her thoughts away from such things. Even if for but a few minutes, Marigold wanted to not dwell on what had been the most dramatic night she had ever witnessed.

Regardless of her intentions, Marigold was still reeling from everything that had happened in the span of just a few short hours over the course of a single night. It had started with a visit to her father, Marscal Tullivan, Warden Lord of the Western Realm of Illiastra, Lord of Fisheries and Oceans, and Minister of the Daol Bay region. His attendance and activity at the Autumn Parliamentary Sessions had taken a toll on his already ailing health due to his consumption sickness. As a result, he had decided to skip the usual feast that concluded the events and get his rest for the train ride home the next day.

Delirious with pain, he had spoken to Marigold of events surrounding the deaths of her mother and baby brother over a decade prior. It had shocked both Marigold and their long-serving house steward, Oire Sellars, to hear these things, as Marscal had always been mum on the subject. Whether or not there was any truth to what he had said, there was no denying that her dying father was wracked with guilt over the untimely loss of Farren and Felixander. It was a matter that Marigold intended to look into further, once she was safely behind the walls of the Tullivan's own manor in Daol Bay.

Once her escort for the evening, the dashingly handsome Captain Freyard Archer of Fort Dornett, had arrived at her father's quarters, Marigold had endeavoured to put that out of her mind. As it were, Pyore Palomb, the twisted seventeen-year-old twin son of Eamon Palomb, Warden Lord of the Eastern Realm of Illiastra, forced Marigold to concern herself with more immediate matters. The boy who was arranged to be her husband had tried to embarrass Marigold before the entire Illiastran Parliament and their families at the feast. If not for his own father's ashamedness, Pyore may well have succeeded in that goal.

That was not his last play of the night though, and when Marigold had refused to kowtow to Pyore's will, he had tried to deliver a backhanded blow to her face.

Tryst Reine had intervened on that occasion, though, Marigold reflected. The speed with which his hand shot up and caught Pyore's wrist in mid-swing had been startling, not just to Marigold, but to everyone seated at the dinner table. Lord Eamon, Pyore's twin brother Eldridge, Lord Mackhol Taves, and even Lord Master Grenjin Howland himself had looked dumbstruck at the sight of Tryst's precise, catty reflexes and vice-like grip. Most of all though, was the look of steel in Tryst's bright, Gildraddi-green eyes. *I can only imagine how fierce he would be in a real battle,* Marigold thought to herself.

Imagining it was the only thing Marigold could do now, though. She and Oire had long been piecing together a plan to free Marigold of her marital bonds and the whole thing had revolved around wooing Tryst Reine. The famous mercenary, recognised internationally by the title of Master of Blades, was without doubt one of the most revered swordsman in the Known World. For four years he had served faithfully as the Lord Master's personal bodyguard and protector and during that time, Marigold had attempted to get close to the man.

Above his remarkable skillset, Marigold thought Tryst to be an honourable and attractive man of some thirty years and most importantly, he was a foreigner of modest birth. As a man who could legally hold no lands or political position in Illiastra and had no pre-existing wealth or titles, he could not usurp Marigold as a ruler. However, he could be her husband and the commander of her army. As Pyore's reaction to Tryst had proven, even the richest and boldest men were fearful in the presence of the Master of Blades.

Yet, all her seasons of planning and plotting had been upended inside of a few hours by the appearance of one woman: Lady Orangecloak, Field Commander of the rebel group known simply as the Thieves, who until that moment had been the most wanted woman in Illiastra. Lady Orangecloak had been brought into the lobby of the Atrebell manor in chains by the renowned bounty hunter, Fletchard Miller and two drunken louts he had hired. The Lord Master consigned Lady Orangecloak to the dungeon beneath the manor and that seemed to mark the final, sad chapter of her life.

Marigold was despondent over Lady Orangecloak's fate and had planned to discuss options to help the poor woman with Tryst when next they spoke. However, Lady Orangecloak, Tryst Reine, and an elf who was also incarcerated in the dungeon went missing, having presumably escaped from its confines before any conversation could occur.

It amazed Marigold that Tryst could so easily turn his cloak on the Lord Master at the very sight of Lady Orangecloak. While Marigold had invested a great deal of time in trying to win Tryst over, he readily sprung Lady Orangecloak from capture within hours of her incarceration.

After dabbing her freshly washed face dry with a plush towel and replacing her hairbrush on the stand beside the washbasin, Marigold returned to the main room.

A long, thick, white bathrobe hung on a hook before the lavatory door. As a shiver ran through her, Marigold grabbed it, slid her arms through, and tied it tight with its accompanying belt. As her body began to warm, she began pacing before the bed, planning out her day in her mind. *First and foremost, I shall go see Father. Oire will have news for me as well. It was a late night for everyone, but it will also be an early morning. After that...*

Marigold had little idea what she would do then. Traditionally, the morning after the summations and closing of the Parliamentary Sessions was nothing more than a figurative parade of the ministers and their families. The lords and the vaunted ministers that were given the honour of residence at the manor would gather in the lobby, say their scripted and empty farewells, and take to their carriages. From there, they would begin the journey to the train station, joined along the way by the lesser ministers who had lodged in the opulent hotels of Atrebell's northern districts.

Ever since she was a young girl, Marigold had been a part of that hollow display of vanity. For the first time that she was aware of, the 'Parade of Parliament', as it was informally known, might be cancelled entirely. The Lord Master had always made the trek to see off his lords and to make a protected appearance amongst the commoners. For the last four years, only Tryst Reine had rode before *that* carriage, seated astride his brown courser and scouting for threats in the crowd all the while. With a man as dangerous as he in the wind, with a turned cloak no less, the Lord Master would likely not bestir himself. There would also doubtlessly be emergency meetings to coordinate contingency plans and arrange armed search parties to hunt down the escapees.

Things had changed, and Marigold suspected that those changes would ripple far and wide across Illiastra.

For the time being though, the manor, or at least Marigold's corner of it, was eerily quiet. The ticking clock on the wall told her it was only just past the seventh hour of the morning. Daylight would be breaking, she knew, and with that, her first glance of what the weather might bring for the day. Her feet went into a pair of warm slippers that had been tucked beneath the bed and she slipped into the servant's hallway.

Outside the wide windows, Marigold could already see the blue sky of what promised to be a chilly, albeit sunny day. There seemed to be nary a cloud and the grass of the manicured lawn shimmered as the rays fell upon its frosted visage. Marigold could see the yard between the kitchen and the staff quarters and the single stone pathway that cut through it to connect the buildings. A man walked alone, bearing a heavy burlap sack on one shoulder. She craned her head to the right, following another stone pathway that led along the side of the building to the rear yards. Further down, she saw a pair of guards, walking slowly beside the outer wall, dressed in the standard issue attire of a blue coat and black trousers.

Marigold moved down the hall to a different window so that she might get a better look at them. From there, she discovered that they were actually examining the brick wall, running their gloved hands over every bit of brick and mortar they could reach. *It would seem that a full-blown investigation has broken out after Tryst and the prisoners disappeared.*

At the end of the hallway was a small window that looked on to the grass and garden on the back of the manor and it was there that Marigold went next. The yard beneath the window was teeming with men in uniform. Most were bluecoats, though speckled among them were the indigo jackets of the Honourable Guardsmen, the elite unit comprised of Illiastra's most prized soldiers. Aside from Tryst Reine, they were the Lord Master's most valued protectors. During any festivities at the manor or on the rare occasions that he ventured outside its walls, the Lord Master called the Honourable Guardsmen together. Now, on account of them already being summoned for the Parliamentary Sessions, they were being used to aid the investigation into the escape of the two prisoners.

The front double doors of the large stables situated near the rear outer gate hung open, and guards in both uniform variations could be seen coming and going. More still were looking over the outer walls and searching through shrubbery. Among the gathered uniforms, Marigold saw two tall, shaggy-haired stablehands leaning against a wall of the stables and surrounded by a few guards who seemed intent on keeping them there.

The iron gates leading to a rear service road generally used for supply deliveries were ajar and being guarded by a dozen men. Just beyond it, Marigold could see half a dozen more soldiers forming up on horseback.

Heavy packs were fastened to the rear of the saddles and the men all bore musket rifles across their backs.

That's a search party, Marigold realised as she continued to observe the organised chaos going on below her. *I wonder how many have been sent out and in what direction they might all be headed.*

Heavy footsteps began to echo off the walls of the tiny hallway and Marigold spun around to see who might own them. Where she expected a butler or another male servant, Marigold's eyes befell a familiar blonde-haired guardsman in an indigo coat.

"Freyard Archer, what brings you here this morning?" Marigold asked him as he approached. "I was actually expecting to find you outside with the other guards."

He smiled at that, or rather his lips did. Freyard was a handsome man just north of thirty with a cleanly shaven face and a moderately muscular build. Outside of his duties as an Honourable Guardsman, he was the Master-at-arms for Fort Dornett and Captain of a renowned cavalry unit known as the Sun's Rangers. The fort was one of several that lined the south side of the Varras River, the wide, snaking body of water that stretched east to west across Illiastra's southerly realm.

"Until a few moments ago, I was, actually," Freyard answered in a voice that was as weary as it was warm and friendly. "Lieutenant Raspen relieved me for an hour so that I might break my fast. I was coming to see if you were awake, I have news that I think you might want to hear."

When last Marigold had seen Freyard, he was dressed in his Captain's uniform, having briefly served as her escort to the Parliamentary feast the night before. Since then he had changed into his Honourable

Guardsman's outfit once more and was put to work in the wake of Tryst Reine's disappearance. As far as he knew, Marigold was completely in the dark on the events that had happened after Lady Orangecloak was consigned to the dungeon. In truth, her steward Oire had dispatched one of the Tullivan's household guards to learn what he could from a member of the Howland household guards that he trusted.

"Tryst is gone. That much I have found out," she answered him sullenly. "Come to my chambers, you can tell me what else you know."

They were quick to enter her room, with her seated upon the edge of the bed and he leaning against the dresser near the servant's entrance.

"So, tell me," Marigold began, leaning back on the bedspread and resting on her hands, "how did Tryst Reine manage to sneak the most wanted person in Illiastra and an elf out of the bowels of the Atrebell manor?"

Freyard shook his head in puzzlement. "That's the strange thing, no one has the foggiest idea how he pulled it off. Neither Lady Orangecloak nor the elf was seen to be leaving the manor. The guard on duty at the stables alleges that he and two stablehands were ordered by Tryst to help him in escorting the bounty hunter off the property. To that end, the hunter's rented jail wagon was hitched up to the two horses that went with it. By the time they finished, they were called to the loft, where they found the drunken louts unconscious."

Having pushed off from the dresser, Freyard started to wander the floor of the chamber. "According to our three witnesses, Fletchard and Tryst both alleged that the sots did not like the deal that Reine was arranging and attempted to turn on both men. A melee ensued and

Fletched and Tryst knocked both attackers unconscious. The lads and the guard helped to load the men into the back of the wagon and the bounty hunter departed through the rear gate shortly after."

Marigold hummed aloud, pondering on what Freyard was telling her. "Did she and the elf somehow find their way into the back of the wagon too?"

"That's what one would think," Freyard said, splaying his arms wide. "However, when Tryst was orchestrating that bit of work, both Lady Orangecloak and the elf, a male named Tyrendil, were under lock and key in the dungeon."

"Alright, so then Tryst sprung the two prisoners after he sent the bounty hunter on his way," Marigold deduced with a shrug. "That seems plain enough."

A shake of the head from Freyard told her that was not as simple as that. "It only gets more complex from there. After he let the bounty hunter go, he made for the dungeon and all the guards he met along the way assumed it was to interrogate Lady Orangecloak. He went into the dungeon, exiled the guards to the top of the stairs, and after a time he returned alone. The guards were given instructions to stay put until he returned once more, so that they would not have to hear the torturer make Orangecloak scream. After that he left through the back door, took his horse from the stable, exited through the rear gate, rode into the forest, and never returned."

While Freyard spoke, Marigold's gaze was on the floor. When he had finished, she met his stare, sharing in the baffled look he wore. "What of the torturer then? What did the guards find when they eventually returned to the dungeon?"

"The torturer had been killed. The guards found him on the cot in his cell, dead of a broken neck," Freyard explained in a tired voice that seemed to beg for sleep. "As for Orangecloak and the elf, they had simply vanished. No guards reported seeing them and there was no trace of where they might have gone. Our first thought was that there was some sort of tunnel or other means of passage, but we could not find a thing. All the cells, the guardroom, and even the bathhouse on the floor above the dungeon show nothing that might allow someone to leave undetected. As it is, though, we still have guards, both from the manor and of the 'Honourable' variety going over every inch of both levels of the basements. There simply must have been a passage down there somewhere for them to fit through. It's just a matter of finding it."

Marigold fell silent as she processed all the information, giving herself a minute to let it all sink in. "Just like that, Tryst Reine is gone," She commented sadly. "The only thing left to wonder now is why he would so wilfully and hastily abandon his post at the sight of Orangecloak."

"Evidently there was more to Tryst Reine than met the eye," Freyard offered in return.

"You knew Tryst Reine better than anyone in the manor, perhaps even more so than the Lord Master himself," Marigold reasoned. "Surely you must have some idea why Tryst would make such a rash decision?"

Freyard exhaled audibly and shook his head slowly at that, taking a few seconds before answering, "I know Tryst passingly well, aye. We were drinking partners and we often spoke at length when I served in the Honourable Guardsmen for one week out of the season. But this..." Freyard's voice trailed off for a moment before he found it again. "I never believed him to be a follower of the policies of the EMP, no more than I suspect you to be. Yet, I had thought he was a man who could be relied on to honour his promises. What are contracts if not promises on paper, after all. That is what he signed when he came into service here. It surprises me as much as it does you that he turned so easily. Perhaps he never valued his contract at all. It might be that he was simply waiting for an opportunity to turn his cloak and the events of last night gave him that. Clearly, if he has a hidden passage within the manor then he has been planning to use it for just that sort of purpose."

That thought sat queerly in Marigold's stomach, but it was hard to deny the logic of what Freyard said. "I knew he had no inclination to support the EMP. I also knew that Tryst Reine was never Grenjin Howland's to control. The man is his own island, independent of a world he was contractually obligated to join. Still, I never expected he could turn on everything so easily. Do you think that either of us ever knew him truly?"

"Tryst Reine is not one to issue his trust easily, that much I can say." Freyard said reassuringly. "I believe that what he showed me and, from what I gather, you as well, was the truth of who he really is. There was just much he left unsaid."

Another thought crept in on Marigold then. "I have to wonder what this will do to the Lord Master. He was paranoid as it was when he thought Tryst was protecting him. Now Tryst Reine has turned his cloak for the other side. The only thing more dangerous than making an enemy of a Master of Blades is making an enemy of one who knows as much about you as Tryst most assuredly knows of Grenjin Howland and his government."

That elicited a hum from Freyard as he considered it for himself. "You raise a fair point. That being said, the old fop will be beside himself over this. I have no doubt that he will send forth everything at his disposal to hunt Tryst down for the rest of his days. Should Tryst emerge at Lady Orangecloak's side, he had best have an army at his back, for Grenjin Howland will most certainly send one to crush him."

He sighed and stepped tiredly toward the servants' entrance of the room. "Anyhow, I have given you all the news I have. I'm quite thoroughly famished and have limited time in which to break my fast. Would you care to join me? We can talk more over a full plate of food."

She was about to stand but caught herself. "Thank you, I am hungry, but it may not be a good idea for us to be seen together for the time being. Pyore was incensed at the sight of you last night and neither he nor his family will take kindly to seeing his bride in the friendly company of another man. I hope you understand."

"But of course. I am sure you have your own duties to attend to this morning as well and I would not keep you. However, once I am relieved of duty, would it be permissible for me to seek you out with further news, should I have any?"

Marigold felt poorly about her choice of words and stood up quickly, giving Freyard's forearm a gentle squeeze. "Yes, of course. We have more in common than a mutual friendship with Tryst Reine. It is important, here and now perhaps more than ever, that we keep in the company of those we can trust. I will learn what I can from the other nobles today and relay it back to you as well. Between us we will have our own little network of information."

"I would not be opposed to that," Freyard nodded with a slight smile while turning towards the door. "Very well then, I shall take my leave of you for now."

After he had gone, Marigold waited until she could no longer hear his footsteps before leaving her room through the guest entrance. The hallway beyond was empty, save for a pair of guards in the black on silver coats of the Palomb household, seated across the hall at the door to Pyore's chamber. Further down were a second pair in the teal of the Tullivan guardsmen, standing watch at the room Marigold's father occupied and it was towards them that she headed.

The two stood up tall at her approach and one tipped his black, beaked hat in greeting. "Good morning, milady. You are awake bright and early, I see."

"I bid a good morning to you, Darrill, and to you as well, Brandyl," Marigold offered in return to the two. "Has Oire arrived from the servant's quarters yet for the morning?"

The second guard, the one named Brandyl answered. "Why yes, my lady, he has been within for the last hour. Unless he ducked out through the servant's door without telling us. Which we all know he is not like to do. Would you like to go in?"

"Yes, thank you," she answered politely.

That request was met by Darrill, a moustachioed man in his early fifties who had been with the Tullivan family guard since Marigold had been but a babe in swaddling clothes. "Please, allow us a moment first to check with Mister Oire and your Lord Father to ensure he is fit to receive, milady."

With a confirmative nod from Marigold, Darrill turned to the door and inserted a key in the hole, knocking with a free hand at the same time. He poked his head within and spoke in a whisper to Oire before retreating again quickly and stepping aside. "You may enter at your leisure, milady."

The door was swung open by Brandyl and Marigold thanked them both and stepped into the room.

Unlike her own guest chambers, Marscal Tullivan's accommodations were located beyond the reach of the servant's hallway and as such, had its own windows. The blue sky quite nearly lit the room of its own accord with a beam of pale light that fell across a wide featherbed, on the end of which sat her father.

The consumption disease had left him sickly thin and gaunt and though he was not quite sixty years old, the disease had aged him at least twenty years more. He was dressed in a tweed overcoat that hung to the floor and a nice, albeit loose, brown suit with a black tie and shoes. Near at hand was his luggage, packed and readied to leave.

"Father and Oire, I bid good morning to you both," Marigold greeted them as she crossed the threshold. She went to Marscal's side and seated herself on the bed. "You are up and about, I see. How are you feeling today?"

"My sweet daughter, a good morning to you as well," he answered in a pain-stricken voice. "I am tired, but I am always tired as of late. However, today I am feeling a little joyous to be putting this forsaken place out of sight and I shan't miss it."

The past week of the Parliamentary Sessions had sapped the strength from her father entirely and the events of last night had taxed him even worse when he heard word.

Marigold had feared for the toll it would take on him, but even still, she was surprised with the haste with which he wanted to vacate Atrebell. "We will be leaving so early, Father," Marigold said concernedly. "Have you spoken with the Lord Master yet? After what happened last night he may want to retain his warden lords for emergency meetings."

"He will," Marscal answered quickly. "That is why I must leave before he has a chance to keep me much longer. I have already dispatched Lewcas to have my cars attached to the next train bound for Obalen. Grenjin knows the state of my health and he won't stop me if I am already in the process of leaving."

"I have not had time to pack, Father," Marigold said as she stood up hurriedly. "I'll have to go at once to my room and even still I shall be rushed. Give me leave to take Brandyl and Darrill to help me and I shall be ready to depart in short order."

A thin hand reached out, gently gripped her wrist, and drew her back down to the bed. "No, Marigold, the only packing you will be doing is to move your things from your current chamber to this one and you will have time enough to do that."

Marigold shot a worried look at Oire, who was busy working mortar and pestle to prepare the Johnahweed her father smoked to lessen his pain. The steward managed to glance at her long enough to give her an assuring wink before putting his attention back into his task.

"You're asking me to stay?" she asked cautiously.

Marscal nodded in reply. "I dictated a letter to Oire and signed it. I have given implicit instructions that you are to substitute for me as my eyes and ears in any further situation that warrants my presence. Furthermore, of our six guards I am only taking three with me back to Daol Bay, the others will stay with you. Do you have any preference of whom you might keep? Lewcas is at the train station as it is and I have already chosen Darrill to come with me. You may have your pick of the other four."

"Very well, Father. If that is your wish then I shall only be happy to obey," Marigold relented to his request. "As for guardsmen, I would like to keep Brandyl, Elden, and Sydnee. They are all larger than Pyore and Eldridge and none less than ten years older than them."

"After what I have heard of last night's events, you shall want two of them about you for the remainder of your time here," Oire added as he joined the father and daughter beside the bed. In his hands was a small envelope he was sealing and tucking into an inside pocket of his jacket. "My lord, we should not delay any further. I will give you and my lady a minute alone, but we can afford no longer. While I wait, I shall issue the guards their instructions and ensure that your carriage is waiting outside. Brandyl and Darrill will escort you out and we will light your Johnahweed when we are safely out of here and within your train car.

Marscal waved at him feebly. "Very well, Oire, that all sounds acceptable. Now please, go on ahead and leave me with my daughter."

The steward nodded and saw himself out without further word, giving them their privacy for a moment.

"Father, are you sure I should stay?" Marigold asked forlornly. "I cannot bear to leave your side like this. I should be at home with you in Daol Bay."

Tenderly he took her hand in his as he answered her. "Daol Bay does not rest when I do. We are the castellans of the west, my darling. It would not do for us to be unrepresented here at such a crucial time for Illiastra."

"We should not worry about that, Father," Marigold reasoned. "Pyore wants to sit in my place so badly, then for today we shall let him. He can think he represents the Tullivans and we will go back to Daol Bay knowing better."

For a brief few seconds it seemed that Marscal was considering what Marigold said, though a sigh heralded the dashing of her hopes. "I have known Eamon Palomb for my entire life. The man is ambitious and greedy and his sons are worse again. You must stay and continue to show your presence. If you run home on my coattails, they will think your courage is only good when I am near at hand. Furthermore, I have a strange suspicion that what is said in the next few days will likely shape the future of our nation. A Tullivan must be present and you are the heir of my legacy now, even if only in name. Serephanie was never suited for this life, but you are your mother through and through. This is a life you were born for and I would not leave you here were I not entirely sure of that."

"If it is your wish, then I promise I shall stay and serve," Marigold declared with a solemn bow of her head.

"I know you will, darling," her father said with as tight a hug as his weakening frame would allow. "It is my promise to you that I shall wait for your return."

As he released her, Marigold met his gaze, furrowing her own brows as she did. "Where else would you go, Father?"

"Nowhere, my dear," he added with a reassuring pat on the shoulder. "Once I am back within the walls of our home I intend to go absolutely nowhere."

Marigold felt a hard pang as she realised exactly what he meant, though she said nothing more of it.

"Will you see me to my carriage?" Marscal asked while feebly making his way to his feet.

She forced a smile and helped him stand. "Yes, Father, of course I shall. Allow me to grab a cloak and shoes to ward off the chill and I will be right with you."

Marigold left him there and went quickly down the hall to her room to garb herself for the cold weather. Inside her room, she found a favourite pair of black, knee-high leather boots and a cloak and donned them both hurriedly. The cloak was her favourite, in a vibrant shade of teal satin, with a white woollen interior and trim, and quilted with goose down. She scarce felt any weather at all when she was wrapped in it.

By the time she had returned to her father, Brandyl and Darrill had been called upon by him and the two stood to either side, waiting on the order to move out. Once she slipped an arm into the crook of her father's elbow, the four began the slow, laboured walk toward the ostentatious staircase that led to the lobby of the manor.

Marscal was weak from sickness, but his pride was too great and he insisted on walking under what was left of his own strength. Even the stairs did not daunt him. With Darrill and Brandyl walking ahead to catch him should he fall, and Marigold beside him to lean on, Marscal Tullivan was able to leave the Atrebell manor for the last time with grace and dignity.

A tight hug, a kiss to both cheeks, and a final farewell were exchanged before Marscal was helped into the carriage and out of sight behind the closed door.

Marigold stood in wait for the carriage to leave, bearing the cold morning while wrapped tightly in her cloak. The third guard to go with Marigold's father, a fellow nearing fifty years of age named Kandell, emerged from the manor beside a pair of servants, all of them carrying luggage. Behind all of them was Oire, carrying a single brown suitcase that Marigold knew to be his lone piece of baggage.

Once all of it was secured away, Kandell climbed aboard the front of the carriage to share a seat with the driver and Darrill slipped inside to sit across from his lord.

Before he could join the two within the carriage, Oire reached inside his coat, produced a brown envelope, and pressed it into Marigold's hands. "Your letter, my lady," he reminded her. "Your lord father almost forgot, though one can hardly fault him for that."

"Thank you, Oire," Marigold said while drawing him into a quick hug. "Safe travels to you and father. I will join you both in Daol Bay the first moment I can."

Oire held the hug and whispered in her ear. "Keep a guard about you at all times. There is no telling what the Palomb's might do if they can get you alone," he released her then, but kept his hands on her shoulders so that they looked one another in the eyes. "I would stay to counsel if I could, but my duty is to your father first, especially now. Lastly, you should gather as much information as you can, but ruffle no feathers and get home to us as soon as possible. You must not take risks right now, not while you are in such a vulnerable position."

"I understand, Oire. I will do proudly by you and father both. Now go, before anyone can stop you two," Marigold said in a voice full of melancholy.

Any time spent away from her father at this stage of his illness brought those feelings on. His time was so precious now and Marigold felt it her duty to spend as much of it with him as she could. It felt wrong for her to be standing beside the carriage and not within, at his side.

During the time that Oire had spoken with Marigold, Brandyl had positioned himself at her side and she turned to face him. "Thank you for staying with me," she said to him, grateful for the company. "I have no doubt you were looking forward to going home to your wife today and I am sorry for delaying that return. It should not be for long, though."

Brandyl was standing at ease, his hands behind his back, his feet apart, and at the ready for a command. As far as Marigold could remember, he was near thirty and had been serving as a guard of the Tullivan household for some five years. There was a dozen or so centimetres in height difference between him and Marigold, and he had a strong body that he kept in fine form. It made for perfect soldiering material and the handsome features of his angular face and wavy, light brown hair had shortlisted him for consideration to the Honourable Guardsmen.

"You need not apologise to me, my lady," Brandyl assured her. "I am a guardian of the Tullivan household and I go where you and your father command me."

They stood there quietly for a time, waiting for the carriage driver to finish inspecting the carriage and the horses. When the stout little fellow was satisfied, he climbed up beside Kandell, took the reins to hand and got them rolling with a sharp crack.

Marigold moved not a muscle during the time that it took for the carriage to leave, waiting where she stood until it had gone beyond the gate and out of sight.

"I assume you started your shift only a few hours ago?" she queried while turning to face him again.

"Yes, milady, I drew the morning shift," Brandyl answered obediently.

The cold began to nip at her face and she began walking back toward the manor to escape it. "I am glad you are well rested, for we are going to have a busy day ahead of us," Marigold told him, apprehension creeping into her voice.

Brandyl followed from a step behind her, speaking up when he was directly at her side. "Might I ask what milady has in mind?"

"For starters, I need to get dressed properly for the day. I am still in my nightgown beneath my cloak and bathrobe. After that, I shall pay a visit to the Lord Master's chambers and let him know of my father's arrangements. After which I suspect that I will be in meetings for most of the morning. As for this afternoon, we will be moving my things from my current quarters to my father's."

They were climbing the steps then, with Brandyl taking two at a time to reach the top first so that he might open the door for Marigold. "Would you have me wake Elden and Sydnee? They both worked the night shift, so they're not long abed."

"No, leave them be," Marigold decided as the wave of warmth from within the manor greeted her. "You will more than suffice to be my guard for the day."

There's more **Gold & Steel**
yet to be discovered.

Stay up to date at
www.thegoldandsteelsaga.com to find
out where you can get the first two
volumes of ***The Gold & Steel Saga***: ***As Fierce as Steel*** and ***The Worth of Gold,***
and to be the first to know when volume
III: ***The Strength of Steel*** will be available.

About the Author

Christopher Walsh hails from the Southern Shore on the Avalon Peninsula of Newfoundland & Labrador, Canada, where he lives with the love of his life, Kyra. After spending several years travelling and living across Canada, he returned home to Newfoundland & Labrador in 2011 and began creating the world of *Gold & Steel*. *As Fierce as Steel,* the inaugural entry in the series, was also his first foray into the published literary world.